Molly's Millions

First published in Great Britain in 2009 by
Allison & Busby Limited
13 Charlotte Mews
London W1T 4EJ
www.allisonandbusby.com

A CIP catalogue record for this book is available from
the British Library.

10 9 8 7 6 5 4 3 2 1

13-ISBN 978-0-7490-7974-1

Typeset in 11/16 pt Sabon by
Terry Shannon

The paper used for this Allison & Busby publication
has been produced from trees that have been legally sourced
from well-managed and credibly certified forests.

PEFC
CATG-PEFC-052
www.pefc.org

Printed and bound in Great Britain by
MPG Books Ltd, Bodmin, Cornwall

VICTORIA CONNELLY grew up in Norfolk and later became a teacher in North Yorkshire. Her love of romantic comedy was fuelled by the diet of Doris Day, Gene Kelly and Marilyn Monroe films she devoured throughout her childhood. Now living in London with her artist husband, Victoria has had great success with her previous novels in Germany, one of which, *Flights of Angels (Unter deinem Stern)*, has been made into a film.

www.victoriaconnelly.com

ALSO BY
VICTORIA CONNELLY
(published in Germany)

Flights of Angels
The Unmasking of Elena Montella
Three Graces

Acknowledgements

To Bridget and Hsin-Yi for reading the early drafts of this book and providing such wonderful feedback.

To Margaret James and all at the RNA London/SE Chapter. Special thanks to Sue Haasler, Jean Fullerton, Janet Gover, Caroline Praed, Jenny Haddon, Rachel Summerson and Pat Walsh.

To Doreen and Martin at The Monument for their time, enthusiasm and insight, and to Clare Donovan for taking part in the Molly experiment at the top!

To Katie Fforde, Liz Young, Deborah Wright, Mags Wheeler, Stephanie Polak, Heather Clark, Louise Nelson, Margaret Connelly, Clare Punchard, Siobhan Curham, Margaret Fotheringham, June Martin, Pat Maud, Yvette Verner and Linda Gillard for encouragement and support. Also to Cam and Kate Boden who always support their local artists!

Special thanks to Susanne O'Leary for her dare! And thanks to my wonderful writing girls: Henriette Gyland, Pia Tapper Fenton, Catriona Robb and Giselle Green for sharing the highs and lows along the way.

Thanks to Louise Watson and all at Allison & Busby.

And my own special Molly for making each day a delight and for taking me away from the keyboard at least twice a day!

Most of all, thank you to my family – my mother, father and brother. And, as ever, to my husband, Roy.

To my husband, Roy,
and my mother, father and dear brother, Allan.
With love.

Chapter One

'That's twenty-six fifty,' the cashier said, looking up expectantly and forgetting to smile in the process.

Molly Bailey opened her purse, her eyes sweeping its depths, knowing there wasn't enough to pay. She bit her lip and took a deep breath.

'I'm ever so sorry. I'm afraid I'm going to have to put something back.'

The cashier's eyes took on a look of the Medusa before she was about to turn some poor soul into stone.

Molly looked at the goods she'd piled into four carrier bags. Something had to go. She knew she shouldn't have bought the wine but it was on special offer and she hadn't had a treat for months.

As she made her decision, she heard a woman behind her groan loudly.

'Maybe if I put this back.' Molly tried to smile as she returned the bottle of wine to the cashier, doing her best to ignore the other people in the queue as her face flushed scarlet.

'Twenty-one fifty-one,' the cashier said, refusing to return Molly's smile.

She still didn't have enough. 'Well, I guess I don't really need this,' Molly said, trying to ignore the woman behind her who'd started up a tutting competition within the queue. 'Far too heavy for me to carry anyway,' she said, making a desperate stab at humour.

The cashier took the four-pack of orange juice back. 'Nineteen seventy-one,' she said, lips barely moving, face devoid of sympathy.

'Great!' Molly pulled out her two crumpled ten-pound notes and handed them over.

'Thank goodness for that,' the tutting woman whispered audibly from behind. Molly could ignore her no longer. She turned round and looked at the woman, who had hyphens for eyes and a mouth to match, and gave her a dazzling smile.

'Thank you *so* much for being so patient,' Molly said, trying her best to sound unfazed by the whole experience and, collecting her change, she beamed at the cashier before heading out into the car park.

It wasn't the first time she'd come out without enough money. Plus her maths wasn't the best in the world. She really should carry a calculator around with her, she thought.

Placing her groceries on the floor of the car, she got into the driver's seat and started the engine, noticing she was short on petrol. She'd have cycled to the supermarket if she hadn't already had to sell her bike.

She sighed. It wasn't that she had aspirations to be rich or anything, it would just be nice not to have to worry so much. She often thought about buying a lottery ticket, but the odds just weren't good enough for her to risk a whole pound coin.

As her Volkswagen Beetle, affectionately known as 'Old Faithful', spluttered out onto the main road, a shaft of brilliant sunlight filled the car. Molly smiled as though it had been sent down from the heavens just for her.

It was as if she knew she was just four hours away from becoming a millionaire.

Once home, she dumped her shopping bags and released a sigh of pure contentment. She might occasionally be short of change but she certainly wasn't short on flowers. Her florist's, aptly named The Bloom Room, was small but perfectly formed. The overpowering smell, which no perfume could ever capture, seeped into her entire body, filling her with a rosy warmth. The olfactory collision of lilies and roses, and the delicacy of freesias, seemed to run through her bloodstream. It saturated her clothes and seeped up through the floorboards into her flat above so that she never needed to buy air fresheners.

She'd never known heaven could come in two hundred square feet. When she'd first moved in, it was nothing but a dusty shell squashed between the baker's and the grocer's, but a couple of weeks of tender loving care, and a few cans of yellow paint, had jollified the place up no end. Or rather 'Mollyfied' the place, as Marty, her brother, loved to say.

Yes, looking round the shop, she could see that it had definitely been Mollyfied. The warm sunshine walls and polished wooden floorboards were the perfect backdrop to the enormous silver buckets of flowers, and the large local watercolours of the nearby Lake District added to the overall calmness of the shop. Perfect.

As the bell above the door tinkled and old Mrs Purdie walked in, Molly was brought back into the present. She'd been expecting her and had rushed back from the trip to the supermarket as Mrs Purdie usually popped in last thing in the afternoon, hoping some of the flowers had been marked down in price.

She was relatively new to the village and nobody seemed to know much about her because she kept herself to herself but she was a regular visitor to The Bloom Room and Molly always looked forward to her visits.

She watched as Mrs Purdie bent, gladiolus-like, over the silver buckets, inhaling the sweet aromas of the bouquets. Yes, she thought, Mrs Purdie was definitely a gladiolus: strong yet yielding. It was kind of a hobby of Molly's to think of people in terms of flowers. It had started when she was about six. She'd been watching her mother walking round their garden one morning, pausing at the fantastic blooms on the rosa mundi and pushing her face deep into their blowsy petals, two-toned, fuchsia and shell pink, so like her personality: gentle yet vibrant.

Molly looked up to see Mrs Purdie standing up to full height after admiring a particularly expensive bouquet.

'Lovely!' she sighed, closing her eyes as she was carried away on the scent.

'I'm marking that one down,' Molly said, 'it's three ninety-nine.'

'Really?' Mrs Purdie's eyes sprang wide in surprise. 'I'll take it.'

As Molly wrapped the flowers in paper she usually charged for, she remembered when Marty had spent a couple of hours in the shop with her one afternoon, and had been astounded when Mrs Purdie had spent one ninety-nine on a bunch of carnations, and had then admired another bunch of flowers at four ninety-nine.

'Here – take them,' Molly had said.

Marty's mouth had dropped open, mirroring the surprise on the woman's face perfectly.

'Molly!' he'd shouted, as soon as the old lady had left the shop. 'That is *not* how you run a business.'

'Oh, twaddle!'

'Don't twaddle your way out of this one!'

'Marty – it's four-thirty in the afternoon; they're not going to sell now, are they? They'll probably end up on the compost heap. Anyway, Mrs Purdie only has her pension. She can't afford many treats.'

'You're meant to be making a living, not running a charity.'

'Oh, you sound just like Dad when you talk like that,' she'd laughed.

And it was true. Much as she tried to deny it, Marty was a Bailey through and through. Slowly, via careful brainwashing from their father, Marty had turned into an old Scrooge.

Molly shook her head as she handed Mrs Purdie her new bouquet. 'Three ninety-nine,' she said with a great deal of satisfaction, secretly wishing Marty was there.

Mrs Purdie handed over her money, a huge smile bisecting her face. 'You'll never guess what I did today,' she began. 'I bought a lottery ticket.'

'Did you?'

'Look!' Mrs Purdie reached into the depths of her voluminous handbag and pulled out the ticket, brandishing it as if it was a sure winner. 'I've never bought one before. Have you?' she asked, her eyes watching Molly carefully.

Molly shook her head, her dark curls knocking against her pink cheeks. 'No. I haven't.'

'The odds are astronomical, of course, but just imagine!' Mrs Purdie's eyes glazed over for a moment. What was she thinking of, Molly wondered? Rooms full of flowers? A retirement that involved a few luxuries?

'What would you do if you won?' Molly asked.

Mrs Purdie looked up, her expression one of perfect surprise. 'If *I* won?' she said, giving a little chuckle. 'I don't know. I *really* don't know. But it would be very nice, wouldn't it?'

Molly smiled and watched as she pushed the ticket back into her handbag and left the shop with her flowers, the bell tinkling as the door shut behind her.

Just imagine!

Mrs Purdie's words echoed around Molly's head like an unforgettable song. But she didn't want to imagine. Not really. She couldn't afford to for a start. The only money she had was in the till and the petty cash box, and she never touched that. Not unless there was a personal emergency.

It would be very nice, wouldn't it?

Mrs Purdie's words, it would seem, weren't going to vacate Molly's head easily, not until she did something about it.

She turned round and looked at the little blue cash box nestling amongst the wrapping paper and, even as her hand closed around it, she knew that it was wrong and foolish but the temptation was just too much. This was a grade one personal emergency.

She bit her lip and opened the box. With rebellious fingers, she picked out a gold pound coin, her eyes, dark as conkers, twinkling mischievously. It wouldn't be missed. She'd return it as soon as she could. This just had to be done; it was as if something was goading her on.

The odds are astronomical.

Yes, Molly thought, but they were still there, weren't they?

Her hand swallowed the coin in a tight fist and, grabbing her front door key, she left the shop, hurrying to the corner store to buy her ticket.

Chapter Two

Carolyn stared down at the sink full of dirty dishes and swore to herself that this would be the last Saturday afternoon she'd spend at Marty's grandfather's.

She turned round and looked into the living room at the sprawling mass of Bailey men. Well, Marty wasn't sprawling; he was on the edge of his seat shouting at some footballer on the television. His father, Magnus, had sunk into the depths of the sofa, a glass of very inexpensive wine in his hand. Carolyn knew it was inexpensive because she'd had a sip of it herself and had instantly remembered the time she'd gone under at the local swimming baths.

And then there was Marty's grandfather, Granville Bailey, head of the great Bailey family. She'd only known him for three years but every time she'd seen him he was sitting in his winged chair as if it were a throne. Did he ever move? Did he sleep in it? From the head-shaped stain on the back, Carolyn suspected that he did.

She stared out of the kitchen window and sighed. What was she doing there? She really had to put her foot down and tell

Marty that she wasn't going to come anymore. She wasn't his skivvy, and she certainly wasn't Magnus and Granville's skivvy either.

In a sudden thrust of determination to get her life back, she threw the dishcloth into the sink. She'd bought it a month ago. Granville Bailey didn't buy things like that, not with the knowledge that somebody else would, and Carolyn felt sure that his meanness was one of the reasons he invited Magnus and Marty over every Saturday. Magnus always bought a bottle of wine, not spending more than two ninety-nine on it, mind, and Marty was responsible for the food, which Carolyn would cook and serve. Then, almost without her noticing, it had become her job to collect up the dishes at the end of the meal, serve dessert and coffee, and wash and dry up. But when had that happened? When exactly had she fallen into that routine?

She walked through the living room but none of the men bothered to lift their eyes from the television screen, so she kept on walking until she found herself in the bathroom. She shook her head in annoyance. If she didn't have the courage to stand up to Marty then she only had herself to blame, but he was a hard man to say no to sometimes.

Take their wedding, for example. Even though her father had given a generous budget, Marty had insisted on scrimping and saving. He had cut corners on virtually everything, which probably explained why they'd had a round wedding cake.

Carolyn had idly dreamt of a dress beaded and bejewelled but Marty had insisted that the money would be better spent on new guttering for the house. She knew he was right, of course, but it had been hard to imagine swooning over photos of new guttering in the years to come.

She gave her hands a wash and fluffed her hair up. That was another thing she'd always done to please Marty: kept her hair at a feminine shoulder-length when she was dying to have it cut pixie-short. She ran her fingers through the butterscotch blonde, wondering how he'd react if she went and had it all chopped off. A little smile lit up her face at the thought. Did she really have it in her? She sometimes felt swollen with rebellion but she'd never carried anything through. Not yet.

She wandered out into the hall and heard a collective groan of annoyance from the living room.

'What *does* that referee think he's doing?'

It was Marty. But Magnus and Granville weren't far behind.

'Idiot!'

'He's *blind*.'

Carolyn sighed a sigh that could have stopped a train. She couldn't face going back in there so decided to have a nose around the spare bedroom at the back of the house. It was stuffed with photographs, and Carolyn could never resist a quick peep. The trouble was, they were the sort of photographs that should have been expensively framed and put on display in the front room but Old Bailey obviously didn't care for that. His front room had a good many photographs all right, but they were all of him: Granville Bailey shaking hands with some toff; Granville Bailey holding a shark-sized salmon on a Scottish fishing trip – all very self-absorbed. There wasn't even a single one of his dearly departed wife. She too was relegated to the back room where the sun never shone: the room of lost photographs.

Carolyn picked up the ten by eight of her and Marty on

their wedding day. It was coming up to their third wedding anniversary and it still wasn't framed. Instead, it remained in its cardboard folder, propped up on the top of an old shelving unit.

Carolyn's eyes swept over the hidden family album. There was Magnus, on *his* wedding day. It was an unusual photo of Magnus on his own. His thick, dark hair and black eyes gave him an almost demonic look, and he wasn't smiling at the photographer, perhaps because he had lost his bride. Prophetically, she was nowhere to be seen. Carolyn had scanned the room several times to try to discover Marty's mysterious mother, but she didn't merit a single photo, even in the back bedroom. 'That bloody Percy woman' was how both Magnus and Granville referred to her in moments of heated anger, and Marty never talked about her at all. It was strongly held that all the misfortunes of the Baileys rested on the day Cynthia Percy had entered the family fold.

Carolyn felt desperate to meet the woman who had seemingly created so much trouble within the family. She instinctively felt that one woman couldn't possibly be as bad as the Bailey men made out. She couldn't be the sole cause of Magnus's jet hair turning silver – after all, he was nudging sixty; nor could she be held completely responsible for Granville's rattling chest, though he was often at pains to say as much. The phrase 'that bloody Percy woman' was as common in the Bailey household as 'you can get that cheaper in Tesco'.

Why couldn't Marty have had a sweet old grandfather? Carolyn wondered. She'd never known her own grandparents, and had been so excited at the prospect of having a grandfather figure but had been bitterly disappointed when

Old Bailey had turned out to be the perfect incarnation of Ebenezer Scrooge. The contents of his cupboards and fridge wouldn't have filled a doll's house, his clothes weren't even fit for the charity bag and during the winter months she always had to plead for the heating to be turned up to a level above tepid.

'You're not cold, are you?' he'd bark from his winged throne.

'Yes, I bloody well am!' Carolyn wanted to bark back but, as with Marty, she'd smile sweetly and say nothing.

One of her greatest fears was that Marty would turn into his grandfather. Magnus had managed it so it seemed inevitable that Marty should follow suit and become a real Bailey. Carolyn pouted. He was well on his way, she had to admit.

'Caro?'

She turned round and saw Marty standing in the doorway.

'You made me jump,' she said, hoping to high heaven that he hadn't been stood there reading her mind.

'What are you doing in here?' He walked towards her and looked down at the photograph she still had in her hand.

'Oh – you know – just looking through the family photos.'

He shook his head. 'You've seen them all a hundred times before.'

'I know. But I get the feeling I'm the only one who looks at them.'

He placed his hands on her shoulders. 'Come on. How about a cup of tea?'

She knew what he meant: it was time for her to make tea for everyone. 'OK,' she said, giving him the benefit of a smile. 'At home.'

Marty's dark eyebrows drew together. 'What?'

'I want to go home.'

'Don't you feel well?'

'I feel absolutely fine. That's why I want to go home.'

Marty stroked his chin, giving her his best perplexed expression. 'What shall I tell them?'

'Tell them your wife wants to go home and ravish her husband.'

Marty's face heated up to a perfect poppy red. 'I'll get my coat,' he said.

Carolyn smiled to herself as he left the room. She was a wicked liar, she thought, but at least she'd got her way for once.

Chapter Three

Buying a lottery ticket gave a strange new structure to Molly's Saturday evening. She wasn't used to having the television on, far preferring to curl up in luxurious silence with a book, so it was odd to have her little flat filled with so much noisy excitement. She'd put the programme on at the beginning and had soon become bored, realising the draw wasn't until the end, so she tinkered around her flat with a pair of baby scissors and a toy watering can, tidying up her beloved plants.

She got so carried away with her miniature jungle that she almost missed the draw completely, running over to the TV just in time to see the first ball rolling out of the bubblegum machine.

Molly screamed as she looked down at her ticket. *Number one.* She had it! How was that for beginner's luck? And what a perfect number for it to be: she'd been so worried about spending a whole one pound on one ticket and now the first ball was number one! She smiled, feeling very smug with herself, but believing it couldn't possibly last as ball number two was revealed. *Number sixteen.* A quick glance down proved her wrong; she had it! *Yes!* This was so easy. Why hadn't she done it before? she wondered.

Ball number three, *ten*, made Molly scream again in delight. That was ten pounds. She'd made a profit of nine pounds, which meant that she'd be able to replace the pound in the petty cash box and go back to the supermarket and collect her fruit juice and wine.

Ball number four: *three*. Molly gasped, unable to scream this time; she just sat staring at the television in stunned silence.

Ball number five: *eighteen*. Molly's dark eyes widened to twice their normal size and, as the sixth ball appeared, *number two*, her mouth dropped open in silent wonder.

One. Two. Three. Four. Five. Six.

SIX!

The pink ticket fluttered in her hand like an autumn leaf about to take flight.

NO!

She blinked. She swallowed. Then the numbers disappeared from the screen. She'd made it up! She was overexcited. She'd never bought a lottery ticket before in her life and had obviously got carried away with the whole thing.

As if sensing her excitement, the ticket dropped from her trembling fingers. Bending down quickly lest it slipped down the gaps between the floorboards, she picked it up. It just couldn't be true. Not her! Not with her first ticket.

Teletext! She'd check teletext. They'd have the numbers up, wouldn't they?

She fumbled for the remote control, which had bedded itself down the side of her sofa and, with hands which no longer seemed connected to her brain, she switched over. What page?

What page? What was she looking for? She giggled. She felt drunk.

Page 555. She waited and, after a few tension-ridden seconds, there they were again:

one, two, three, ten, sixteen and eighteen.

The same six numbers. Her eyes checked them over on her ticket. No, she hadn't made it up; there was absolutely no mistake and they looked so beautifully simple. The easy flow of one, two and three. How unlikely it seemed for them to appear and yet – statistically – they were as likely as any other combination. The simple strength of number ten. How sturdy it looked – the first double numeral. Sweet sixteen had proved very sweet indeed. And eighteen – the age that made everything legal.

Molly looked at them jostling together like happy friends. Was it unusual to have all six numbers under twenty? There they stood, like beautifully obedient soldiers waiting for her command, but she had absolutely no idea what to do.

She walked round her little flat, feeling that, if her smile got any bigger, her face would crack open completely. And it wasn't just her who was smiling; the whole world seemed to be smiling: the plates on her draining board, the apples in her fruit bowl, her coffee table, her bookshelves – everything suddenly looked happier. Even her pot plants were in on the act.

'Congratulations, Molly!' the spider plant waved from the window sill.

'Don't spend it all at once,' the parlour palm warned from its corner by the bookcase.

Molly laughed a wonderful glittery laugh that bounced and hopped around the room. She felt as if she'd swallowed a great bubble of happiness, and it all seemed so ridiculous because less than ten minutes ago she'd been Molly Bailey, florist with a mortgage, a loan and a seriously starved bank account. How could six numbers change all that? It wasn't as if she'd even chosen them with any care. They weren't birthdays or lucky numbers or anything. Her pen had merely chosen them at random – as if driven by a force of its own. There'd been no thought process as her pen made the vertical strokes, and yet they'd had the power to change everything. The only question was, how much had she won? How much were her six numbers actually worth? She couldn't remember what they'd said on the programme, but there was the possibility of a number of winners, which would mean dividing the jackpot. But, even with that eventuality, it would probably be more money than she knew what to do with.

Just imagine! Mrs Purdie had said. Molly gasped. She was imagining all right: imagining shopping trips where she wouldn't be embarrassed at the till; imagining not falling into panic mode at every strange noise Old Faithful made, or worrying each year when the MOT was due, imagining…

But her reason was trying to communicate with her: *Earth to Molly! Earth to Molly!*

Molly's heart raced. She knew there had to be a glitch. There was bound to be a spanner, or three, in the works.

The Bailey men. Her mouth dropped open at the thought of them: Marty, Magnus and Granville – three names to strike terror into the heart of any new millionaire – and, all at once, her imagining drained away.

Heaven only knew what they'd do once they found out about her win.

* * *

Molly's mouth had made a silent and perfect 'o' as she was told how much she'd won. Four point two million pounds. For her. And her alone.

She'd been told by the winners' adviser not to make any rash decisions; to take a holiday and give herself plenty of time to think things through. But she didn't need time. She knew she couldn't possibly keep all that money, especially with the men in her family. The trouble had been in deciding exactly what she was going to do with it.

So, Molly had spent two long weeks mulling over her options whilst slowly coming to terms with the fact that she was a millionaire.

A millionaire, for goodness' sake! In the peace of the shop, it was still hard to take in and it didn't really make any difference to her daily routine. Chrysanthemums didn't care if you were a millionaire: they still wanted watering, which was just the way she wanted it. She wasn't into exotic holidays, fancy cars or champagne, and her fingers, with their boyishly short nails, would look ridiculous if she were to dress them with large diamonds. Besides, that sort of ostentation had always been frowned upon in her family, and money had been the source of every single family argument. As far back as she could remember, her mother and father had fought over it. Holidays never got more luxurious than static caravans, and birthdays were kept to a bare minimum, usually involving reference books and sensible clothes.

'Presents should be practical,' her father used to say.

Her mother had never agreed. 'Books and clothes aren't presents, they're punishments!'

Then the arguing would start, and it would always end the

same way: with Cynthia giving in to Magnus. Well, that's how it appeared on the surface. What Magnus didn't see was Cynthia picking Molly and Marty up from school and driving them into town for hot chocolate and cake, followed by a trip to the toy shop to pick out a present, which would be bought on the understanding that their father was never to lay eyes on it. For years, Marty had had to keep his train set tucked under his bed, and Molly's doll's house was hidden at the back of her wardrobe.

For Molly, even today, the filthiest word in the English language was *money*. Forget anything with four letters, the word *money* was really quite hateful to her. Ever since she was a child, she'd blamed money for bad behaviour in people. Her father had made their lives miserable at home with his penny-pinching ways. She and Marty had been the only children at school not to be given pocket money. Instead of freely handing out his cash, their father would ask them what they wanted. He would then ask whether it was absolutely necessary and, if they insisted that it was, which they rarely did through fear, he'd give them half of the money they actually needed and told them to find some odd jobs round the house in order to raise the rest.

The only time they ever got any half-decent presents was at Christmas, and that was only because their mother's family erred on the generous side.

'They're *children*, dear,' Cynthia would chide when she thought Molly and Marty were out of earshot. 'And you're only a child once. What possible harm can a little bit of spoiling do to them?'

But Magnus Bailey was never convinced by his wife's sweet reasoning. 'It wasn't the way *I* was brought up,' he'd growl back, and Molly and Marty, hiding behind the door, would draw their eyebrows together and wave their forefingers in the air in perfect impersonation of their father. They'd always managed to laugh at their father's behaviour. Until the day their mother had walked out.

Molly shook her head at the memory. If there was one lesson she'd learnt from the past, it was that money was to be enjoyed. Yes, bills had to be paid, and provisions made for the future, but her father's way of saving and depriving had done nothing but create barriers, and she was determined that that was never going to happen again.

Yes, she thought, if the Bailey men got wind of her win, they'd have *plenty* to say about it. They'd have it ISA'd and bonded, split over sure-fire shares and packaged off into a pension before you could say 'shopping spree'. And that was just Molly's share of it.

She wouldn't get to keep it all herself, of course. Not that she wanted to anyway. She'd give her family a share: a *small* share each. They didn't need any more money, she was quite sure of that. They were all as comfortable as old armchairs, and Molly knew that her winnings would only lie useless in a bank, accumulating even more wealth to be fought over and never actually enjoyed.

Anyway, what on earth could one person possibly want with so much money? It really was quite obscene. Sure, she'd had years of scraping by to make ends meet, and it would be lovely not to have to worry anymore, but four point two million pounds? She had more than she knew what to do with with the interest alone.

So she'd come to a decision. After sorting out her own finances at The Bloom Room, and putting a little aside for each family member as a token of goodwill, she was going to get rid of it.

As she rearranged the rainbow display of carnations, she realised how hard it was going to be leaving the shop, even for a short while. It had become such a huge part of her life that it was hard to imagine being anywhere else. But one just couldn't be a millionaire in a place as small as Kirkby Milthwaite, and she wouldn't be gone for long; just long enough, she thought, a smile lighting her rosy face; long enough to spread a little happiness.

'I hear you're going away?' a voice startled Molly out of her reverie.

She blinked as she saw Mrs Purdie standing in the centre of the shop. How could she know that, Molly wondered, and then she remembered that this was Kirkby Milthwaite and that news travelled faster than a summer swallow.

'Is it true?' Mrs Purdie asked.

'Yes,' Molly said, 'but I won't be away for long.'

'It's a bit sudden, isn't it?'

Molly nodded. 'It is.'

The old lady's eyes crinkled at the edges. 'A young man, is it?' Mrs Purdie gazed at Molly and, for a moment, Molly thought that the old woman knew the truth. She *knew*! But how could she? Molly hadn't told a soul. She was just getting paranoid. Maybe that's what winning a large sum did to a person.

'*Not* a young man, then?' Mrs Purdie tried again, her eyes twinkling.

Molly didn't bother to say that it was because of a whole bunch of men that she was going away. The Bailey men: brother, Marty; father, Magnus; and, at the top of the hoarding hierarchy, Granville – 'Old Bailey' himself. Each one would swoop down on her millions, like starved vultures, if they got to hear about it, and she wasn't about to let that happen. Molly was going on a spending spree but it was going to be like no other spending spree before. And, in the process, she was going to change the route of the Baileys once and for all.

Chapter Four

Tom Mackenzie stood outside the George Hotel, wincing as the rain finally found its way down his collar. He looked up at the pearly grey sky. So much for summer, he thought. This was one of the loveliest parts of the country – when the sun was shining. He loved the gently rolling fields with their mile-high hedgerows, and the villages with more ducks than people. He loved the quietness of the land: the way the flint churches seemed to grow out of the ebony soil. Yet it was this very quietness that he found so hateful in his job because, lovely as it all was, rolling fields and candy-coloured cottages didn't exactly provide riveting copy. He'd long grown tired of the absurd annual tractor race, the endless debates over new bypasses, and local shop robberies. They just weren't the kind of news stories to stir his blood and make his fingers race feverishly over his keyboard.

In short, he was bored, and it was beginning to show in his work. Only last week the editor had shouted across the small open-plan office, 'Mackenzie, you great arse! You've got Brenda Myhill married to her own brother here!'

Tom hadn't bothered to apologise. He'd rewritten his copy and gone home. But it couldn't go on like this. He'd often asked himself why he was letting his life leak away when he knew there could be so much more. But where? Where was this life he wanted to lead? One thing was for certain: it wasn't hanging around outside hotels in the hope that a D-list celebrity might show his head and make a comment about his relationship with his much younger co-star in last year's Christmas panto.

So what was it that kept him going? That big story that would make his name? The splash that would propel him into the world of the big players? It wasn't really likely to happen in a backwater of East Anglia. But you never could tell, and that's what kept him sane: the promise of something bigger and better just over the horizon. In the meantime, he was freezing his butt off in the middle of a Suffolk summer.

Sod it, he thought. He was going to do his shopping. Shaking a hand through his dark-blond hair, which had almost turned black in the persistent drizzle, he headed for his car.

There weren't many advantages to living in the middle of the country but farm shops were one of them. Tom loved the fact that the goods for sale were grown only a few yards away and wouldn't have been flown across oceans with the possibility of foreign creepy-crawlies as travelling companions.

As he drove along the country lanes, he felt himself begin to thaw out. It had crossed his mind that he could probably get away with spending his entire career in his car, just driving around the county, making the stories up in his head.

'After a night of torrential rain, Mr Mandrake was shocked to find the river running through his sock drawer.' Or 'For centuries, this village has been the home of the annual duck and teaspoon race.' Nobody would notice because they were exactly the kinds of things the local paper was full of each week.

Tom turned off the road into what was really still part of a field but which passed for a car park when it wasn't a bog. He took care to avoid the potholes and kept half an eye on his rear-view mirror, making sure his guitar wasn't getting a rough ride. Perhaps he should have put it on the back seat and secured the safety belt around it rather than leaving it to roll around on the floor.

He parked the car and leant back to inspect it for damage. Being second hand, it already had one or two imperfections, so he really couldn't afford any more. He knew he should be more careful with it yet, because he could never bear to be without it, it was constantly flung from living room to car as he moved around, enabling him to strum whenever opportunity and urge coincided. But now he had potatoes on his mind so, repositioning the pale-bodied instrument to prevent further damage, he headed into the shop.

There was nobody about, which was just how he liked it. For a reporter, he found general, everyday conversation hard. The 'hello, how are you' stuff always seemed stilted and unnecessary. People normally weren't interested anyway, so why bother? It was another of the reasons why he favoured this shop, because the man who ran it liked conversation about as much as Tom did.

His name was Pike. Tom had once asked his name and, whilst pouring the contents of a man-sized bag of potatoes into a display, he'd simply said 'Pike'. Was it his surname or first name? Tom was never quite sure but one thing was certain, he was a man of very few words, most of them blasphemous or cripplingly rude. But somewhere, under the fleece body warmer, checked shirt and thermals, which he wore despite the change of the seasons, there was a heart of gold. Tom was almost sure of it.

Either way, Pike was quite a character. Tom had always thought it rather fitting that he should have a cauliflower ear and a nose like a Maris Piper, and he loved the way he moved over the shop floor, his shoulders hunched to within kissing-distance of his ears, and his heavy boots grazing the bare floorboards.

Piling his basket high with fruit and veg, he took it to the till. Pike was on the phone but nodded to let him know he wouldn't be long.

'You jammy bastard!' he was saying. 'I wish my honesty box was as full.'

Tom's ears pricked up. It was the occupational hazard of being a journalist.

'And you've no idea who could've left it?' Pike sucked in a good amount of air very noisily. '*Je*-sus!' There was a pause and a good deal of head-shaking. 'Well send some down this way if you don't know what to do with it. All right. Talk soon.'

'Everything all right?' Tom asked as Pike ran his massive hands through his sparse, sandy hair. He looked slightly drunk on the news he'd just received.

'That jammy bastard, Wilfred, has just had a windfall. Seems he found five thousand pounds in his honesty box this morning.'

'Really?'

'*One hundred* fifty-pound notes. Can you believe it!'

'What on earth does he sell to warrant that much?'

'That's just it!' Pike said, shaking his head in wonder. 'He only had a couple of caulis by the side of the road.'

'Blimey,' Tom agreed. 'Not a bad return.'

'Who the hell would do something like that?' Pike asked, weighing Tom's goods and writing the prices down on a large piece of yellowing paper. The till had obviously broken again or hadn't been repaired since the last time.

Tom shrugged. 'Who indeed?'

'Certainly nobody round here. Bunch of mean gits.'

'Where was it, then?'

'Up in the Eden Valley in Cumbria.'

'Oh.' Tom couldn't disguise his disappointment. Just his luck that the first piece of exciting news to come his way happened to be over three hundred miles away. Nothing newsworthy ever happened within a fifty-mile radius of his newspaper. News was something that happened elsewhere; big stories broke in other reporters' neighbourhoods. And what did that mean for Tom? He pondered for a moment as Pike placed his goods into a carrier bag. If the story didn't find him, maybe he should go in search of the story.

'Pike,' he said, the name sounding strange on his tongue, 'can you ask your mate if he's reported that story to the local newspaper yet?'

Chapter Five

A tank full of petrol was a beautiful thing, Molly thought. It was partly the novelty, of course, because, previous to her win, her tank had never been above half-full. But it was the symbolism of it too; it was filled with endless possibilities. The road lay ahead, blissfully unexplored. The map on the back seat lay open, page after page of discoveries to be made. Left or right? Motorway or B-roads? Town or country? The decisions were endless, and Molly had all the time in the world to make them.

The first decision she'd made, though, had been to visit the local dogs' home. Ever since she'd moved to Kirkby Milthwaite, she'd been meaning to buy a dog, but her profits from the florist's were barely enough to feed her, let alone a dog as well, so she'd made do with weekly visits and helping out with the feeding and walking.

That's when she'd met Fizz. He had come to the kennels when a puppy and had looked like an out-of-control snowball. From the day Molly first clapped eyes on him, she knew he was meant to be hers and, because the owner of the kennels couldn't justify keeping him there until Molly could afford to look after him, she'd absolutely dreaded the thought that he might become somebody else's pet. But she hadn't had to wait long.

He was sitting beside her now in the passenger seat. As good as gold and far more precious. She wondered how they'd get along together on her mission. Would he make a good travelling companion? He certainly wouldn't be bothered about the distribution of her wealth. There wouldn't be any sanctimonious pleading as to whether she was doing the right thing. For a moment, she tried to imagine what it would be like to have Marty travelling with her.

'It's irresponsible and childish, Molly,' he'd say, shaking his head. 'It won't make you a better person, you know. People won't thank you for it, and just think how much interest you could make – *we* could make – if you invested it all wisely. You'd never have to work again.'

'But I love my work,' Molly said aloud, as if really answering him back.

He'd glower at her in disbelief. 'That's not the point.'

And Molly could argue all she liked but she knew that there was no winning with Marty. No verbal winning, anyway. So, over the years, she'd learnt to keep her thoughts to herself as she'd listened to her big brother's advice, and then went and did exactly what she wanted.

One thing was for sure, she thought, looking down at Fizz, she'd chosen her travelling companion well. She smiled to herself. At long last, she'd found the perfect male companion.

She pulled over into a lay-by for a moment, Old Faithful making a peculiar noise as she did so. The car was, of course, another thing her brother would have made a scene about. Why did she insist on driving a clapped-out old Beetle when she had a mountain of money in the bank? Why indeed? The car was old and temperamental, but it would be like losing a limb if she parted with it. At least she had the money to get it fixed now if it did decide to break down.

She grabbed the map off the back seat, quickly finding where they were. This was the sort of mapscape she loved: more green than brown, more space than roads, and not a hint of blue motorway. She looked down and examined the roads before her. Green, red, yellow or white. From Carlisle, the green was straight as a piece of taut ribbon in places, and the yellow too, whereas the reds and whites curved and crinkled like caterpillars. In true Dorothy Gale mode, she chose to follow the yellow road, sincerely hoping, for her old car's sake, that it wasn't made of bricks.

She'd never taken that road before, but the red castellations of Hadrian's Wall marked on her map looked so pretty that she wanted no other route. It was a strange feeling, though, having so much freedom. She was no longer bound by her daily routine at the shop. There was nothing she absolutely *had* to do and that felt peculiar. All she had to worry about was looking after herself, Fizz and Old Faithful. And the money.

After making the necessary arrangements for her own relatively modest future, she'd opened several bank accounts and split her win up into more manageable amounts. This enabled her to make daily withdrawals from a number of cash machines as she moved around the country. That way, she could keep her secret stash of cash in the car topped up, and the money she *deposited* on her mission would not be sequential. She wanted to remain untraceable, so she wasn't going to take any chances.

She gave a great sigh of contentment. Wasn't time the best thing money could buy? It stretched out as beautiful and enticing as the road ahead, and Molly intended to enjoy every minute of it.

Of course, she *had* been tempted by thoughts of a mad shopping spree. What woman with a few million in her bank account wouldn't be tempted to blow the whole lot? There'd been a very dodgy moment when she'd shut up shop one day and just hopped on the first train to London. Normally, the price of the ticket would have been prohibitive but she'd handed over her credit card without a second thought and headed for the big city.

What an experience that had been. Growing up in the Lake District hadn't quite prepared Molly for the level of noise in the capital. She could well understand how it had got its name the Big Smoke because she soon felt as if she'd ingested most of the pollution around her.

Then there were the crowds to contend with. Molly wasn't used to rugby-scrum streets or armpit travelling on the tube and, in her initial panic, had travelled in completely the wrong direction on the Central line and spent half an hour getting back to where she'd begun. It had been most exhausting.

Once she'd surfaced, it had been with a strange sense of unease that she'd walked down the place she'd reckoned on spending some of her winnings: New Bond Street. She felt rather like a red rose in a field of buttercups; everybody seemed to be blonde and slim with straight-cut hair, straight-cut figures and straight-cut shopping bags. Molly, with her head of dark curls and bouncy bosom, felt alarmingly alien.

And they were all so confident-looking, as if this was the most natural way to spend time, but Molly just couldn't get the hang of it. Her idea of clothes shopping was the winter and summer sales in Carlisle's department stores; shops which weren't the least bit intimidating but, here, she didn't even dare venture into some of the shops for fear of being frogmarched out again. They were all so immaculate. Even the shop assistants looked as if they graced *Vogue* in their spare time.

Then there were the price tags. Honestly, some of them had more figures than a telephone number. But everything was so beautiful, especially the jewellers with their marquise-cut diamonds, square-cut emeralds, flower-shaped rubies, and sapphires the size of lakes. Molly's eyes were dazzled and dazed. She even tried a ring on in Tiffany's, slipping an egg-sized sapphire on her finger.

'It's beeeeaaauutiful!' she cooed, her vision dissolving into its blue depths.

'And it suits you,' the assistant said, dripping compliments on her in a steady flow.

Molly held her hand up to the light, watching as the diamonds surrounding the sapphire winked at her most becomingly.

'H-how much is it?' she dared to ask, not having a clue seeing as the only item of jewellery she owned was a pair of large silver hoop earrings.

'Twelve thousand,' the assistant said without batting an eyelid, his tongue used to such dizzying figures.

Molly gulped and tried very hard not to blush. It was a mere splash in her ocean of winnings, of course, but it was still twelve thousand pounds. That was a hell of a lot of money to spend in one go on herself for a single item. What had she been thinking of? What did she want with such baubles? She was a florist! Florists didn't wear rings like that. They belonged on the fingers of film stars.

Molly slipped the ring off and handed it back to the assistant. 'It's very lovely,' she said, 'but I think I'll have a look round before making my mind up.' And, avoiding eye contact with the rows of eye-socking solitaires and gold necklaces as thick as wrists, Molly left the shop.

As soon as she was out in the street, a woman waltzed passed her, casually knocking Molly's shin with a sharp and expensive-looking carrier bag. Molly turned to watch as the high heels clicked past on the pavement. Stopping to peer in one of the designer shops, she gave her icy-blonde hair a quick flick, her hand then reaching up to stroke the gold necklace on her throat. Molly grimaced. Who really wanted to wear such a vulgar dog collar? Wasn't gold just cold? Wasn't it nicer to wear a woolly scarf against your skin? And, as for diamonds, they weren't called ice for nothing, were they?

Molly was in the wrong place. There was nothing in these shops that she wanted to buy and she certainly didn't want to turn into one of these New Bond Street clones. So, after getting on the wrong tube once again before finally finding her way back to King's Cross, she bade farewell to the city and headed north.

It had been such a relief to get back to Kirkby Milthwaite; to a life where people weren't obsessed by possessions and where the air was as rich as wine. She knew she'd made the right decision in not spending any of her money on such foolish luxuries. It wasn't in her nature to spend so freely – not on herself anyway. It was so unnatural; so unsavourily selfish, and that was partly what had given her the idea of what she should do with the bulk of her money.

Now, cranking Old Faithful up again, she pulled out of the lay-by and, hitting the accelerator, headed for Housesteads.

Tom had never been to Cumbria before. Come to think of it, he'd never been further north than Derbyshire, and that trip had only been because of a family funeral. He'd found that most people in East Anglia were the same. 'I never leave the county if I can help it,' his elderly neighbour had once told him as if it was something to be intensely proud of. 'I went to Cambridge once,' she'd elaborated, 'but I didn't like it.'

Tom was profoundly ashamed of how little he'd seen of the country. His road atlas was practically untouched. He didn't even keep it in his car because the stories he had to cover were in places he'd be able to find if blindfolded.

So where was the atlas now? He pulled a face worthy of a gurning competition as he looked round his study. Study, he thought grimly. It was his 'everything' room really. Sure, there was his computer and books but that was all that comprised the study element of the room. Then there was the chest of drawers and wardrobe which hadn't fitted in the bedroom because that's where he kept his family of smashed-up guitars. There was the second-hand futon which doubled up as a spare bed; a rowing machine which had probably forgotten it was a rowing machine and more likely thought of itself as a still life; and a huge standard lamp inherited from his grandmother. Added to that were the heaps of what he called 'unhomed items': old shirts he hadn't quite finished with but which weren't fit to be hung in the wardrobe; notepads scattered on the floor like stepping stones; picture frames he wasn't sure how to hang; rucksacks and old hiking boots; and odd-looking tools his father kept buying him in the vain hope that he'd get his house sorted out. It wasn't a pretty picture.

He started by tentatively probing one of the mountains of unhomed items with his toe but it didn't look very promising so he moved on to the next one. But there was nothing but rubbish.

At last, under an avalanche of old receipts and notepads, the road atlas was found. He bent down to pick it up and opened it, quickly finding the page he wanted. Cumbria.

'Bloomin' heck!' he whispered, giving a long, low whistle. It was a long way up north. His eyes scanned the page quickly. Other than Carlisle and the M6, there really wasn't much to it. It was all empty space up there. Did people really live there? Could a story really begin in such an unlikely place? And was it worth the travel? It was at least three hundred miles. That was a lot of driving and a lot of petrol. A lot of time too. Time he knew he wouldn't be able to get off work.

He flopped down onto the futon and puffed his cheeks out in a dragonesque sigh. He knew what his options were and it was a dangerous choice. He thought for a moment. What did he have to go on? Someone had placed an obscene amount of money in a farmer's honesty box. So what? They might be insane. They might have trespassed on the farmer's property at some point and felt an overwhelming sense of guilt.

But what if it went the other way? Maybe it wasn't just a one-off act of kindness, but the beginning of a spate. Maybe this person had found out they were dying and wanted to go out in style? Perhaps they'd inherited, or even won, a large amount of money and wanted to share their good fortune. That's what got Tom excited: the knowledge that this sort of thing didn't happen every day, and that the person behind the donation must definitely be worth writing about. But what made him think that it could pan out into a story? His guts? Maybe that was just indigestion.

He scratched his chin. It was an enormous risk but, then again, wasn't that what life was all about? It surely beat stagnating at his local news desk. He knew that if he stayed there much longer he would work himself into early dementia. There had to be more to life than writing about cemetery extensions and stolen power tools, and it was up to him to go out in search of it. He would be out on his own, yes, with absolutely no assurance that he would be successful.

Tom grinned as he suddenly realised how utterly delicious that sounded.

Chapter Six

Carolyn was trying to read the Saturday TV listings but it was virtually impossible with the noise Marty was making over the post. It was the usual early morning ritual. It didn't matter that it was the weekend, Marty's stress level was still at boiling point.

'*God almighty!*' he seethed, his eyes scanning the phone bill which ran into half a dozen pages. 'Bloody hell,' he exclaimed over the Visa bill.

'Everything all right?' Carolyn dared to ask, knowing full well what the answer would be.

Marty shook his head, his eyes narrowed, as if refusing to take all the information in. 'Look at this,' he said, pushing the phone bill towards her.

'What?'

'All these calls.'

'What about them?'

'There are *hundreds* of them!'

Carolyn put the TV guide down and reluctantly examined the phone bill. 'Oh, Marty – they're to your own sister,' she said, pushing the bill back to him and returning her eyes to the film listings.

'It would be cheaper to get in a taxi and visit her.'

Carolyn tutted. Sometimes a tut was the only possible response to Marty.

'What do you two talk about, anyway?' he asked.

'*You*, of course!' Carolyn said, trying to force a little smile out of him, but it didn't work.

'That isn't funny. And neither is the cost of this quarter's bill.'

'Let me see.' Carolyn pulled the sheets of paper out of his hand. 'Well, most of this is service charge,' she said. 'I don't know what you're fussing about. It's not as if we go out on the town all the time, is it?'

'What do you mean?'

'I mean, we never eat out like other couples. We never go to the theatre or cinema or clubs.'

'You want to go clubbing?'

'No,' Carolyn sighed, 'that's not what I meant. It's just we don't exactly spend a fortune on ourselves, do we?'

Marty's eyes wrinkled up until they were tiny chinks of brown. 'Why would we do that?'

Carolyn stared at him. She sometimes wondered if he was having her on but, more often than not, he was deadly serious. 'People do occasionally go out, you know.' She smiled encouragingly. 'When was the last time we went out? And—' she raised her hand in the air, 'you're not allowed to include going round Old Bailey's.'

Marty shook his head and looked down at the bills that had now obscured most of the coffee table.

'Come on!' Carolyn said. 'When was it?'

He shrugged his shoulders in defeat. 'I don't know.'

'Exactly! I think the last social event we attended was our own wedding and my dad paid for that.'

'You don't have to spend money in order to have fun,' Marty pointed out.

'I know,' Carolyn sighed, 'but we don't spend *any* money, do we? And just look at the state of this house! There's paint flaking off the front door, and these carpets are really disgusting.'

Marty glowered at her. 'You want to spend more money?'

'No!' Carolyn was starting to become exasperated. He wasn't understanding her at all, was he? 'I just think we should lighten up in our attitude towards money.' By *we*, she did, of course, mean Marty. 'You know Molly and I get along really well and I don't think you should make such a big deal about the odd phone call.' Carolyn could see the words 'odd phone call' on the tip of Marty's tongue but he bit it and nodded instead. 'After all,' she continued, 'we hardly see her.'

'She shouldn't live in the middle of nowhere,' Marty said, shaking his head in a manner that was scarily like his grandfather.

'She doesn't live in the middle of nowhere,' Carolyn said. 'Just because you don't like the countryside, doesn't mean you shouldn't visit her now and again.' Carolyn tried to stop herself from smiling as she thought of the last time they'd visited Molly and had gone out for a walk in the woods. Carolyn had never seen anybody so startled by the sight of mud before. Marty had taken at least ten minutes to leave the safety of the car and had walked through the wood like a flamingo on stilts.

'I visit!' Marty defended himself. 'But she seems to take great pleasure in my discomfort. She deliberately winds me up. She's just like—' He stopped.

Carolyn stared at him, his mouth open but refusing to finish the sentence he'd begun. Was he thinking about her-who-shall-remain-unnamed? Was he thinking about his mother – the mysterious Cynthia? Carolyn had guessed, long ago, that Molly must surely take after her mother as there didn't seem to be an ounce of Bailey in her. But Marty had never confirmed her suspicions either way.

'Molly has a sense of humour, that's all,' Carolyn said.

'More like a sense of the ridiculous.'

'Oh, don't you just sound like the older brother?' she teased, ruffling his dark hair affectionately.

'Caro!' he complained, pulling away from her.

'Shut up and give me a kiss,' she said, undeterred by the monstrous mood he was in. She saw a gentle softening around his eyes as he turned to face her. That, she thought, was the Marty she'd fallen in love with and married, but what had happened to him? Why didn't she see him so often these days? Why did he hide himself behind a wall of bills and worries?

'Give us a kiss,' she whispered into his ear. 'And don't stop until I tell you.'

He drew closer to her and she closed her eyes as his mouth reached hers. Several seconds ticked by, slowly turning into minutes.

'Caro?' Marty said, drawing away for a brief moment.

Carolyn pulled him back towards her. 'I said, *don't stop until I tell you*!'

Marty relented and Carolyn held his face in her hands as she kissed him again. Sometimes, she thought, a woman just had to take charge.

*   *   *

Tom's arms flailed at the sound of his alarm clock. He'd forgotten to cancel it again. How many Saturday mornings had he been rudely awoken because he'd forgotten to cancel his alarm?

He sat up and yawned like a cave, and then he felt his head throbbing as if it had been slammed in a door. Not that he'd been drinking. He hadn't even a bottle of red wine vinegar in the house but he had had rather a restless night; one of those strange, sleepless, dreamless nights when you shut your eyes but the brain doesn't quite find oblivion.

He thought briefly about trying to go back to sleep again – he'd just managed about an hour before the alarm had gone off – but he dismissed it when he heard the post arrive. Flinging a housecoat around his body, he padded barefoot downstairs to see what had landed on the doormat.

One Visa bill, one phone bill, one envelope claiming he'd won some money, and another with something solid inside. He ripped it open. It was a charity begging for money and they'd included a pen to help him fill in their direct debit form. Tom sighed. As bad as he felt about it, he couldn't afford to make any donations at the moment so he put the form into his recycling bag and popped the pen into his jacket hanging up in the hallway. He was always losing pens.

Wandering through to the kitchen to make a cup of coffee, he thought about the events that had led up to his sleepless night. It had begun on Friday morning. He'd awoken with a great sense of foreboding: he had to go to work. Now, there was nothing unusual about that but, for the first time, he realised it was in his power to change the course of events. After all, if *he* didn't do it, nobody else would, would they? Everybody in this life is accountable for himself alone.

Nobody else gives a damn – really. Or, that was how Tom was feeling about things at the moment.

So he'd gone into work with heavy feet and a heavier heart. I don't want to be here, I don't want to be here, he'd chanted, until his head was filled with the noise of his own agitation, and that was when he'd done something about it. He'd got up from his desk, neatly pushing his chair under for what he knew would be the last time, and walked calmly to his boss's desk.

'Is it ready?' Bill Matthews asked without looking up from his computer.

'No,' Tom replied.

Bill looked up at him. 'What?'

'I'm leaving.'

'What for?'

'Good.'

Bill's eyebrows had crashed into each other. '*What?*'

'I've got another job,' Tom lied. Well, it was only a half-lie, really.

Bill's huge mouth had dropped open. The rest of his colleagues in the open-plan office had, by now, sussed that something interesting was happening and had downed tools.

'Since when?' Bill barked.

'Now.'

'*What?*'

'Yes,' Tom had said, casually stroking his chin, savouring the moment. 'So I'll be off then.' And he'd turned on his heels and simply walked out of the office.

'Tom Mackenzie!' Bill Matthews shouted after him. 'You won't be getting a reference out of me!'

'Don't need one!' Tom shouted back.

'You're in breach of contract!'

He was also, he thought, in breach of his brains. It had been a mad thing to do. Mad and wonderful. But what now? Was there really any money to be made from this oddball in Cumbria? He picked up his road atlas and opened it up again. His fate now lay in a stranger's hands.

In the meantime, his credit card company and the telephone company weren't going to bend sympathetic ears towards someone who'd jacked in their job on a whim. He had to make some money somehow and, as time was money, he thought he'd better make a move straight away.

He suddenly felt a wave of vigour coursing through his body, flushing out any niggling doubts or insecurities. Something told him that he could make this work; that his future began here and now.

Just then, the doorbell went. He tightened the belt on his housecoat, wondering who would call at eight o'clock on a Saturday morning. The post had already been but it could be an oversized parcel.

He opened the door. It was a parcel all right. In the shape of a little girl holding a candy-coloured suitcase in her hand.

'Hi, Daddy,' she said in a voice between a whisper and a yawn.

'*Flora!* What on earth are you doing here?'

The girl looked up through a thick blonde fringe, her eyes wide and apologetic. 'Mummy says I'm to spend the summer holidays with you.'

Chapter Seven

'How did Mummy know I'd be in?' Tom asked, having made hot chocolate for two instead of strong coffee for one.

'She said you're always in at the weekends.'

'Oh.' Tom shook his head as he cleared the clutter away from the kitchen table to make some room for his daughter. Bloody Anise, he thought, always taking advantage of his reliability. But what was he to do now? Where exactly did that leave him with his planned trip? It was one thing taking off at a moment's notice on your own but taking a ten-year-old along for the ride was a different matter altogether.

It wasn't the first time that Anise had dumped their daughter on him last minute either. There was that time when she'd shown up at the office claiming she had roaring toothache and couldn't cope with Flora. The office had come to a complete standstill: the men staring goggle-eyed at Anise whilst the women clucked and cooed over three-year-old Flora. He'd had to take the rest of the day off work.

Then there'd been the evening he'd prepared a meal for Samantha, the girl he'd been seeing, on and off, for two months. They'd just been about to embark on dessert when a knock at the door and a seven-year-old in her pyjamas had put paid to that.

Tom had never hidden the fact that he'd had a daughter: there were photos of her all over the house, but the reality of it had been too much for Samantha so she'd sashayed out of his life for ever.

'She said you never go away on holidays,' Flora said, bringing her father back into the present. He watched as she blew her hot chocolate into brown waves.

'She did, did she?'

Flora nodded. 'Yes.'

'What else did Mummy say?'

Flora looked pensive. 'She said you're always on about not seeing enough of me, and that you can bloody well see plenty of me this summer.'

Tom frowned. 'Watch your language!'

'But that's what she said.'

'I believe you.'

Flora cupped her hands round the teddy bear mug Tom kept in his cupboard for her. It hadn't occurred to him that it was the summer holidays. This wasn't going to be easy.

'The thing is, Flora, I have to work. Surely Mummy knows that?'

Flora gazed into her mug. 'She told me she's going away. She says she'll be away all summer.'

'*All* summer?'

Flora nodded. 'She's leaving tomorrow.'

'And I suppose she's going with Jean-Philippe?' Tom gritted his teeth as he realised how bitter he sounded. It wasn't a nice trait in a father, especially at the breakfast table.

'Don't you or Mummy want me?' Flora suddenly said.

'Of *course* we do.' Tom felt his heart swell. What on earth was he thinking of? He was probably laying the foundations for years of very expensive therapy. 'I'd do *any*thing for you!' He gave her little body a huge hug and kissed her cheek with a resounding smack. 'The only problem is, I'm going away too.'

'Where?'

'Well, I don't really know yet. But I'm not sure you'd want to come. It's a long way, you see.'

'I don't mind long ways,' she said enthusiastically, as if she were aware that she had to promote herself.

Tom sat down opposite her. 'It's a long way, it won't be much fun, and I'll be working. I'll be staying in horribly cheap hotels, getting up at the crack of dawn, eating on the hoof, and I'll probably be in a constant foul mood.'

'So what's new?'

Tom laughed. 'You sound just like your mother sometimes.'

Flora smiled back at him. 'So when do we leave?'

How did the Romans put up with the intense cold of Northumberland? Molly wondered, winding her window up. And how did they manage it in tunics and sandals when she was shivering in jumper and jeans? They must have been awfully homesick. It was a lonely kind of countryside too and, in a way, it was beginning to depress her. Maybe it was time to head south.

She'd done a lot of thinking over the last few hours. Her trip to the Roman fort of Housesteads had provided her with the opportunity to just sit and think. She shook her head as she remembered how she'd felt sitting on an uncomfortable piece of Roman wall. Surely there was no lonelier place than Housesteads? It was such a strange, sparse landscape occupied by triangular hills and conspiring copses – the sort MacDuff's army might have moved behind – and the great stretches of Hadrian's Wall dominated the landscape. Other than those features, there was little else except the wind. It had been the perfect place for contemplation; for thinking about her journey and what lay ahead. She'd even gone as far as getting her notepad out but had only succeeded in doodling a little picture of Fizz.

Had she really wanted to make a plan? Probably not. Surely that would have taken all the fun out of things. For a moment, she weighed up the pros and cons of planning; thinking, inevitably, of her mother and father.

She remembered when she'd first noticed the difference between them. At their family home, her father had always been in charge of the front garden and it was the picture of neatness: a narrow brick path leading in a regimentally straight line to the door; the grass permanently mown to billiard table baldness, and two conifers that didn't dare to grow out of alignment for fear of the shears. The back garden had belonged to her mother. Molly had once asked her how she arranged the flowers and her mother had looked at her as if she was quite mad. 'Arrange flowers?' Cynthia had laughed her musical laugh. 'Molly, *my darling*, you don't think I'm the sort to arrange flowers, do you? Heaven forbid! They arrange themselves. Look!' She'd pointed to the profusion of pinks, blues, whites and mauves which knitted together in a blowsy bounty. It was heavenly.

Molly could still almost smell the garden as if a naughty wind had caught hold of it from her past and was winging it to her. It was then that she'd decided she wasn't going to have a plan. She'd got as far as writing one to ten on it: a good, strong plan – her father would have been proud of her. But she was her mother's daughter. So she'd torn it out neatly and then ripped it up into little pieces, sending the recycled shreds into the wind to disperse as freely as her mother's flowers.

No, she didn't want to start timetabling things. It would be no good trying to compartmentalise counties and divide her winnings up into likely numbers of beneficiaries. That would take all the fun out of things.

No, she was going to suppress her father's organisational genes and give free rein to her mother's spontaneous genes instead.

Chapter Eight

Tom was running around like a man possessed. He'd almost forgotten Flora was sitting in the front room in his hurry to get things organised.

'The first thing we've got to do is pack,' he said, beating the palm of his left hand with his right as if choreographing a group of invisible dancers.

Flora picked up her pink suitcase and pointed to it. 'I've packed already – look!'

'Yes. Good,' Tom said absent-mindedly. 'Now, what do *I* need?'

'Clothes?'

'Clothes,' Tom repeated. 'Yes,' he said, as if methodically packing in his brain.

Flora followed him upstairs and watched as he emptied his worldly goods out onto the bed. It was terrible. It was as if all the rejects from the local charity shop had been dumped onto his duvet.

'There's a big hole in this one,' Flora said, picking up an old denim shirt.

'And there's an even bigger one in this one!' Tom said.

Flora giggled as he wiggled his finger through it. 'Shall we go shopping?' she suggested, the credit-card-pushing genes of her mother already apparent.

'No. We haven't time,' Tom said, not bothering to add that he didn't have the money either. 'Chuck these in that sports bag over there,' he said, selecting six shirts that had seen better days five years ago, 'and empty that top drawer too.'

Tom ventured into the 'everything' room and began to sift through the mountains of notepads on the floor. How many would he need? All of them? He knelt down to choose.

'Daddy!' Flora gasped as she poked her head round the door. 'You really should tidy your room!'

He turned round and saw her stern face. 'Who's the parent here?' he asked, but he couldn't keep the laugh out of his voice.

'If this was *my* room, Mummy wouldn't let me have any tea until I'd tidied it.'

'Well, I don't live with Mummy anymore, do I?' he said somewhat tersely, and instantly regretted it as he saw a dark shadow pass over Flora's face.

He got up off the floor and walked across the room to ruffle her hair. 'Sorry,' he whispered, kissing the top of her head. 'I shouldn't have said that.'

''Sokay,' she said. 'None of my friends' parents live together. I don't mind.'

Tom gave her a squeeze. God, he thought, what a mess, and he wasn't talking about the state of his room.

'It means I get to have two homes instead of just one,' she added.

Tom looked down at her. Was this child for real? How could one be so rational at the age of ten? He was sure he hadn't been half as wise when he was a child.

'Well, for the next couple of weeks or so, we're not going to have a proper home,' he told her. 'Are you sure you still want to come with me?'

'You wouldn't want to go on your own, would you?' she asked, looking up at him with questioning eyes.

'Nah!' he said. 'That wouldn't be much fun, would it?'

'So when do we go?'

'After lunch,' Tom said and then frowned. Was there actually any food in the house?

They went downstairs to find out. He knew Flora was used to eating out of tins when she stayed with him but he'd like to be able to offer her something a bit different just once.

'What would you like?' he asked over his shoulder, crossing his fingers that he'd be able to find it.

'I'm not really that hungry,' she said, 'but I wouldn't mind some tomato soup.'

Tom smiled as he opened a cupboard. Tomato soup was the right answer.

Molly could smell soup – tomato soup – floating up through the floorboards of the bed and breakfast. It was ten-thirty in the evening and the owner was probably sitting down to tea at last.

Molly closed her eyes and floated back into her past on the scent. She was sat at the enormous kitchen table in their house. She was ten years old.

It was a wet Saturday afternoon and Molly and Marty had had enough of each other's company so Cynthia had called them into the kitchen.

Without saying a word, she placed a piece of paper before each of them, together with a pencil.

'I'm too old to draw,' Marty whined.

'So am I,' Molly said.

'We're not going to draw. We're going to write,' Cynthia said.

'We write at school. I'm not writing on a Saturday,' Marty complained.

Cynthia smiled at him. 'It's not school writing I want you to do.'

Molly looked up at her mother. 'What, then?'

'I want you to make a wish list of everything you want in the world.'

'A wish list?' Molly repeated.

'Yes.'

'What's a wish list?'

Cynthia paused for a moment, her eyes wide and wise. 'It's a list of everything you want. For example, it could have things on it – like toys and games and bikes, but it must also have other things too – like happiness, a fulfilling job and good luck.'

'That sounds like a strange list to me,' Marty observed.

'The stranger the better,' Cynthia laughed. 'I want you to *really* think about everything you want in the world.'

Molly and Marty stared at their mother. How did she come up with these ideas? Did she have a secret book somewhere on how to keep children amused on wet afternoons?

'I'll make us some soup whilst you're doing it,' she said, leaving them to look at their blank sheets of paper with bemused faces.

As Cynthia was heating the soup, Molly and Marty covered

their sheets of paper in an endless stream of wishes. The thick smell of tomato rose from the hob and flooded their nostrils with a homely warmth. It was only an ordinary can of tomato soup but something mysterious and wonderful happened in between opening the can and serving it which made it taste like nothing else in the world.

'Have you written your lists?' Cynthia asked, pausing a few minutes later with their bowls of soup, as if she meant to trade them for their wishes.

'Yes,' Molly said, her mouth practically watering at the savoury scent.

'I've got nearly thirty!' Marty boasted.

'Good,' Cynthia said. 'Now, before you have your soup, I want you to read your lists to yourself, but I don't want to know what's on them.'

Molly and Marty obeyed, Molly wondering if her mother was about to perform some magic trick on them and guess their lists.

'Have you read them?' she asked, and Molly and Marty nodded. 'Know them by heart?' Again they nodded. 'Right. Now tear them up.'

'What?' Marty's eyes narrowed.

'Really?' Molly's eyes widened.

'Yes.'

'Why?' Marty asked.

'Because I don't want you to think about what *you* want, because that's not always the most important thing in the world.' She smiled as she saw their faces cloud over. 'What I *really* want you to do is to make a wish list for somebody else, listing what you wish *them* to have in their lives. You could do each other's if you like.' She put the soup down in front of them and then handed them another piece of paper each.

Marty pulled a sour face and Molly pulled one back at him.

'I'm going to do yours,' Molly told her mum.

'All right,' she said, handing them a spoon each. 'Whose are you going to do, Marty?'

He looked thoughtful for a moment. Molly watched him closely, trying to read the thoughts somersaulting round his brain.

'Nobody's,' he said, his voice short and surly. 'It's a waste of time.'

Nothing had changed there then, Molly thought, bending to tickle Fizz's ears and getting another whiff of soup from the kitchen below her bedroom. Even today, whenever Molly smelt tomato soup, she couldn't help but think of her wish list. Had that been her mother's intention, she wondered? Did Marty still think of it too? She'd never found out what had been on her brother's list but it had certainly been a great deal longer than her own. He'd almost worn his pencil down writing it.

She tried to remember what she'd put on her list. There'd been the obvious kid stuff but what had the other wishes been, and what had been on her list for her mother? It hadn't included a life without them, had it? She hadn't wished for her mother to leave them the very next year.

Molly looked out of her window. Darkness had claimed the land. The hills were now part of the sky but she could still feel their presence, brooding and bruising. Somewhere, out in all that darkness, was her mother. What would she advise her to do now, Molly wondered? Was this journey the most perfect wish list ever?

Chapter Nine

'I still don't understand why you have to give up Dylan,' Flora said, strapping herself into the passenger seat in the front of the car.

Tom got in next to her and sighed. 'Because there's no way I'm giving up Presley or Isaak.'

Flora puffed her cheeks out. 'What does Mike want with Dylan, anyway?'

Tom put his seat belt on and started up the car. 'It's what's called collateral.'

'Collaterwhat?'

'Collateral. It's like an exchange: I swap something precious of mine for something precious of his because I can't afford to pay him any money.'

'Doesn't he trust you, then?'

'No.'

Flora's mouth formed a perfect 'o'. 'Why?'

'Don't ask.'

Flora's 'o' turned into a stern line. How could somebody not trust her father?

'Anyway,' he said, 'Dylan isn't as precious as Presley or Isaak, and I need his laptop. I can't write a story on a guitar, can I? Anyway, a laptop's smaller. I couldn't fit all the guitars in this car.'

'Why don't you get a bigger car?' Flora asked with the innocence of someone who's never had to earn any money.

'Because I like this one,' Tom lied, wishing Flora didn't have quite so many questions that needed answering.

'Jean-Philippe's is much bigger.'

'I've no doubt it is,' Tom said through gritted teeth.

'He lets me call him JP,' Flora added, as if that was the epitome of cool.

'Does he?'

Flora nodded. 'And he has a cushion for me for the front seat.'

'You want a cushion?' Tom slowed the car down. There was a cushion somewhere in the car and, if Jean-Philippe gave his daughter a cushion, it was the least he could do.

'It's all right, Daddy.'

'No, Flo, if you want a cushion, I can get you a cushion.' He pulled over and parked, undoing his seat belt so that he could gymnast behind his seat.

'But I don't really need one.'

Tom pulled himself up from the strange position he'd got himself into and looked at her. 'You *don't* want a cushion?'

'Nah!' she said, shaking her head. 'Cushions are for babies. JP has no idea, really, does he?'

Tom laughed as he did his seat belt up again. 'No. He doesn't,' he said. 'How could he possibly have mistaken you for anything other than a young lady?'

Twenty minutes later, with Dylan duly swapped for Mike's

laptop, they hit the road. It was the perfect day to travel, Tom thought, driving with the window wound down, the warm wind blowing the cobwebs away, and his job had provided him ample opportunities to collect cobwebs. His whole body felt full of them. Well, now it was time to break free and to go in search of the person he knew he could be.

He tried not to think of the hundreds of miles that lay ahead of them: of the possible delays, accidents, roadworks, nasty service areas and petrol cost. Instead, he focused on the positive things: the sense of freedom, the glorious sunshine, the possibility of an exciting story. And his daughter, Flora.

He glanced quickly at her. She was staring out of her window, humming to a song on the radio he'd never heard before. Probably some band who needed at least five members to sing a song. Not like his great idols. Not like Chris Isaak.

The only thing he hadn't banked on with having his daughter with him was the number of stops she would request. Were all girls the same? he wondered, as he pulled into the third service station. The journey was going to take far longer than he'd anticipated if they had to stop every hour or so.

Flicking through a magazine in a shop that sold everything, Tom waited for Flora to surface from the Ladies'. He wasn't keen on her going in there on her own but what choice did he have? She wasn't small enough for him to take her into the Gents' with him, and he'd get himself into terrible trouble if he followed her into the Ladies' so he positioned himself in the shop from where he could keep an eye on things.

He watched an old lady wander in. She was probably all right: no threat there. Then, a teenager with a nose ring sashayed in behind her. Tom felt a wave of panic rippling through his body. He put the magazine back on the rack but ended up dropping it because he didn't want to remove his eyes from the ladies' toilets. Was this teenager a potential kidnapper? A murderer? All sorts of wild thoughts whipped through his brain as he left the shop, legging it across the hallway to stand outside the toilets, craning to hear signs of Flora.

He heard a hand-dryer. Flora? It was impossible to tell with the amount of noise around him. But no, it wasn't Flora; it was the old woman.

'Excuse me,' Tom said, his voice croaky in his dry throat. 'Did you see a little girl in there?'

The old woman glared at him as if he were some kind of pervert.

'She's my daughter,' he explained, but the old woman wasn't interested.

He had no choice but to wait. What was taking her so long? What did the female of the species do in toilets? With men, it was in and out in two shakes, so to speak, but he had a feeling that women had a hairdo and manicure somewhere between the hand-drying and the departing bit.

Another toilet flushed. Tom felt his heartbeat accelerate.

'Flora?' he called out as he heard the sound of water again. Then the hand-dryer. God, what a nightmare. He was never letting his daughter out of his sight again.

'Daddy?'

Tom's eyes doubled in size as he saw her walking out.

'Flora? *Where* have you been?'

She looked at him as if he had completely lost his head. 'I've been to the toilet,' she said. 'I told you.'

Tom nodded, his heartbeat slowly returning to normality.

She'd been to the toilet, that was all. She was fine; he was stupid. This was what being a parent was all about, wasn't it?

He scratched his head and almost went flying when the teenager with the nose ring and attitude knocked into him.

'Cool!' Flora sighed. 'Did you see her nose ring?'

'Yes. It's disgusting.'

'Can I have one?'

'No, you can't,' Tom said, placing a very firm hand in the small of Flora's back and propelling her out to the car park.

It was Saturday again and Carolyn opened her eyes and shut them immediately as a heavenly column of sun flooded the bedroom. They'd only had an opportunity to partially close the curtains as they'd charged into the bedroom after a marathon kissing session on the sofa, and the startling sunshine hurt her eyes after her blissful doze.

She allowed herself a little smile as she looked at Marty. His face was as flushed as a summer strawberry but that wasn't surprising really. For the best part of an hour, she'd had his undivided attention. No money talk. No bill talk. Just bliss.

She traced her finger along his jawline and did a little tap dance with her fingers on his mouth, giggling as he flinched.

'Wake up, sleepyhead,' she whispered, watching as his eyes opened. She'd never seen eyes quite so brown before. They were like the bitterest chocolate and his lashes were the sort women spent a fortune trying to achieve. Why was that? Why were men given eyelashes like that? Carolyn wondered. Her own were as pale as daisies.

'What time is it?' Marty asked.

Carolyn yawned and leant up on an elbow to see her alarm clock. 'Just after one.'

'NO!'

'Yes!'

'Damnation!' Marty was up and out of the bed in a flash – quite literally.

'Marty! Where are you going?'

'We're late for Granddad's,' he said, streaking into the en suite.

Carolyn groaned. She'd almost forgotten about their weekly date with doom. Almost, but not quite. How could one forget the social low-spot of the week?

'Marty?' she shouted above the hiss of the shower. He couldn't hear so she padded through. 'What are you rushing for? We've got all day.' She pulled back the shower curtain.

'Caro! Don't do that! The floor will get wet.'

She bit her lip and tried again. 'I'm not going with you, you know.'

Marty stopped lathering-up for a moment. 'What?'

'You heard me. I'm not coming with you.'

He turned the shower off and stood dripping for a moment. Carolyn passed him his towel. 'We always go over on a Saturday,' he said slowly, patting his hair dry.

'You don't have to tell *me* that.'

'So what's different about this weekend?'

Carolyn chewed her bottom lip as she tried to find the words to express how she really felt. 'Nothing's different about this weekend. It's just that I'm fed up of the same old routine.'

'Why haven't you said anything before?'

Carolyn started. What was this? A caring Marty? It didn't

seem very likely. 'Well, I know how much it means to you.'

Marty stepped out of the shower, quickly drying himself. 'OK,' he said, very calmly and very quietly. 'We won't go.'

Carolyn felt herself smiling. This was unbelievable. She'd never thought he'd be so understanding. If she'd thought, for half a minute, that all she had to do to get out of their boring routine was to say something, she wouldn't have suffered in silence for so long.

'Great,' she said, watching as he hung his towel up and threw his body into his housecoat. He then stepped forward and planted a kiss on her forehead.

'But we'll have to go next weekend,' he said. 'We can't miss two weekends in a row.'

Chapter Ten

'Wake up, Flora!' Tom whispered. She looked so peaceful that it seemed almost a crime to disturb her but they had to make a start. It was eight o'clock and Tom was keen to get to the farm and start hunting down his story.

Her grey eyes opened. 'I'm sleepy.'

'You can sleep in the car. But we've got to get moving. Go and have a wash and get dressed.'

'OK,' Flora said, yawning like a lion.

Tom finished packing his overnight bag and sat down on the bed, picking up Isaak and strumming. He would never dream of leaving his beloved guitars in the car unattended. Flora had teased him the night before by asking if the second bed in the room was for her or the guitars.

He played a few bars of 'Yellow Bird' and had just stopped when a head popped round from the bathroom door.

'Don't stop!' Flora said. 'That was lovely.'

Tom smiled. It was nice to be appreciated. Anise used to tell him to pack it in and grow up; said he was an outdated hippie and that he should get a proper pastime like DIY.

She'd rather have had him plumbing than strumming.

Once Flora had washed, dressed and packed, they went downstairs to eat and then left the bed and breakfast and headed for the Eden Valley. It was a warm morning and they wound the windows down, luxuriating in the velvet-soft air. The countryside itself was a paradise of rivers, sandstone bridges and rolling fields. Tom wondered why he'd never heard of it before, but he guessed that the close proximity of the Lake District probably accounted for it.

He reached in the glove compartment for the address Pike had given him. They couldn't be far away now.

Sure enough, a few more bends in the road and Gilt View Farm revealed itself. Tom slowed down to take the unmade road and was soon greeted by a huddle of outbuildings. He parked under the shade of an enormous sycamore tree.

'Are you coming, Flo?'

Flora nodded. 'You don't want me to keep an eye on the guitars.'

'They should be all right. We're in the middle of nowhere,' Tom smiled.

They got out of the car and Tom rolled his sleeves up above his elbows. He hadn't caught the sun so far this summer, not with the endless East Anglian rain, and his skin was disappointingly pale, but a few days like this and he'd be sporting a golden glow in no time.

He walked towards the farmyard followed by Flora. He was on time, but there was no sign of Wilfred Barton. Tom eyed the outbuildings, and wondered if it was worth making his way to the farmhouse. He didn't know much about farming but guessed that most farmers didn't spend that much time indoors, so decided to hang around the farmyard and hope somebody would show up.

No sooner had they both made themselves comfortable against an old gate than they saw someone appear from one of the outbuildings.

'Hello?' Tom shouted across the yard. 'Mr Barton?'

The man in a green cap with a white moustache nodded.

'I'm Tom Mackenzie. Friend of Pike's. And this is my daughter, Flo.'

'Aye. I was told you'd be comin'.'

'Thanks for making time to see me.' Tom tried hard not to stare at the farmer's moustache but it was so astonishingly white that he couldn't take his eyes off it. It was as if a little pile of snow had settled along the top of the farmer's mouth.

'So, what is it you want to know?' Mr Barton asked, joining them at the gate.

'I'm rather interested in finding out who left you the money in your honesty box.'

'Yes,' Mr Barton chuckled. 'So am I!'

'You mean, you have no idea?'

'No,' he said, scratching his chin and shaking his head slowly.

'You've no way of finding out?'

'How could I find out?'

Tom shrugged. 'No security cameras?'

'No money for that sort of equipment. *Good God!*'

'And nobody saw anything?'

'Round here? Nope.'

Tom nodded. He supposed that the houses were far too well detached for anything like neighbourhood watch to be successful.

'So how do you know the money was a gift – that it was meant for you?'

'Well,' Barton scratched his chin again. 'I don't, do I?'

'And there was nothing to give away the person who left it?'

'No,' Barton said. ''Cept if you count a flower. There was a yellow flower in with the money.'

Tom's eyes widened with promise. 'Can I see it?'

Barton shrugged. 'Wife wanted to press it. She's sentimental like.'

'What kind of flower is it?'

Barton scratched his chin again. 'I don't rightly know – some sort of daisy, maybe. But not a wild flower. I'd say it were definitely a bought one.'

He led the way, in a strange half-shuffle, across the courtyard to the farmhouse. It was little more than a shack really, and didn't even look as substantial as some of the outbuildings.

Inside seemed incredibly dark after the intense light of the summer day but, as soon as Tom's eyes had adjusted, he was able to take in his surroundings. There wasn't much to see really. A few old wooden chairs stood around a large kitchen table, a cat sat quietly licking itself in a corner, and an old clock chimed sonorously. Flora went to make a fuss of the cat and Barton moved over to a large dresser stacked with mugs and papers.

'It's 'ere somewhere,' he said, his thick hands paddling through the unopened bills and booklets covered in muddy footprints. Tom grinned.

''Ere!' Barton said at last, sending a cascade of envelopes onto the flagged floor.

Tom reached out and took what looked like a diary from his hands. 'May I?' he asked. Barton nodded, and Tom opened it. Page after page of tiny writing in black ink greeted his eyes. Someone kept themselves busy, he thought, but he wasn't here to read the secret journal of a farmer's wife.

'It's at back,' Barton said.

Tom turned to the back, and there, as bright as summer sunshine, was the flower.

'You can take it out if yer like,' Barton nodded.

Tom picked it up. It still looked fresh, despite having its life force pressed out of it prematurely. It was the most beautiful yellow he'd ever seen: warm and glowing, happy and hopeful.

'It's lovely,' he said, replacing it in the diary. 'Thank you for letting me see it.'

'Does it help?'

Tom frowned. 'I'm not sure yet.'

'Wish I knew who it was. You've no idea what a godsend that money was.'

'What will you be using it for?'

Barton chuckled. 'Have you seen the state of this place?'

Tom smiled.

Barton shook his head slowly and looked down at his boots. 'It's bin a strange old time. We've never bin out of the papers recently, what with foot and mouth and other disasters.'

'You mean you're a bit of a local celebrity?'

He chuckled again. 'Don't know about that!'

'But enough for someone to hear about you and want to help you?'

Barton stared at him as if the thought had never occurred to him. 'Maybe,' he said at length.

* * *

After having his hand crunched in Barton's enormous one, Tom and Flora left the farm. They drove back down the farm track and, because it was such a glorious day, decided to stop by the river and have a bit of open-air brunch.

'Did you get your story, Daddy?' Flora asked once they'd found a grassy bank and opened an economy packet of crisps and a bottle of Coke.

Tom sucked in a great lungful of sweet air and then sighed it out. 'I'm not sure yet. I'm going to write this up and sell it to *Vive!*. I've had a word with one of my old contacts and he's told me they can use it.'

Flora wrinkled her nose.

'What?' Tom asked.

'Mummy says *Vive!*'s only good for wrapping fish and chips.'

Tom tutted. *Vive!* had only been in business for a year but had already gained a reputation for being a little under par when it came to scruples.

'Flora,' he explained, 'this is just the kind of story *Vive!* go for. I can't be too choosy, you know, or I'll miss out altogether and not get paid.'

'So *Vive!* will pay you?'

'Oh yes. It's not going to be much, but it might well lead to other things.'

'And do you know who we're after now?'

Tom shook his head. 'No. But I think the field's narrowed down somewhat.'

'How?'

'What kind of a person would leave a yellow flower behind, do you think?'

Flora screwed her eyes up in thought. 'A kind lady.'

'Exactly!'

She stared at her father. 'But how does that help?'

'Because we've narrowed the field down by fifty per cent – we're looking for a woman.'

'Oh.' Flora didn't sound overly excited by the prospect.

'Either that or a gay man.'

Flora's eyes widened but, for once, she didn't ask any questions. 'So what do we do now?'

Tom looked down into the river. It would be tempting to just follow the river and spend a few lazy days doing nothing but living, but then he remembered the bills on his floor at home and the fact that they didn't have much to live *on*.

'I guess we keep on travelling until something else turns up.'

As much as Molly adored her travelling companion, there was just no conversation to be had with a mongrel. She'd left Northumberland via Weardale and Teesdale, and had sneaked into North Yorkshire via Swaledale. Her whole route had provided no conversation whatsoever. She'd stopped several times: to refill the car, to walk Fizz and to buy a bag of toffees, but nobody had wanted to talk to her.

Molly, who was a natural chatterbox, was beginning to believe that she'd lost the power of speech. She seriously thought that her vocal chords must have seized up by now, and that her tongue was in grave danger of going rusty. She *had* to speak to somebody.

In one of those weird moments that life often flings at people, Molly spotted a telephone box. Not having bought herself a mobile phone yet, she parked the car alongside a village green and dug around in her pockets for some change. Silence hit her as she got out of the car. It was a silence she wanted to fill with noise but, resisting the urge to shout and scream and startle the locals, she walked over to the phone box and picked up the receiver. She knew who she was going to call. It was her best friend. The dearest friend she had ever known. She wasn't quite sure what she was going to say, after all, she'd told no one of her recent good fortune, but she just wanted to wrap herself in the warmth of conversation again.

'Carolyn?' Molly yelled the name down the phone, delighted that she still had the power of speech after all.

'Molly?'

Molly frowned. Her sister-in-law sounded so far away. She also sounded seriously depressed. 'Caro? Are you OK?'

There was a pause at the other end of the phone. 'Molly,' a little voice said at last. 'I think I'm going to leave Marty.'

Chapter Eleven

Molly felt a cold shiver travel the length of her spine. What was happening? *Leaving.* Who was leaving? She turned to look at Marty at the foot of the stairs. His face was white. She'd never seen him look so pale. He was a little ghost in a pair of blue-checked pyjamas.

Her father looked up to where she stood: a little higher up the stairs than Marty; in that no-man's land that is neither upstairs nor downstairs.

'Did you hear that, Molly?'

Molly felt her mouth open but no words offered to come out. They'd all disappeared, so she shook her head.

'Your mother's left.'

There was a space of silence that felt like a fourth person in the hallway.

Marty was the one to break it. 'When will she be back?'

Their father looked at them, his face strange – it was more like an effigy than a real face. 'She won't be coming back,' he said and, folding his arms neatly behind his back, he disappeared into the living room, leaving Molly and Marty on the stairs.

* * *

'Molly?'

Molly opened her eyes at Carolyn's voice.

'Are you still there?'

'Yes,' Molly said, shaking her head and freeing herself up to the present. 'Sorry, I just—'

'Did you hear what I said?' Carolyn asked in a shy voice.

Molly felt as if she had one ear in the past and one in the present. 'Yes,' she said, digging around in her pocket for some more change and feeding the hungry mouth of the telephone. 'But why? When did all this happen? I've only been away a few days.'

'Away? Where are you?'

Molly peered out of the phone box. 'I'm not exactly sure. Swaledale.'

'*Swale*dale?'

'Yorkshire – North Yorkshire.'

'What are you doing there?'

Molly gritted her teeth. 'I'm having a holiday.'

'Oh,' Carolyn said. 'That's nice.'

'But never mind about *me*. What's happening with *you*?' Molly could almost see Carolyn at the other end of the phone. She'd be twisting a strand of blonde hair around her fingers and her pale eyebrows would have arrowed prettily over her nose.

'I don't know, Moll. I wish you were here.'

'Where's Marty?'

'Out. He went out. I don't know where.'

'Did you fight? What happened?' Molly asked, knowing Carolyn had slipped away into herself and that she'd take some prodding before she revealed anything.

'Oh, it's the usual things,' she said in a voice which sounded strangely muted.

'Money?' Molly suggested. 'Or the time he spends with you?'

Molly felt her brain filling with images like an overactive kaleidoscope. It was happening again, wasn't it? The past had found a route into the present and was in grave danger of repeating itself.

'I can't let this happen,' Molly said, the words fleeing the safety of her mouth with little intervention from her brain.

'What?'

'Caro! You've got to try and sort this out. Marty isn't a bad man.'

'I know. I *know*!'

'He can just be a bit of an idiot sometimes but he's not beyond redemption, is he? You don't seriously believe that he can't be saved – that you've given up on him?' Molly's voice was beginning to sound anxious, overdramatic even, but she and Carolyn had had this conversation a hundred times before. At first, it had all been a big joke.

'Marty's turning into his father,' Molly would tease.

'He's a real Scrooge!' Carolyn would laugh.

'He wouldn't be able to spend money recklessly if you paid him.'

And on it would go but, as the years went on, Marty's character had intensified until he'd slowly turned into the man Molly and Carolyn had dreaded and it was no laughing matter anymore.

'You haven't really given up on him, have you?' Molly tried again after an ominous silence.

'I really don't know what to do. He just doesn't listen to me. He doesn't even try to understand what I want.'

Molly sighed. It was tough to hear such words said against

your own brother. 'Caro, listen. Don't do anything drastic. You haven't, have you?'

'Well, we argued but that's normal. And now he's gone out in a huff.'

'OK,' Molly said, trying to sound in control. 'That will give you both time to cool down a bit.'

'And then what?' Carolyn asked as if genuinely expecting Molly to hold the answer.

Wait for a miracle, Molly wanted to suggest.

'Just—' Molly wasn't sure what she was going to say but she suddenly heard pips. 'Caro! Just a minute.' She plunged her hand into her pocket but there was nothing in it but a tatty fiver. 'I've run out of change, Caro. Listen – I'll ring you soon.'

'Moll?'

The phone went dead. Molly stood looking at it for a moment, wondering if Carolyn would press 1471 and call her back. She hadn't had time to suggest that. It was ridiculous. She had over four million pounds in the bank but she didn't have any change, and that meant she'd left Carolyn in one of her peculiar moods. She'd seen them before. Carolyn might look as serene as the Venus de Milo but Molly knew that it was all a front.

With a frown you could plant potatoes in, Molly left the phone box determining two things: that she couldn't let Marty and Carolyn's marriage go the same way as her parents', and that she really should get a mobile phone.

Down by the River Eden, Tom decided that he should find a florist's before he did anything else. Like the farmer, he wasn't terribly good when it came to flowers and thought it would probably be best to try and identify the sunshine daisy before he forgot what it looked like.

Packing up their picnic, Tom and Flora took the road back towards Penrith. They hadn't gone far when Flora spotted a florist's.

'Excellent,' Tom said, pulling up and getting out of the car.

The shop was sandwiched between two old stone cottages. Trays of colourful bedding plants littered the paving and Tom had to walk in sideways to avoid knocking over a variety of gaudy displays.

A quick scan round the shop and it didn't look very promising. He couldn't see anything that looked like the sunshine daisy.

'Can I help?' asked a middle-aged lady wearing a jumper with a field of sheep on it, despite the intensity of the sun outside.

'Yes,' Tom began, giving her his best smile. 'I'm looking for a particular flower. It's kind of like a big daisy.'

'Any particular colour?'

'Yellow – like a summer sun.'

The lady came out from behind the counter and bent over some buckets at the back of the shop whereupon Tom noticed a hungry-looking sheepdog climbing up her spine.

'How about these?' she said, standing up with a bunch of the sunshine daisies in her hand.

'That's them!' Tom said, a smile filling his face at how easy his first task had been. 'What exactly are they?'

'Gerbera,' the lady said.

'Gerbera? Could you write that down for me, please?'

The lady pulled out a business card and wrote the name down.

'Are they quite common?'

'Oh yes!' the lady enthused. 'Different colours too if you want. Pink, red, orange—'

'No, no – yellow's what I want.'

'How many bunches?'

'Just one.'

'One bunch?'

'Er – no, just one, please.'

'One flower?'

'Yes please,' Tom flexed his charmer smile again, 'if that's all right.'

The lady blushed and handed Tom a single flower and the business card. 'Thank you very much,' he said as he paid. 'So these are quite popular at the moment?'

The lady nodded.

'And have you had many orders for the yellow ones? I mean, from one person?'

She eyed him, as if realising that he wasn't just interested in the flowers. 'How do you mean?'

'Has anyone been ordering these yellow gerbera?'

There was a pause as the lady thought. 'Oh!' she suddenly said, 'have you got a secret admirer, then?'

Tom laughed but, before staunchly denying it, thought he could use it to his benefit. 'As a matter of fact, yes.'

'I see!' the lady smiled, blushing again. 'And you want me to disclose who the young lady is?'

Tom widened his eyes most appealingly. 'That would be extremely kind of you.'

'Well,' the lady said, straightening her back and squaring her shoulders as if suddenly feeling important, 'I can tell you that I've had no such requests. I've sold a couple of bunches but they were to men.'

'Oh,' Tom said, the smile slipping from his face, and his eyes narrowing down to their normal size. 'Nobody else?'

She shook her head. 'Sorry to disappoint you. Perhaps you could try The Bloom Room – in Kirkby Milthwaite.'

Tom nodded. 'Thanks for your help,' he said and then, just for the hell of it, beamed her a smile again, just to see her blush.

'Any news?' Flora asked as Tom got back into the car.

'Well, I've found out that this is called a gerbera,' he said, handing her the flower.

Flora screwed up her nose. 'What a horrible name.'

'Yes,' Tom said, 'a horrible name for such a beautiful flower. I'm just going to call it a sunshine daisy.'

'That's much nicer,' Flora agreed.

After finding Kirkby Milthwaite in the road atlas, Tom pulled out and, once again, navigated round the labyrinthine lanes that laced across the Eden Valley. Flora sat twirling the sunshine daisy like a beautiful wand and Tom wondered what he was going to do with the flower. It wouldn't last very long in the heat of the car. Should he press it like Barton's wife had done? He could always buy another – the lady in the florist's had said that they were popular enough, but that meant watching this one dry out and die. Ah well, he thought, it was all in the name of research.

'Look!' Flora suddenly shouted, 'there's a florist's. Can I come in with you this time?'

'Well,' Tom said, pulling up alongside the kerb, 'you could if it wasn't closed.' Tom sighed. Just as he'd been thinking things were going his way for a change. 'Bugger.'

'Daddy!'

Tom bit his tongue. That was mild coming from him. He

was going to have to rein in his language this summer, that was for sure.

He was just about to pull out again when a young woman stopped outside the florist's and fished a key out of her pocket.

Tom leant out of his car window. 'Excuse me. Are you opening?'

The young woman turned round. 'Oh! No,' she said. 'I'm looking after it for a friend. Why?'

'I was wondering if you could help me. I've got a query about some gerbera.'

The woman smiled. 'That's the best opening line I've heard for a while.'

Tom grinned and got out of the car, nodding to Flora to stay put.

'Come on in,' the woman said. 'I don't know if I'll be able to help. This isn't my shop but I am a florist.'

Tom frowned a little as he followed her into the shop. How many florists were there in the Eden Valley?

It was a small shop with wooden floorboards and an army of silver buckets that looked sadly empty, like gaping mouths begging to be fed. On the wall, there were a number of watercolours of local scenes.

'So how come you're looking after this place?' Tom asked, trying to sound casual.

'Molly's on holiday.'

'Molly?'

'Molly Bailey. She's the owner.'

'How long is she away for?'

The woman looked at him. 'You're not a burglar or anything, are you?'

Tom laughed and shook his head. 'God! Why did you ask that? I don't look like one, do I?'

The woman smiled. 'No,' she said. 'Actually, I've never seen anyone look less like a burglar. Far too handsome. What are you, then?'

Tom looked back at the watercolours, stalling for time, wondering if he should answer. 'I'm a reporter.'

'Oh!' the woman almost screamed, as if that were far worse than being a burglar.

Tom knew that his job description often had that effect on people. Sometimes, they'd just clam up completely.

'You're not after Molly, are you? She's not in some sort of trouble, is she?'

'No, no! Nothing like that. I don't even know if it's her I want.'

The woman looked puzzled. 'Then what is it?'

Again, Tom wasn't sure if he should answer the question. He had no proof that this Molly person could help him with his story. 'I'm not sure, but I may need to be able to contact her.'

'I see,' the lady said, looking pensive.

'Does she have a mobile?'

'Molly? You must be joking. It's all she can do to keep her landline operational! Just a minute,' she suddenly said. 'There is a number here somewhere. Her brother's. He lives nearby.' She opened a drawer and produced a card. 'Here,' she said, 'I'll write it down for you.'

'Thanks,' Tom said.

'Now, what was it about gerbera?' the woman asked, a giggle colouring her voice.

'I don't suppose you'd know of anyone who's been ordering yellow gerbera recently, would you?'

The woman looked thoughtful. 'I've sold a few,' she said, 'but there's nothing unusual about that.'

'Anyone out of the ordinary?'

She shook her head. 'Usual customers.'

'So no long-term orders on them?'

'No,' she said, placing the post she'd picked up by the door onto a small filing cabinet behind the counter.

'And nothing's been ordered from here?'

'Molly went away last week.'

'I see. How long's she away for?' Tom asked. 'If it's all right me asking.'

'It's funny you should mention that, because she said she didn't know. A fortnight to begin with,' the woman said, 'but she had a dangerous sparkle in her eyes, and when Molly gets the sparkles, well, there's no telling really. I may be collecting her post for months.'

Tom grinned. 'Well, thanks for your help.'

'Is that all?' the woman asked, looking slightly disappointed.

Tom nodded, noticing for the first time how pretty she was. 'Got to go,' he said, returning her smile. 'Things to do, people to see.'

'Good luck!' the woman said.

'Thanks.'

He was just about to leave the shop when something, other than the pretty woman behind the counter, caught his eye. In the gloom of the unlit space hung a painting. But it wasn't a watercolour landscape like those in the rest of the shop. It was a painting of a single sunny gerbera.

Chapter Twelve

Molly was making the most of her new-found freedom on the North Yorkshire roads: driving round quite haphazardly; taking a right turn here, a left turn there, doubling back if there was something she'd missed, content in the realisation that the real power of money lay in freedom of choice and the ability to do exactly what you wanted.

It was then that something quite spectacular caught her eye. Standing with an unrivalled view over Swaledale was Whitton Castle. Molly had noticed it coming up on her map and gasped at her first sighting. It might have had great chunks blown out of it during the Civil War but it was still a sight to behold. Four medieval square turrets stretched high into a periwinkle sky, and the few windows lucky enough to be glassed winked in the sunshine. It was definitely time for a break from behind the wheel.

Molly followed the high-banked lane round the side of the castle and parked before putting Fizz on his lead. She wasn't sure if dogs were allowed in the castle grounds but it was worth a try.

It seemed rather quiet for a Sunday afternoon in summer, but Molly wasn't complaining. Paying her entrance fee, she headed straight for the gardens, Fizz slipping in quite unnoticed. The gardens were picture-book beautiful with the kind of view that sold jigsaws. Gently sloping, with borders full to the brim with pinks and mauves, they were easy on the eye and delightful to the nose, with low stone walls allowing the visitor's gaze to escape and wander over the expanse of Swaledale.

Spotting a stone seat in a secluded corner, Molly led the way, giving Fizz a little slack so that he could poke his head into a border stuffed with herbs.

Sitting down, she let her shoulders slump and exhaled slowly. All her worries seemed to be in that exhale: her worry about Carolyn; her concern for Marty; her fear for the future, and the constant questions she had about Cynthia. She was beginning to realise that, even with four point two million pounds in the bank, a person still couldn't banish worries.

She closed her eyes, lifting her head towards the sun. Oven-warm, she felt as if she was being slowly baked, floating in a weightless, wordless world. The universe evaporated until there was nothing but the scent of herbs and the sun on her skin to tell her she was alive.

And the faint smell of a cigar.

Molly frowned. She opened her eyes, trying to fathom where the smoke was coming from. At first, the light of the afternoon blinded her and she shut her eyes again, screwing her face up and then looking down to the ground. She was faintly aware that somebody was approaching her and looked up in time to see a tall, well-built man striding across the lawn towards her. Molly panicked. He had a definite purpose in his stride and, seeing that there was nobody else around, there was no doubt that it was *her* he wanted to talk to.

Shielding her eyes from the sun, she decided to be bold.

'Can I help you?' she asked, her voice sounding far braver than she felt. What if he was a lunatic about to strangle her with a hollyhock? Or an irate farmer who didn't appreciate Fizz in the vicinity?

'Just come to say "afternoon",' the gentleman said, in a very gentlemanly voice.

'Oh,' Molly said, taken somewhat off-guard, particularly as her eyes rested on a rather handsome face.

'Enjoying your visit?' he asked, taking a puff on his cigar and letting the smoke stream out of his mouth to vie with the herb garden for fragrance.

'Yes,' Molly replied, still not sure that she should encourage him to make conversation with her.

'Hewson,' the man said, suddenly extending a hand. 'Henry. Lord Henry.'

Molly's eyes widened. His mop of unbrushed hair and holey tank top didn't exactly conjure up her image of what a lord looked like but, as he was smiling at her so winsomely, she decided to shake hands.

'Molly,' she said.

'Pleased to meet you, Molly,' he said, winking a blue eye at her before sitting down on the stone bench. Molly moved up a fraction. There really wasn't enough room for two.

'So what do you think of my castle?' Lord Hewson asked.

Molly had to stop herself from laughing. It was certainly a line she'd never heard before but, coming from him, it didn't seem the least pretentious. It was rather cute really; rather like saying – is it all right? It's not *too* bad, is it?

'I think it's beautiful.'

'You've been inside?'

'Not yet,' Molly admitted. 'I think I'm a bit late now,' she said, glancing at her watch.

'Late? Who said? If you want to look round, I can personally guarantee you all the time you want.'

Molly stared at him for a moment. She wasn't used to being given castles. 'Thank you,' she said.

'On one condition.'

Molly had guessed that there would be a catch. 'What's that?' she asked, responding with a smile as she saw the twinkle in his eye. If he was flirting with her, she was jolly well going to flirt back.

Henry Hewson stood up, dropping his cigar to the ground and stubbing it out with a thick boot before offering Molly his arm. 'The condition is that you let *me* show you around.'

When Molly had rung off, Carolyn had found it impossible to stop herself from crying. She wished Molly hadn't chosen now to go on holiday, and that she could pop over to The Bloom Room for a cuddle and some sister-in-law-type sympathy. Molly had always understood her. Growing up with Marty as a brother had never been easy and Carolyn had always felt that she had been next in the Marty relay race when she'd married him: Molly had passed on all those niggling concerns and full-blown gripes when Carolyn had said 'I do'. But Molly still took an active interest in Marty's faults and the two women had bonded together in an attempt to iron them out for ever.

Wiping her eyes and giving her nose a good blow, Carolyn got up and walked into the kitchen. She refused, point-blank, to feel sorry for herself and switched on the kettle and grabbed a mug from off the dresser. She grimaced as she remembered the fuss that had been made about buying the dresser. She'd wanted one since she was a little girl and as soon as they'd moved in to their house had started the hunt. Marty, however, had thought the idea ridiculous.

'Why do you want things on show like that? Mugs belong in cupboards, which we've already got!'

What he'd meant was that the cupboards were already there. You didn't have to spend money when you already had built-in units. Carolyn had tried arguing but had been forced to save up the money by herself and scour the local papers for a second-hand one.

She looked at it now and sighed. It was beautiful: a piece of furniture that seemed to smile at her every time she walked into the kitchen. It was the only thing in the house that *was* smiling at the moment, she thought ruefully.

She was just about to pour hot water into her mug when there was a loud rap at the door. Was it Marty? Was he back to say sorry and that he loved her and that everything would be all right? It wouldn't be the first time. It was the same thing over and over again: Carolyn would allow things to build up before finally erupting; Marty would storm out; Carolyn would have a good cry; Marty would return with a cheap bunch of flowers by way of an apology, saying it would never happen again. Until next time. Still, even though they'd been through it all time and time again, Carolyn couldn't help praying that it was Marty at the door. But why would he be knocking? Had he forgotten his key?

Running through the living room, she opened the front door. It was Marty all right but he hadn't been the one to knock. By the look of him, he was practically knocked out.

'Carolyn, isn't it?' a young man asked, holding Marty up as best as he could.

'Yes,' Carolyn nodded.

'I'm Alec – a friend of Marty's,' he said, giving a shy half-smile. 'Well, kind of a friend. I thought I'd better help him home. I think he's had one too many.'

Carolyn's eyes widened in astonishment. 'Come in!' she said quickly and watched in horror as Marty tripped over the doorstep.

'Do you want me to help him upstairs?'

'I don't need any help,' Marty slurred.

Carolyn nodded. 'Yes, please,' she said quietly, and watched as Alec dragged a reluctant Marty up the stairs. Carolyn followed, listening to the unfamiliar groans coming from her husband. As far as she'd known, he'd never been drunk in his life. It was something he just never did. It cost too much money for a start.

'Do you know how much he's had?' Carolyn asked Alec, rather dreading the response.

'Well, I wasn't keeping track but he drank me dry,' Alec said as Marty fell onto the bed.

'You mean, you paid for him to get in this state?'

'Well,' Alec said, turning round and looking rather sheepish, 'I didn't think this would happen. I don't know,' he shrugged, 'we had a few, and a few became a lot.'

'So who drove you here?'

'I called for a taxi – it's outside. Marty's car's still at the pub.'

Carolyn shook her head.

'I'm sorry,' Alec said again.

'But you're not drunk at all?' Carolyn noticed.

'I guess I'm used to the odd drink.' Alec shuffled uneasily from one foot to the other, obviously not used to being in a strange couple's bedroom in the middle of a Sunday afternoon. 'I'd better get going – the taxi's waiting.'

They walked back downstairs.

'I'm sorry if I was a bit abrupt,' Carolyn said as he stood in the hallway. 'It's just I'm not used to seeing Marty like that.'

'No worries.'

They stood, wondering how to end the conversation with the least embarrassment possible.

'He didn't say anything to you, did he?' Carolyn asked, anxiety lacing her voice.

'About what?'

She tried to read his face, but it was a perfect blank. 'Nothing,' she said. 'Thanks for seeing him home safely.'

When the taxi pulled away, Carolyn went back upstairs to check on Marty but he was dead to the world, lost in an alcohol-induced sleep. She wondered if he'd told Alec about their argument. Was this Alec really a friend or one of those anonymous people you tell all your woes to in a moment of madness? Either way, it was typical of Marty that he had found a way to avoid paying for his own drinks and taxi home.

The coldness of the castle was giving Molly goosebumps after the warmth of the sunny garden.

'Is Fizz OK coming in?'

'Of course,' Henry said cheerily. 'As long as he doesn't cock a leg against any walls. We've got quite enough damp as it is.'

Molly smiled. 'This way?' she asked.

'After you,' he said and, rather uneasily, Molly led the way up the stone steps that spiralled out of view. Was it her imagination or was he eyeing up her expanse of bare flesh that her very short shorts revealed? If she hadn't had Fizz's lead in one hand, and her other on the cold stone wall, she would have glanced back.

'Just keep going,' Henry said from behind as they passed a chamber on their left. 'We want to go all the way,' he said.

Molly stifled the urge to giggle and tut at the same time. She was all alone in a tumbling castle with a handsome lord who seemed more than keen to entertain her. She couldn't help but smile. Nobody in the world knew where she was and that liberating thought made her feel rather naughty.

The steps seemed to go on for ever and she had a feeling that she might have stumbled across the stairway to heaven, which wasn't a bad guess as, when they reached a doorway, she realised that they'd climbed to the very top of the castle.

Stepping out into the dazzling sunlight, Molly gasped. The whole of Swaledale sprawled beneath them. She held on to a piece of wall, which didn't look altogether safe, and stared out across the fields and hills bleached with sunshine.

'Like it?' Henry asked, a strong breeze lifting his hair, trying to send it in every direction at once.

'Love it!'

'I come up here when I want to get away from it all.'

Molly turned round and saw the tiny hamlet of Whitton far below them.

'What could you possibly want to get away from when you have all this?' Molly asked, keeping a tight hold on Fizz's lead in case he decided to have a look over the battlements.

'All this is precisely what I want to get away from.'

Molly glanced back at him. 'Really?'

He gave a lopsided smile. 'Sometimes. When the bills start piling up.'

Molly nodded. 'I guess it must be rather a money pit.'

'Try money dungeon!'

'Oh dear,' Molly said, watching his face as he gazed out over the dales. He had one of those faces that was impossible to age. His skin was lightly tanned by the sun, which made his blue eyes all the more striking. Molly pondered. Late forties? There were certainly a few silver strands in his hair but she could see that it had been raven-black in his prime.

He turned round and caught her staring at him. Molly felt herself blushing but he merely smiled, and that's when it clicked. She'd thought there was something vaguely familiar about him, and now she knew whom he reminded her of. His eyes were exactly like those of Andrew Fellowes. Molly felt a smile growing in her stomach at the memory. Beautiful Andrew Fellowes, with the day-dark stubble and eyes like bright moons. She'd met him at a horticultural training day and their relationship had bloomed as quickly as a summer rose. Pity it hadn't lasted as long, Molly thought wistfully.

'Come on,' Henry said, startling Molly out of her romantic reverie as he turned and headed back down the staircase into the heart of the castle. Molly followed.

When they reached the chamber on the first floor, which had been overlooked on their way to the top, Henry motioned to Molly.

'This is what I mean,' he said. Molly glanced around. She didn't know much about medieval architecture, but it certainly looked in need of some sort of restoration programme.

Fizz gave a little whimper. 'I don't think he likes it in here,' Molly said.

'He's got good taste, then,' Henry said. 'It's horrible, isn't it?'

'I've seen happier-looking rooms,' Molly admitted with a smile.

'Follow me,' he said, 'and I'll show you a slightly happier room. Maybe we can even find a drink there.'

Going down more stairs and walking through the great hall, he ushered her into a room at the end of a short corridor, tucked away from the prying eyes of tourists. It was an office. An ancient computer slumbered on a rickety-looking desk strewn with papers. Henry obviously didn't have a secretary or, if he did, they were very slovenly because there was mess everywhere.

Molly's eyes settled on a pile of empty bottles in a glorious glassy mountain in the corner of the room.

'No recycling facilities near here, then?' she smiled.

Henry turned sharply and saw where she was looking. 'Er, no,' he said. 'We're a little out of the way. Now, I'm sure there's an untouched bottle here somewhere.' He bent down to search underneath the desk and Molly found herself staring at the rather shapely view he presented to her. Why was her heart beating like jungle drums? Was she still thinking about Andrew Fellowes? She must be. She couldn't possibly be fantasising about Lord Henry, could she, even if he did have the most dazzling eyes and the sexiest of smiles?

'Here we are!' he said, standing up with a bottle of white in his hands. 'Fancy a glass – or a mug?'

Molly nodded, trying to hide her grin. No wonder there were so many bottles if he made a habit of chatting up stray tourists.

Had she stumbled across the local Lothario? The bevy of bottles in the corner was probably the result of dozens of secret sessions at Whitton, but it was none of her business what a lord got up to in his own castle. She tried, instead, to focus on what she'd seen of the castle so far: walls that were in serious need of repointing; the lack of any furniture, which didn't exactly help to recreate what the castle must once have looked like; and encroaching damp in the second-floor bedchamber.

'Listen,' she said, her voice darkly quiet, 'I'd very much like to make a donation.'

Henry walked across the room and offered her a Snoopy mug of white wine.

'Thank you,' Molly said, aware that he had inched into her personal space in a rather predatory way, his head almost touching hers.

'You smell of lavender,' he said.

'Do I?' Molly replied, knowing full well that she didn't.

'It's trapped in your hair from the gardens.'

'Is it?' Molly said, not believing him for a moment. 'Look,' she said, trying to get back to the matter in hand, 'this donation – it's got to be confidential.'

'Of course,' he grinned, his features blurring as his forehead touched hers oh-so-lightly.

'That's absolutely clear?' she said, suddenly feeling as if she'd drunk a whole bottle of wine rather than half a Snoopy mug.

'So, tell me,' Henry said, his breath warm on her face, 'is it a nice, voluptuous figure?'

Molly could feel herself blushing again, and felt a warm shiver travel the length of her spine as his arm encircled her waist. 'Well,' she said, 'I don't think you'll be disappointed.'

Molly's Millions

VICTORIA CONNELLY

Chapter Thirteen

Wasn't it all just a little too easy, Tom wondered as they pulled away from The Bloom Room? He always got a little suspicious if things went too smoothly, as if the gods were leading him on, waiting for the right moment before throwing a colossal spanner in the works. He just couldn't shake off the fact that it had all been incredibly straightforward so far. The flower had led to a florist who'd told him of another florist – the florist's possibly owned by the person he was after, and now he'd got a contact number for this woman's brother. It just seemed far too easy. Still, he had no proof that this Molly Bailey was the one who'd left Barton five grand richer.

He looked down at the business card the lady from The Bloom Room had given him. Molly Bailey. He flipped it over. Marty Bailey. Molly and Marty. Tom smiled. Maybe they were twins. Whatever they were, they were the only lead he had so far.

He reached for his mobile phone and rang Marty's number.

'Hello?' It was a woman's voice, and she didn't sound at all happy at being disturbed on a Sunday afternoon.

'Hello,' Tom began, 'I was hoping to speak to Marty Bailey.'

'He's not available at the moment. Can I take a message?' the woman asked, sounding as clipped as a professional secretary. Tom imagined her sat at a highly polished desk with a memo pad in front of her and a very sharp pencil hovering for his message. He thought for a second. What could he say? That he was possibly chasing after this man's sister for a possible story which might possibly be big?

'Yes,' he said. 'Could he call me back?' Tom gave his mobile number and thanked her.

'Who was that?' Flora asked.

'An angry wife,' Tom said.

'Are all wives angry?'

Tom laughed. 'Most of them are most of the time.'

'Why?' Flora asked.

He started the car up. 'Because they have husbands.'

Tom and Flora spent the rest of Sunday afternoon driving round the Eden Valley before heading into Penrith for a nutritious chip supper. I'm a terrible father, Tom thought. If the upbringing of his daughter had been left to him alone, Flora would starve one moment, on a diet of baked beans and soup, and have a cholesterol problem the next with endless bags of chips and takeaways. That, he thought, was the real reason for having two parents. A child had to have a fair shot of being looked after properly.

They ate their chips and wandered around the shops, the evening light mellow on their bare arms. It was then that Tom remembered something.

'Come on,' he said, leading the way.

Tom and Flora walked towards the church of St Andrew's.

'I once read something rather interesting about this place,' he said, eyeing the beautiful red sandstone of the buildings, which were positively glowing in the rosy light of evening. 'There!'

Flora gazed over into the churchyard. 'What is it?'

'What do you think?' he asked, wanting her to try and work it out for herself.

'Is it a grave?'

'Yes.'

'But it's enormous.'

Tom nodded.

'There must be a lot of people in it,' she said, her face a mixture of wonder and horror.

'Or one very big one,' Tom said, looking across at the four hogback tomb covers carved from red sandstone and covered in intricate designs.

Flora looked up at him. 'A man – *that* big?'

'A real giant, apparently. Fifteen foot tall.'

There was a large intake of breath from Flora. 'But he wouldn't be able to fit in any of the shops.'

'Oh, he lived a long time ago – hundreds and hundreds of years ago – when they didn't have shops.'

'That was lucky, then.'

'Yes,' Tom replied, loving his daughter's innocent logic.

They turned to walk back towards the car, each thinking giant thoughts. Tom wondered what would happen if they dug the grave up to find no body there at all – just a load of old myth. It was best left undisturbed, wasn't it, so it would continue to fill people's imaginations?

He stifled the urge to laugh. Wasn't he a kind of archaeologist? Wasn't he in the very process of trying to dig some dirt about Molly Bailey, or whoever it was who had left Barton five grand? Would it all be best left to the imagination – the safe, secretive place beyond public scrutiny? Probably, but that wouldn't pay the bills, he thought. Dirt was meant to be dug. Stories weren't stories until they were told. He was the mere teller, that was all.

It was a strange job when you thought about it. He was a professional nosy parker. He'd often wondered what he'd do if he wasn't a reporter, but nothing had ever tempted him.

'You want to keep your options as open as possible at this stage,' the middle-aged careers officer at school had told him, her breath stinking of cheese and onion crisps. He had, of course, made the grave mistake of telling her that he wanted to be a writer.

'That's not a career option,' she'd told him, not noticing that he was slowly inching his chair away from her. 'You can't just become a writer.'

Tom had wanted to ask why not, but realised that that would probably necessitate a long answer and prolong his death by cheese and onion, so he quickly mumbled something about becoming a journalist. It was a word he'd always liked and the images on TV of crowds of people hanging round trendy places to thrust a tape recorder at some celebrity had always struck him as fun.

The careers officer had seemed better impressed by the word 'journalist' than 'writer', and had thrown some leaflets at him. And that had been that. Fourteen years later, and he still hadn't pushed his tape recorder into a celebrity's face.

Walking back to the car, Tom said, 'So what do you want to be, Flo? When you grow up?'

'Oh, Dad!' she groaned. 'That's sooooo boring!'

Tom grinned. He remembered how he'd hated that question when he was young. It had seemed an obsession with adults, as if they were jealous that they no longer had their youth, and their only consolation was to remind children that theirs wouldn't last for ever either.

'Sorry,' he said as they got back in the car.

'It's all right,' she said in a very adult way. 'And, if you *really* want to know, I'm going to be a writer.'

Tom tried not to splutter. 'A writer?'

Flora nodded. 'Like Julia Golding.'

'I see,' Tom said, a little disappointed that she'd not said 'I want to be a writer like my father'. She didn't see him as a writer, did she? His stories didn't count because they were nothing more than fact, and pretty fatuous fact at that. Most of the time he hated writing it, so he couldn't really expect anyone to enjoy reading it, could he?

That was the whole point of this journey now. He was a man in search of a story – a decent story – a story worth writing and reading. A tale to stir the public imagination, and to waken them to the possibilities in life. But none of that was going to happen until he'd found the person he was after, and that wasn't going to happen until he'd spoken to Marty Bailey.

Tom sighed and picked up his mobile phone.

'Hello?' the uncertain voice of the woman he'd spoken to before greeted him.

'Hello,' Tom echoed, 'It's Tom Mackenzie. I rang earlier to speak to Marty Bailey.'

There was a pause where Tom expected some sort of explanation as to why Marty Bailey hadn't phoned him back.

'Hello?' Tom said again.

'I'm sorry. He's still not available.'

'Oh,' Tom said, tapping his foot on the floor of the car and thinking that time was money and he wasn't earning any at the moment. 'Maybe you could help me? Am I talking to Mrs Bailey?'

'Yes,' the lady said, her voice threaded through with suspicion.

'So Molly Bailey is your sister-in-law?'

'Yes.'

'OK,' Tom said. 'Would it be possible to come round and have a chat?'

'I don't understand what this is all about.'

'That's why I think it would be best to have a chat. It would really help me out and wouldn't take long,' Tom said. 'You'd be doing Molly a favour too,' he lied, wincing slightly at his boldness. Still, it seemed to do the trick.

'Where are you?' she asked.

'Penrith.'

'And do you know where we are?'

'No.' Tom took a pen out of his shirt pocket and scribbled down the address as she dictated it quickly.

'It's about a ten-minute drive from Penrith,' she explained.

'Thanks,' Tom said. 'I'll see you soon.'

Tom found the place easily enough. He was getting used to the winding country lanes and huddles of stone cottages. It really was a beautiful county, he thought. He could just imagine himself in a little whitewashed cottage with extensive views over the sheep-scattered fells, bashing away at his laptop – Tom's dream sequences invariably involved his own private laptop – before pulling on a pair of stout walking boots and heading, Wordsworth-like, to the nearest pub.

'Am I allowed to come too?' Flora said, pulling Tom out of his dream sequence.

'Er,' he hesitated. He wasn't used to working with a kid alongside him. She might just put this Mrs Bailey off. 'Best not, Flo. Not this time. This woman didn't exactly seem friendly on the phone.'

'OK,' she said, not sounding unduly hurt.

'You just—' He was about to tell her to make a nosedive into a book but she already had. 'I won't be long.'

Tom got out of the car and opened the waist-high gate. Well, he *tried* to open it but it almost fell off its hinges. He looked up, half expecting someone to shout at him from one of the windows. Who did he think he was – breaking the gate like that? Nervously he tried again, managing to inch it open successfully.

Walking up the path, his boots scuffed on the uneven surface. Looking down, he noticed that the path didn't really have a surface; it was more like an unmade road. He grimaced, and then his eyes caught something: a huge hanging basket full of flowers. Tom didn't normally go for that sort of thing; he always thought flowers didn't quite work when suspended. Weren't they meant to be rooted in the earth? But at least it looked as if somebody had tried to make the best of their home. Somebody cared even if they couldn't afford to have their pathway resurfaced or their gate fixed.

Tom pressed the doorbell and waited. He was glad there was a bell because the paint on the front door looked as if it had acute eczema. He didn't have to wait long until the door was opened by a young woman.

'Mrs Bailey?'

'Mr Mackenzie?'

Tom nodded and extended his hand towards her, noticing how pretty her hazel eyes were but also how red they looked, as if she'd been crying.

'Come in,' she said somewhat formally, leading him through a grim-looking hallway which looked as if it hadn't seen a lick of paint for a good few years.

'I'm afraid my husband isn't able to see you,' she said, her eyes fixed to the floor and her cheeks seeming to flush red. 'He's unwell.'

'I'm sorry to hear that.'

Mrs Bailey looked up at him, and Tom almost felt his eyes watering in response to hers. She looked so sad.

'Can I—?' He moved a step towards her but she held up a hand and waved him away.

'I'm sorry,' she said. 'It's not been an easy day. I'll make us some tea, OK?'

Tom nodded and watched as she disappeared into the kitchen. It was a pattern he was used to. During his early days as a reporter, Tom had paid numerous house visits in order to interview people and no sooner would he get through the door than the kettle would go on. He liked that because it gave him a few valuable moments to absorb the atmosphere of the house and get a feel of the people who lived there. He'd soon got the art of dissecting a room down to two minutes flat: staring at photographs, looking for papers and magazines, and reading the spines of any books, CDs or films on show. You could tell a lot about people before asking any questions. But this lady didn't know he was a reporter so wasn't it a bit odd that she should offer to make him a cup of tea before finding out what it was he wanted? Or had it been to allow herself a few moments to regain her composure?

When she came back through to the living room with two mugs of tea, Tom noticed that her face wasn't quite so flushed.

'Oh, please sit down,' she said. Tom sat down on the sofa, his bottom immediately sucked in so deep that he almost hit the floor.

Mrs Bailey gave a nervous little laugh. 'I'm sorry about that. It's rather old. We keep meaning to replace it but just haven't got round to it. Please, why don't you sit on that chair?' She motioned to a wooden chair in the corner of the room, a blush of embarrassment colouring her face.

'No, no!' Tom said quickly. 'I'm very comfortable here, thank you.'

'I rather doubt that,' Mrs Bailey said brightly, her face lighting up at last.

There was a couple of seconds' awkward silence. Tom was the first to speak.

'I'd better tell you why I'm here,' he said, attempting to sit forward in the sofa but finding it an impossibility.

'You said something about Molly.'

'Yes. I'm a journalist,' he said, deciding to be absolutely honest, 'and I think Molly might have a rather interesting story to tell.'

'Story? Is Molly in some sort of trouble?'

'No, no!' Tom said quickly, knowing that people always jumped to the worst possible conclusion as soon as the media started to show an interest. 'But I think she might have recently...' Tom paused. How much information was he going to have to give away in order to be able to get in touch with this Molly Bailey? 'Mrs Bailey,' he began again, 'do you know where I can find Molly?'

Mrs Bailey's pretty hazel eyes crinkled at the edges as if she was trying to weigh him up. He waited a moment without pressing her further.

'She's on holiday,' she said at last, 'but why should I tell you where she is? I don't know you from Adam.'

Tom smiled. 'I think you'd be interested to know her story.'

'What story? She's on holiday!'

'Not just any old holiday, though,' Tom said, hoping that it would be enough to drop hints and that maybe, that way, he could get the information he required.

'What do you mean? There's nothing special about Swaledale.'

Bingo! Tom tried to hide his joy. Swaledale. Well, that narrowed things down a little. He'd just have to find out where Swaledale actually was.

'There might not be anything special about Swaledale but I still need to talk to Molly.'

'And you want me or my husband to tell you exactly where she is?'

'It would be most helpful.'

'But why should I?'

Tom gave an inward sigh. Mrs Bailey was proving to be a rather cool customer. 'Because it might benefit you.'

'Benefit? How?'

Tom could see he was going to have to be more direct. 'Mrs Bailey, has Molly come into any money recently?'

'How do you mean?'

'Inherited any, for example?'

'Inherited? God!' She gave a hearty laugh. 'You obviously don't know the Baileys.'

'Or won any, maybe?'

'Won? Like the lottery?'

Tom nodded. 'Anything's possible.'

'But she would have said something, wouldn't she?'

'You'd be surprised what people do when they win,' Tom said, as if he knew.

'How do you know about this?'

'Just a lead I was given.'

Mrs Bailey screwed her face up in confusion. 'You've got it all wrong. She would have told us if she'd come into money.'

Tom shifted uneasily in the sofa. He could sense that he wasn't going to get any more information out of this woman. 'Has she a mobile phone I can contact her on?' he tried with limited optimism.

'Molly? You must be joking. She can't afford one of those.' As soon as the words were out of her mouth Tom could almost see her brain tick-ticking away, weighing the possibilities.

'I'd better make a move,' Tom said, making an effort to separate his bottom from the sunken middle of the sofa. 'Thank you for your time, Mrs Bailey.'

She stared at him, eyes wide with wonder.

'Bye then,' he said, holding his hand out to shake hers. She took it silently and he let himself out of the house.

Most peculiar, Carolyn thought, as soon as the door was shut. Molly – come into money? No! It was ridiculous. She definitely would have said something. They didn't have any secrets from each other. Did they? Carolyn shook her head. She supposed she should check on Marty.

Heading out of the living room, she almost jumped out

of her skin as she collided with him at the bottom of the stairs.

'*Marty!*'

'Who the hell was that man?' he growled. 'And what's all this about Molly and money?'

Chapter Fourteen

After scuffing his shoes on the dodgy path again, Tom got back in the car and reached for his road atlas.

'OK?' Flora asked without lifting her nose from out of her book.

'Fine,' Tom said, quickly finding out that Swaledale was in North Yorkshire. He sighed. More petrol. Still, he supposed he should be grateful it wasn't in North Wales.

'Flo, we're moving.'

'OK,' she said, closing her book and doing up her seat belt. 'Where are we going?'

'Swaledale.'

Flora giggled.

'I know. There are some ridiculously named places round here.'

'I like it.'

'Let's hope so,' Tom said, pulling out and heading towards the A66.

* * *

It was almost dark by the time they checked into a small hotel in Hawes. They'd been turned away by a fair few bed and breakfasts, and had been advised to try Hawes which wasn't exactly in the right direction. Still, he couldn't have his girl sleeping in the car, could he?

After sharing a packet of Mini Cheddars, and marching Flora into the shower, he thought it time he made a move. He didn't like leaving Flora alone. Anise would kill him if she ever found out, but what other choice did he have? He'd made sure she had his mobile phone number if anything happened and had told her he'd be back as soon as possible, and certainly no later than midnight.

'I'll be all right, Dad. Stop fussing!' she said.

'You've got my number right there.'

'I know!'

Tom ruffled her hair and bent down to kiss her cheek. She smelt of apple blossom. All fresh and fragrant.

'I won't be long.'

'*Go!*'

'OK. Night-night.'

'Night, Dad.'

Tom left the hotel and got back in the car. To be honest, he could have done with a quiet night in: just him, Flo and his guitars. He smiled, remembering summer holidays past when they'd get all hippie after a barbecue: him strumming and Flo singing. He could do with a dose of that right now. He didn't feel like trailing round pubs in what might prove a fruitless search for a story he might never end up writing or selling. And what would happen then? He didn't have a job to go back to. He was out in the world without even a decent reference to his name. The pressure was on him to find this Molly.

Switching the car light on, he gazed down at the map. There was only one main road through Swaledale, an ambling, rambling road which followed the River Swale. It was fairly long. Where would he start? He stroked his chin. He didn't suppose it mattered where he started as long as he got a move on.

Marty's face was as dark as a storm cloud as he banged kitchen cupboards and drawers in his attempt to make himself a cup of coffee.

'Have you got a headache?' Carolyn dared to ask.

He nodded. 'Where's the sugar?'

Carolyn pointed to the canister standing where it always did, arms crossed against her chest, waiting for him to say something first. The trouble was, Marty had overheard the last part of Tom Mackenzie's questioning and wouldn't let it go now, which meant that he'd completely forgotten about their own argument that morning. After the reporter had left, Marty had demanded Carolyn told him everything that had been said then looked as if he didn't believe a single word of it. But the strange thing was, she didn't feel like shouting at him anymore. That moment had passed. Somewhere between the frustration and the crying, her anger had simply bled away. She felt exhausted with it all. What she needed was a long, hot soak in the bath.

'I'm going for a bath,' Marty said abruptly and, for a brief moment, Carolyn was tempted to tell him to put his head under the water three times and take it out twice, but she managed to resist.

There was certainly no difficulty finding a pub in Swaledale and, after visiting The Heifer and The Ram's Head, Tom found The Miner's Inn . A cosy, cottage-like pub, it had all the requirements: dark beams studded with horse brasses, an inglenook fireplace and an atmosphere soaked with ale.

Tom had been under the impression that it would be a quiet, sleepy sort of place but he couldn't have been more wrong. The noise level almost knocked him over. He approached the bar through a crowd of people who were ordering drinks like there was no tomorrow. The barman, who was rather red in the face, was doing his best to cope.

Tom waited his turn, watching as the bar slowly became less congested. Finally, the barman turned to Tom.

'Hope you've not been waiting too long,' he said, the colour still high in his cheeks.

'No,' Tom said. 'Is it usually this busy?'

'If it was, I'd be retired by now,' he chuckled. 'Pint?'

'Half, thanks,' Tom said, remembering he might have to cover quite a few pubs before he actually found out anything about where Molly Bailey might be.

As the barman placed the glass in front of him, Tom looked round at the locals. There were small groups of people nestled round tables but, in the corner by the fireplace, was a larger group. They were talking loudly and one chap, in particular, seemed to be the centre of attention.

'Who's that?' Tom asked. 'Is he the man buying everyone a round?'

The barman didn't seem to have heard and continued polishing glasses. Tom was just about to repeat his question when the barman looked up.

'Lord Henry. Owns Whitton Castle further up the dale.'

'This is his regular?'

'Well,' the barman said grinning, 'I wouldn't quite put it like that. He drops in occasionally, same as most folk round here, but he prefers to entertain in the castle, if you know what I mean.'

Tom nodded, noticing the naughty gleam in the barman's eyes.

'Wealthy, is he?'

The barman chortled. 'You've not seen Whitton Castle, have you?'

'No, I'm afraid not.'

'It's not exactly Buckingham Palace.'

'I see.'

'Mouldy old shell of a place. It's usually everyone else who has to buy him a drink, not the other way round.'

Tom turned round and looked across at the impoverished lord.

'Another round of drinks, Dave!' a ruby-cheeked Lord Henry bellowed across the pub, then, staggering to his feet, he made an unsteady route towards the bar. 'And a bag of nuts for me,' he added, burping loudly. And then he noticed Tom. 'Hello there!' he said. 'Henry Hewson! How do you do?'

'Tom Mackenzie. How do you do?'

'Very well, Tom Macrenzie. Very well indeed.'

Tom was almost knocked off his stool with the smell of alcohol. He'd obviously been knocking back the drinks for some time now.

'So what brings Tom Macrenzie to our little local?'

Tom took a swig of ale, measuring his answer. 'Holiday,' he said.

'Ah!' Lord Henry waved a finger in the air. 'Then you'll be visiting my place, will you? Up the dale? Bloody big castle: battlements, dungeons – the damned lot – can't miss it!'

'I'd be delighted.'

'Good! Good!'

The barman gave him his bag of peanuts and Tom watched as he struggled to open them.

'Blasted things,' he said, his thick fingers slipping down the packet. 'A man could starve to death whilst trying to get into them.' He tried again and in a split second the whole bag had ripped, causing a peanut volcano to erupt over Tom. 'Bugger! God. I am sorry. Here,' he said, stumbling forward. 'Let me.' Lord Henry was just about to collect the peanuts that had settled in Tom's lap when Tom stopped him.

'No. It's fine. Let me buy you another packet.'

'Gracious, no! Wouldn't hear of it. Look!' Lord Henry flashed a wad of notes at him. 'Flush – today!' he said, waving a wad of fifty-pound notes under Tom's nose.

'Makes a change!' the barman laughed.

Lord Henry chortled. 'It certainly does.'

'Won the pools or something?' the barman asked.

'You could say that!' Lord Henry beamed.

Tom was immediately on red alert. A down-on-his-luck lord in Swaledale who'd suddenly got a wad of fifty-pound notes.

'Let me tell you a little sh-secret,' Lord Henry slurred, leaning in a little closer to Tom and encompassing him in a shroud of alcoholic fumes. 'Women are amazing!'

Tom grinned. 'You don't need to tell me,' he said, quietly thinking of his own little lady asleep at the hotel and how he wished he could get back to her as quickly as possible.

'I'm shure I don't,' Lord Henry said with a wicked wink. 'Look!' he said, waving the wad of fifty-pound notes again. 'A woman gave me this!'

Tom felt his spine tingle in anticipation. 'Really?'

'Shertainly did! Couldn't believe my eyes.'

'She just gave you all that?'

'No. There's more. But that's at home,' Lord Henry said, patting his nose with a finger. 'Got to save a bit for the old house.'

'She must be quite a woman!' Tom said, carefully feeding him a line in the hope for more information.

'Quite a woman! You're not wrong there. And she was beautiful too! Beautiful and loaded! Bloody good mix, that!'

'However did you find her?'

'In my garden! Was out having a smoke and there she was – just sitting in the sun with her dog. Bare legs up to her armpits and a bosom to die for!'

'Great Scott!'

'Molly!'

'Molly?'

'Her name was Molly. Molly the dolly!' Lord Henry guffawed. 'And her hair! Big, black, bouncy curls like I've never seen before.' His red face glazed over and, for a moment, Tom thought he was going to swoon right off his bar stool.

'So how come she ended up at your castle?' Tom asked, trying to keep Lord Henry on track.

'No idea!' he said, sighing loudly. 'God, it's swarm in here,' he said, reaching into his trouser pocket and pulling out an enormous hanky. As he did so, something dropped onto the floor.

'What's that?' Tom asked, spying a glimpse of yellow.

'*She* gave it to me,' Lord Henry said, picking up a flower and spinning it round in his hand. ''Fraid it's not taken kindly to living in my pocket.'

Tom smiled. It was a sunshine daisy. Lord Henry had been

Mollied, that was for sure. 'So where is she now?' he asked.

'Ah!' Lord Henry waved a finger in the air as if he wanted to keep it a secret but then he shrugged his shoulders. 'No idea!' he conceded. 'Didn't like to ask where she was going. She's just one of those people, I guess. Never shaw her before and will never shee her again.'

'Shame.'

'Shame,' Lord Henry agreed. 'But she said something about Bradford. Asked me the best route.'

'Bradford?'

'Yes. Guess she's heading to the big city. Not much for a young gal out in these parts apart from randy old lords like me, eh?'

'Guess not,' Tom said. 'So you've no idea where she's staying.'

Lord Henry stared at him. 'Why? Fancy a piece for yourself, do you?'

Tom couldn't help but smile. 'You could say that!'

'You dirty old bugger! Here!' he yelled to the barman. 'Another drink for my mate—'

'No, thanks. I've really got to go, but thanks all the same.'

'Pleasure! And don't forget to visit my humble home,' Lord Henry said, pointing in the direction somewhere beyond the gents' toilets.

'I won't forget,' he said, thinking that he'd have to make a move to Bradford first thing in the morning. It was a shame really. It would have been nice to amble around the Dales for a day but this was no holiday.

Tom left the pub, a wicked grin lighting his face. 'Got you, Molly Bailey!' he said out loud. 'You're mine!'

* * *

As Molly's head hit the rather lumpy pillow in the bed and breakfast, she grimaced. Not because she was pining for her marshmallow-soft pillow at home but because she was beginning to regret her actions earlier that day.

She hadn't meant to sleep with Lord Henry – truly she hadn't – but a strange, compelling mix of charm and wine had been spurring her on. She'd become completely absorbed by the moment. The countryside, the gardens, the castle, the lord: all had merged into one magical, mesmerising moment, and she'd grasped it – him – with both hands.

It had been the weirdest experience. She'd never done it on a trestle table before. It was one of those things that you read about in bad romantic books. *The thick stone walls of the castle exuded cold whilst their hot flesh melted into each other; the table smooth and warm against her back* – that sort of thing. The truth of the matter was that it had been the most uncomfortable encounter she'd had since being short of money in the supermarket, and one she certainly wouldn't be repeating.

Still, it had been good fun. She wasn't sure if it had been her own ample charms or the charms of her ample fist full of money that had caused Lord Henry to become amorous, but she didn't really mind. It had seemed an age since her last encounter and it had felt nice to be appreciated again. And he had certainly been appreciative.

'Good lord!' he'd hollered when she'd got up to leave. 'I don't know what to say.' He'd peered down at her through his thick fringe. 'Golly, Molly!' he'd said, which had made her laugh. 'That was really something, and I'm not just saying that.'

Molly had smiled at him, allowing him to lie to her without

batting an eyelid. If the stack of empty wine bottles was anything to go by, then Lord Henry was definitely not short of lady friends.

Now, Molly sighed the sigh of a sated woman. She liked men, which was just as well because they seemed to like her. Since she was fourteen, she hadn't been able to walk to the local shops without being tooted or whistled at, and the once shy girl had courted the attention too: hitching her school skirt up a few inches before she walked through the school gate and smudging kohl round her already enormous eyes. Her poor perplexed father hadn't been able to cope.

'You need a mother,' he'd mumble under his breath whilst shaking his head in despair. Molly had always noted his use of the phrase *a mother* rather than *your mother*.

For Molly, romance had been a release; it was something carefree and beautiful, a world away from the restraint and restrictions of the Bailey household. And that's what this afternoon had been: a wonderful romantic release. She giggled at the memory. Trouble was, she couldn't sleep now.

She swung her legs out of bed and padded across the thick carpet to the window. Drawing back the curtains, she heaved the sash window up and stuck her head out. The air was deliciously cool and she shivered as if a thousand frostbitten fingers had tickled her all over. The sky was clear and dark and stuffed with stars. Molly stared up into them until she felt her vision blurring. Were they guiding her? Did they really hold her destiny? Molly didn't like to believe in fate; she liked to believe that she, and she alone, held the power to determine her own future.

Still, looking up at the heavens, it was easy to believe otherwise.

Chapter Fifteen

It was over fifteen years since Molly had visited Bradford. It had been an annual event throughout her childhood but, shortly after her mother had left, Molly had lost touch with the Percy side of the family. She'd heard her father say that he thought Auntie Clara had moved to Leeds but nothing was ever confirmed and she had never spoken to her auntie or cousin again. But she had never forgotten them.

She remembered being put on a train in Carlisle, with her baby suitcase, for the journey south. Bradford was still in the north of England, but Molly's father had always referred to his wife's relatives as 'those southerners'. Still, Molly had always enjoyed the train ride: through the dales and valleys of Cumbria, and across the bridges and becks of Yorkshire until the moors would give way to regimental stone terraces, which, in turn, would morph into factories of black stone and cities of chimneys.

Auntie Clara and cousin Jess would meet her at Leeds so she didn't have to change trains on her own. From there, it was a short train ride and a long bus ride, via a bag of chips and a doughnut, to the flat which seemed to Molly to be as high in the sky as you could possibly live without being an angel.

Sitting in her car now, she looked up at the tower block. God, it was ugly. It hadn't been her childhood imagination that had painted it in such miserable colours. It was truly an eyesore to rival all eyesores.

She could still see it all, and smell it all too. The corridors had smelt like a zoo where the cleaners had gone on strike, and they were as stark, echoey and frightening as a new school.

'Never use the lifts!' Auntie Clara warned Molly on her first visit.

'But I thought you lived on the top floor?' Molly said.

'That's right – fourteenth.'

Molly's mouth dropped open.

'Exercise is good for you,' Auntie Clara had smiled, giving her trademark rattly cough which Molly's father referred to as 'smoker's smog'.

Molly thought that someone with a name as regal as Clara Percy should have lived in a stately home rather than on an estate, and the flat came as a complete shock to her. For a start, there was barely any furniture in it. The living room housed a TV no bigger than a shoebox, an old brown sofa and a couple of tables with cup ring marks where coasters should have been.

'Make yourself at home,' Auntie Clara said, disappearing into the kitchen. Jess sat next to Molly on the sofa, waiting for her to speak first.

Molly looked round the room, desperately trying to find

something she could comment on. There was a row of unframed photographs on the fireplace, curling and browning like autumn leaves.

'You've got a nice house,' Molly said hesitantly.

Jess glared at her. 'Crap.'

'What?'

'That's a load of crap.'

Molly gasped. She'd never heard such language before, and then she remembered something her father had said. 'Mouths like sewers those kids.' He'd been talking about the nameless, faceless children on the estate who'd let his car tyres down the one time he'd deigned to visit with Molly's mum.

'Is that sewer talk?' Molly asked Jess.

Jess glared at her again. 'What?'

'*Crap?*'

Auntie Clara's head popped round the kitchen door. 'Who said that? You been swearing at Molly already?' She came into the room and clipped Jess round the ear. 'She's only been here five minutes and she sounds like a carbon copy of you.' Auntie Clara sucked hard on her cigarette until Molly felt sure her cheeks would disappear down her throat.

'What's a carbon copy, Auntie Clara?'

'A mistake, Molly,' she said, shaking her head. 'A *huge* mistake.'

It didn't take long for Molly and Jess to become firm friends. Whenever Molly was invited, they'd sit and talk: old-fashioned, honest-to-goodness talking. It was always a strange experience for Molly because talking was something that her family didn't ever do. There was moaning. One could always rely on at least three moans a day in the Bailey household, but talking? That was unheard of.

'So, Moll, what do you think?' Auntie Clara would often ask, and Molly would feel herself blushing at being asked for her opinion on something. Did it really matter what she thought of something? Could her opinion make a difference? The intensity in her aunt's eyes and the concentration etched across her brow would seem to say so, and that made Molly feel oh-so-special.

Something else that was rare in the Bailey household, but in abundance at Auntie Clara's, was laughter. The silliest things would set the three of them off until the couch was put under so much pressure with them rolling around that they'd have to stop before there was an accident.

There was the time when they'd wanted to play snakes and ladders but realised they didn't have one.

'Must have given it away,' Auntie Clara said.

'Given it away?' Jess shouted. 'We never had one.'

Auntie Clara had shaken her head. 'We'll have to make our own.' She then walked round the house gathering all the socks she could find. 'These are the snakes,' she said, laying them down on the threadbare carpet. 'And these,' she said, 'are the ladders.'

'What are they?' Molly asked.

'Oh, *Mum*!' Jess wailed. 'You can't use those!'

'What's wrong with them? They're clean.'

'What are they?' Molly asked again, her eyes screwed up in wonder.

'Stockings,' Auntie Clara had explained. 'They're like tights but without the saggy bit in the middle.'

There'd then been the strangest game of snakes and ladders Molly had ever played. Nobody had any real idea of the score, but it didn't seem to matter as they erupted in laughter every time somebody went down a sock-snake with one of Auntie Clara's button earrings which were being used as counters, and the whole game had ended in a big sock fight.

It was then that it had happened. The incident that Molly would never forget.

They didn't hear the knock on the door at first because they'd been laughing so much, but they couldn't miss the second knock.

'It's Maud,' Auntie Clara said. 'That's her warning knock.'

'Warning knock?' Molly turned to Jess whose face had turned white in an astonishing short space of time since it had been bright red.

Jess put her finger up to her lips. 'Listen.'

Molly listened as Auntie Clara opened the front door, but she couldn't make out what was being said.

Finally, Auntie Clara came back into the living room. 'Quick,' she said. The laughter had drained from her body and her voice sounded steely, almost afraid. 'Phil Phipps is on the prowl. Get behind the sofa.'

Molly started. Had she heard right? What did she mean? Was this some sort of new game involving the neighbours?

Molly had never been behind a sofa before and it was a strange experience. Quite a new perspective on the world.

'Auntie Clara, what are we doing?' she asked as she huddled into a human ball.

'You can see straight into this room from the front door. I keep meaning to get it replaced but haven't had the money. Just get behind the sofa and don't make a noise.'

There was a loud banging at the front door, and Molly had to do her best not to scream out in fear. She looked at her aunt who was bent double next to her, her forehead pressed against a dirty antimacassar as she tried to keep her balance.

'Don't make a sound, Moll.'

Molly wasn't going to; she was too scared. This wasn't a very fun game, if it were, indeed, a game, so she watched and waited, wincing each time there was a knocking on the door.

'Why don't they just go away?' Jess asked.

'They will,' Auntie Clara told her. 'As long as we're quiet.'

They waited for what seemed like an eternity, until Molly felt sure that they would have to set up a permanent home behind the sofa.

Finally, Jess nudged her mum. 'They're going away,' she said in an excited whisper.

'Are you sure?'

'Listen.'

They all listened as heavy boots shuffled along the passageway outside.

'He'll be going to Kerry Anderson's,' Auntie Clara said.

'Who?' Molly asked. '*Who* will be going to Kerry Anderson?'

Auntie Clara smiled down at her and ruffled a hand through her thick curls. 'You don't ever want to know, Moll.'

'But I do. Who is *he*?'

'He's the man everybody owes money to,' Jess explained.

Molly's mouth dropped before she fished around in her trouser pocket. There were two fifty-pence pieces there, and she handed them to Auntie Clara.

'Bless you, Moll, but it'll take more than that, I'm afraid.'

'But what do you owe him money for?' Molly asked. She'd already seen the flat, and knew there was nothing in it that they'd spent any money on recently.

'The telephone,' Auntie Clara said.

'But you don't have a telephone,' Molly pointed out.

'No. Not since we were disconnected.'

'Why don't you explain that you can't pay him?'

Auntie Clara gave a laugh that was half cackle, half rumble. ''Cause you don't *explain* to people like Phil Phipps. The only language they understand is money.'

Molly looked up at the flats and wondered if Phil Phipps still haunted the residents. She'd never actually seen him but had a picture of what he must be like. He'd be the sort of man whose neck was as thick as his head, with red, roughened, lizard-like skin and the kind of knuckles with which you could knock down a house.

Molly got out of the car, Fizz dancing at her heels in anticipation of a walk.

'You really wouldn't want a walk round here,' she said to him, his face as innocent as a snowdrop. 'I don't think you'd like the neighbourhood dogs. They're all bodybuilders and have nose studs and tattoos. Anyway, we've work to do.'

She had the envelopes ready; each stuffed with notes and a single yellow gerbera. All she had to do was post them but that was easier said than done. She no sooner opened the door into the flats than Fizz started to whimper. Could he smell the other dogs already or was it the smell of humans that he didn't like? The *stench* of humans, Molly thought, her nose wrinkling in disgust. Why did flats always smell like that? All of the nastiest of human smells seemed to congregate there, like a perfume section of a department store which had gone horribly wrong.

'We'd better make this fast,' she said, and headed straight

for the stairs, her hand closing over the thick creamy envelopes. She took a deep breath, but not too deep, and then began the long, laborious climb to the fourteenth floor.

Chapter Sixteen

Tom and Flora walked hand in hand towards the nearest newsagent's. It seemed hard to imagine *Vive!* selling in the Yorkshire market town but it was there on the shelves along with all the other papers. It would seem that people wanted to read the latest gossip no matter where they lived.

'Do you want to look for it, Flo?' Tom asked after paying for it and leaving the shop.

Flora took the paper from him. 'Are you nervous?'

Tom nodded.

'Don't be, Daddy.'

But he couldn't help it. He could tell that he wasn't on pages two or three already. His heart beat faster as Flora turned another page. Had they not used his piece? Had he been taken out last minute or had they not thought it newsworthy in the first place? Was he washed up already? Had his great adventure ended before it had even begun?

'You got a facing page, Daddy!' Flora beamed. She knew all the jargon.

'Where?' Tom grabbed the paper from her.

'Page seven!' she said.

'*Seven?*'

'That's good, isn't it?'

Tom quickly scanned the stories that had taken precedence over his own and then slowly nodded. 'It's not bad,' he said. 'To begin with.'

'I think it's wonderful. *Honesty Box Bonanza!*'

'So you don't mind me writing for *Vive!* now, do you?'

'No, I don't mind. I think it's exciting!'

Tom quickly read through his article checking for errors but it was word-perfect. It was rather a novelty to see his work in a national and he felt intensely proud of it but he'd have to get a move on with the next piece if he wanted to keep both editor and readers interested. At least he had a name he could now link to his story. Molly Bailey. She was his and he was going to turn her into a breakfast phenomenon.

'Here's that Molly Bailey again,' the nation would chirp over their cornflakes. 'That Tom Mackenzie's hot on her trail now.' Yes, he thought, their names would be instantly recognisable before too long: thrown together in the media event of the year. But he mustn't get too ahead of himself; he had his next piece to write.

Whitton Castle's Windfall. Donation Dame Strikes Again. Hmmm, he'd have to come up with something better than that if he was to graduate from page seven.

In the meantime, they had to start making tracks to Bradford.

Carolyn woke up on Monday morning with a feeling that something was wrong. She stared at her alarm clock. It was ten to seven. She always woke up exactly ten minutes before the alarm was due to go off, which gave her head a few minutes to untangle from dreamland before starting the day.

Rolling over, she looked at Marty. He was still fast asleep. After his bath the night before, he'd gone straight to bed without speaking to her, and the thing that occurred to her was that she hadn't been the least bit surprised. It was all part and parcel of their argumentative cycles.

She'd be glad to get out of the house and escape to work. It wasn't that she loved her job at the call centre but it did provide a temporary escape from her problems. It was always so much nicer listening to other people rather than dwelling on herself. She'd recently been promoted too, which she still got a kick out of. She didn't get her own office or anything posh like that but it did, at least, mean a little more money.

Sighing into her pillow, Carolyn remembered the evening she'd come home from work with the good news. She'd bustled round the kitchen organising a romantic meal, even opening a bottle of wine in celebration. Then, somewhere between the main course and dessert, she had broken the good news.

'How much are you on now?' had been Marty's only response.

She looked across at him again. His thick hair was so dark against the cream pillow, and his beautiful lashes swept his skin as he began to wake. How could someone so handsome be so disagreeable most of the time? she wondered. It just didn't seem possible. And then she remembered. She couldn't escape to work. She'd booked leave; *they'd* booked leave, for the next two weeks. She felt a groan growing in the pit of her stomach. She'd been so looking forward to spending some relaxing time with Marty. Heaven knew they needed it. But now? After their continuing rowing, the holiday would be more like a prison sentence.

Luckily, they hadn't booked anything so Carolyn would probably be able to escape to her friend's house and sit out the holiday with her.

Marty stirred beside her and Carolyn felt her body tense. 'God!' he groaned, pushing the duvet down his body and swinging his legs out of bed. 'I said I'd go round to Granddad's today.'

'Why?'

Marty turned to look at Carolyn, his eyes big and brown and still half drowsy from sleep. 'Because he's eighty-six and doesn't get out much. He likes to have a bit of company.'

Carolyn would have laughed if Marty hadn't looked so serious. The thought of Granville Bailey liking company was a bit much. He was nothing but an old grouch. Besides, he saw Marty every weekend and Magnus at least twice a week.

'You can come with me if you like,' Marty said.

She bit her lip. Hadn't she vowed that she wouldn't be pushed into that again?

'You don't have to come,' Marty said, his voice soft and gentle. 'But I'd like you to.'

Carolyn felt weighed down by sudden obligation. Marty knew all the tricks in the book, didn't he? The big brown eyes, the gentle voice, the non-didactic plea for her company.

'OK,' she said, knowing she'd probably regret the decision sooner rather than later. 'As long as we're not round there all day.'

Tom had never been interviewed on radio before but, he'd reasoned, Bradford was too big a place to find Molly Bailey in without a little bit of help. It wasn't as if he could just go into a pub and stumble over a local who'd met her. He wasn't in

Swaledale anymore so the idea of an appeal by local radio had occurred to him. He wasn't sure if it would work but it was worth a go.

It was quite exciting, really. Flora was allowed to go with him too and he kept glancing at her as she sat, eyes wide in excitement, as DJ Dan Dooley ran through his questions quickly.

'We don't normally do interviews in the lunchtime slot,' he said in a tone of voice that heavily implied he was doing Tom a huge favour, 'but your story does sound rather interesting.' Dan Dooley was talking over a tuneless love duet that reminded Tom why he never listened to local radio.

'I really appreciate your time,' Tom said, quite willing to butter him up even though he was greasy enough already.

'You're very welcome, young man. Very welcome.' Dan Dooley turned away as the record ended. '"A Love Supreme" there, requested by Mrs Patricia Forbes from Shipley. Hope that brought back some of the old memories for you, Patricia,' he said in a voice like out-of-date syrup. 'You're listening to Dan Dooley Daily.'

Flora giggled, causing Dan to give her a reprimanding look. Tom also gave her one of his own but was finding it hard to suppress the giggles himself.

'It's not every day you meet a millionaire,' Dan Dooley began, 'and it's even less likely that you meet a millionaire whose mission seems to be to give her entire fortune away, but that's exactly what happened to my next guest, Tom Mackenzie. Welcome to Dan Dooley Daily, Tom.'

Flora giggled again, her cheeks flushing pink with hysterics.

'Thank you,' Tom said, trying desperately to curb the laughter in his voice.

'You're a freelance reporter, aren't you?'

'Yes, currently working for *Vive!*,' Tom said, scoring an instant point for his current employer and not doing himself any harm in the process.

'*Vive!* I think we've got quite a few *Vive!* fans listening today, haven't we?' Dan Dooley said, his thick lips hovering over the mic like an insistent lover. 'So tell us what it is you're up to at the moment.'

'Well, I got wind of a possible story a few days ago. Up in Cumbria, a farmer came across five thousand pounds in his honesty box.'

'Five *thousand* pounds?'

'Yes. Not the sort of thing you hear every day.'

'Certainly not round here,' Dan Dooley chortled into his mic.

'So, I asked around a bit and it turns out that a local girl, Molly Bailey, seems to have come into quite a lot of money.'

'You mean won the lottery?'

'We're not absolutely sure at the moment but one thing's for sure: it's not been inherited from her family.'

'So why would this Molly Bailey want to give her money away?'

'Again, that's something we've got to find out but the last lead I had told me she was heading to Bradford. I don't know what her plans are or where she's heading next but there's one clue: when she leaves money for people, she has a rather unusual calling card.'

'What's that, Tom?'

'A single yellow gerbera – it's like a very large daisy.'

Dan Dooley nodded. 'And that's where you come in, listeners. If any of you out there have been left a sudden windfall in cash, with a single yellow—'

'Gerbera. It's like a large daisy.'

'—large daisy, give us a call. You know the number,' Dan Dooley said, repeating it twice, 'we want to hear from you and try to track down this modern-day Robin Hood.'

Bastard! Tom thought. *He's stolen my line.*

'So get calling,' he said, as he began playing another God-awful love ballad.

As soon as the music started, the phones started too. Tom looked across at where a little lady in a white blouse covered in strawberries was scribbling on a piece of paper and nodding into the phone. What was going on? Was this a hoax? Were these people attention seekers or had they really encountered Molly?

Dan Dooley nodded over to the little lady as the song ended.

'I have a Mrs Esther Cobbs on the line. You're through to Dan Dooley Daily.'

Flora giggled.

'Where are you calling from, Esther love?'

'Moor View, Bradford.'

'The flats?'

'Yeah.'

'And would you like to tell the listeners what happened to you?'

'Well, I wus just doing a bit of ironing when I heard a rattle at the letter box. I thought it wus one of those leaflet people messing me flat up again and I was just about to have a go at whoever it was when I saw the envelope.'

'Was it addressed to you?'

'No, it weren't. It wus completely blank. And it wus far too good quality to have any of them begging letters in, so I opens it.'

'And what was inside, Esther?'

'Five hundred pounds – in fifty-pound notes.'

'And you've no idea who left it?'

'Well, I thought I'd see if I could spot someone but there didn't seem to be anyone around so I knocked on my neighbour's door to see if she'd seen anything and she'd been left an envelope too.'

'With the same amount of money in it?'

'The same.'

'Was there anything else inside the envelope?' Tom asked.

'Yes, there wus as a matter of fact. A flower.'

'Yellow?'

'Yeah!'

Dan Dooley glared at Tom, obviously not liking his slot being taken over. 'That's all we've got time for, I'm afraid. Esther – thank you for your call. Keep tuning in to Dan Dooley Daily.'

Flora giggled.

Before they left the studio, the little woman in the strawberry-print blouse came up to Tom and presented him with the A4 sheet of paper she'd been scribbling on. 'I don't know if this is of any use to you, but there was another woman who rang in from the Moor View flats who thinks she might have seen this Molly Bailey. I've highlighted the number there. She said she'd be happy to talk to you.'

Tom looked down at the name and number. 'Thank you,' he said.

'And here's a little something for your girl,' she said, presenting her with a large red, yellow and blue sticker with *Dan Dooley Daily* written on it.

Flora giggled.

They walked down the corridor away from the studio, their faces pulled tight from the exertion of not laughing but it all became too much when they saw a life-sized cardboard cut-out of Dan Dooley in reception. *The Dan Dooley Daily Roadshow – coming to you this summer!*

Tom and Flora looked at each other and immediately broke out into uncontrollable laughter.

'*Vive!* Who brought that rag into this house?' Granville Bailey barked from his winged chair.

'It was cheaper than the others,' Marty's father, Magnus, explained. 'I only wanted it for the TV guide.'

A likely story, Carolyn smirked. Everyone knew that *Vive!* had more gorgeous girls than *The Sun* and more gossip than a women's glossy. Bored to tears by the men's conversation, Carolyn picked up *Vive!* and flicked through it, her eyes soon out on stalks at the amount of flesh on display. It was like taking a trip to the local deli.

She was just about to toss the paper onto the floor in disgust when she saw a familiar name. Tom Mackenzie. Was that the same Tom Mackenzie who'd paid a visit to their home asking about Molly? So he *was* a reporter after all, not a stalker as she'd first suspected.

Carolyn read the short article. Five thousand pounds. Gilt View Farm. A single yellow gerbera.

Mrs Bailey, has Molly come into any money recently?

Carolyn blinked as she remembered Tom Mackenzie's question. But this story couldn't be connected with Molly, could it? What possible motivation could she have for giving five thousand pounds to a complete stranger? And then she remembered something. Carolyn had visited The Bloom

Room a few weeks ago and Molly and she had gone out for a walk and she distinctly remembered how sad Molly had been. It wasn't surprising really. Molly had always adored the countryside, and it was heartbreaking to see most of the local footpaths closed off due to foot and mouth. The fields had become like ghost towns without the sheep and cattle, and Molly and Carolyn had had to stick to the roads for most of their walk.

'I wish there was something I could do,' Molly had said.

I wish there was something I could do. That was just *so Molly*, Carolyn thought, but she knew her sister-in-law didn't have five thousand pounds even to help herself, let alone somebody else. Or did she?

Chapter Seventeen

Molly looked down at the absurdly small mobile phone and frowned. How hard could it be? She pressed a few buttons and smiled. Action! It certainly beat phone boxes and, after her recent disaster in Swaledale, there was one person she owed a call to now: Carolyn.

But there was no answer. Funny, she thought, she could have sworn Marty said they'd booked leave for this week. Maybe they were out. Or maybe they were paying a visit. She tapped in Old Bailey's phone number and waited.

'Hello, Dad?'

'Molly! How are you?' Magnus said sounding unusually cheerful.

'I'm fine.'

'I've not seen you for a while.'

'I'm away at the moment – taking an impromptu holiday.'

'Oh. Where?'

'Just around, you know,' she said, not wanting to say that she'd just visited Moor View flats in Bradford. Her father wouldn't have been happy with that. 'Is Carolyn with you?'

'Yes, she is. Hang on a minute.'

There was a pause as Magnus put the phone down and Molly could just make out Old Bailey muttering something in the background about the price of whisky at his local convenience store.

Finally, Carolyn came to the phone. 'Molly?'

'Hi, Caro! Sorry about yesterday. I ran right out of change but I've got a mobile phone now.'

'Moll – I'll just take the call in the back room, OK?'

'OK,' Molly said, picturing Carolyn moving through the tiny flat to the dark room at the back. The land of lost photographs.

'Molly? Just a minute,' Carolyn said, and then there was a click. 'Right, we can talk now. I just wanted to make sure the other phone had been put down before I told you what happened yesterday.'

'Have you and Marty made up?' Molly asked, thinking that they must have done in order for Carolyn to be round Old Bailey's during her holiday.

'Not exactly, but listen, Moll,' Carolyn said urgently, 'there was a reporter here yesterday evening – asking all sorts of questions about you.'

'A reporter? What did he want?'

'I'm not sure. He seemed to think you'd come in to some money? Said he wanted to catch up with you.'

'To interview me, you mean?'

'Well, I guess so.'

There was a pause whilst both women wondered what to say next.

'Molly?'

'Yes.'

'*Have* you come into some money?' Carolyn asked quietly. 'Moll? Are you still there?'

'Yes. I'm still here,' Molly said, chewing her lower lip and wondering how she could break her news.

'Come on then,' Carolyn pushed.

'What would you say,' Molly began slowly, 'if I told you I'd won the lottery?'

It was typical that the only person to have seen Tom's Robin Hood lived in the highest place in Bradford. You could have wrung the pair of them out and got at least a couple of pints of sweat from them by the time they'd reached the fourteenth floor. Poor Flora was pink in the face and Tom dreaded to think what he looked like. On entering the flats, they'd been about to hop into the lift but had thought better of it on first smell. Far preferable to risk a heart attack, Tom had thought.

Finally, they reached the flat of Ms Amanda Gunton, and Tom, not wanting to waste any more time, knocked loudly.

After what seemed an interminable wait, the door was answered by a woman with bottle-blonde hair and a cough like a sick hyena.

'Ms Gunton?'

'You the reporter?'

'Tom Mackenzie,' he said, holding out his hand to have it shaken by her stubby yellow fingers. 'And my daughter, Flora.'

'Hello,' Ms Gunton said without smiling.

'Hello,' Flora said shyly, eyeing up the woman's jewellery: a nasty gold ring on every finger.

'Come on in. I've got the kettle on, but you'll have to excuse the mess. The bloody washing machine's just flooded the kitchen.'

Tom and Flora followed her into the dark, narrow hallway and were shown into a living room with a carpet covered in hypnotic swirls and wallpaper with more flowers than *Gardeners' World*.

Ms Gunton disappeared into the adjacent kitchen and Tom watched her through the Seventies serving hatch as she coughed into the sink before stubbing out her cigarette on the draining board. He turned away in disgust and noticed the line of photographs on the fireplace.

'Are these all your children?' Tom asked.

Ms Gunton came back through with two mugs of tea and an orange juice on a tray.

'The rogues' gallery,' she cackled. 'Jen, Cath and Jane. If you want to take any of them off my hands, you're welcome. I can't seem to shift any of them. Oh, sorry, you're married, right?'

Tom blushed but didn't bother to explain his marital situation in front of Flora.

'So you'll be wanting to ask some questions, right?'

'Please. If you don't mind,' Tom said, sipping the tea and trying not to grimace at the mug which tasted of cigarettes.

'Here's the envelope,' Ms Gunton said, producing it from a coffee table covered in old tabloids open at the racing pages. 'I've put the money somewhere safe.'

'And it was all in fifty-pound notes, was it?'

'That's right.'

'And the flower?'

Ms Gunton nodded into the adjoining kitchen where the beautiful sunshine daisy was stood in a miniature vase of water, its happy face doing its best to jollify the gloom.

'The lady at the radio station said you'd seen something?' Tom said.

Ms Gunton nodded again. 'I did that,' she said. 'I heard the letter box go and when I saw what was in the envelope I thought I'd have a look around. Thought there'd been some mistake.' She paused to give her hyena cough, the wrinkles round her eyes deepening into ditches. 'But I couldn't see anything. So I hung around, figuring the person couldn't have gotten far. Then, I thought I'd take a trip down to the bins in the basement. You wouldn't believe the amount of rubbish we make here. And that's when I saw her.' She paused for effect, edging up to her big moment.

'What did you see?'

'A young woman with dark curly hair and a little white dog – some sort of terrier, I'd say.'

'Did you speak to her?'

Ms Gunton shook her head. 'No. She got into her car so fast, I didn't have time.'

'What kind of car did she have?' Tom asked, trying not to get too excited.

'One of them old VW Beetles. A bright yellow one.'

Tom's eyebrows raised.

'She had a bit of trouble starting it, but managed to get it going before I could get over to her.'

'So how do you know this was the woman who delivered the envelopes?'

Ms Gunton reached down the side of her chair and produced a packet of cigarettes, offering one to Tom before she lit up. 'I don't,' she said, 'but you get to know the people who come and go round here and the girl in the Beetle was definitely a stranger. Never seen her before.'

'I don't suppose you got the registration number?'

Ms Gunton chuckled. 'You must be joking. I'm useless when it comes to things like that. Can't even remember my own phone number. But it was a bright yellow car – just like that daisy, in fact.'

Tom nodded. 'Well, thank you very much for your time.' He glanced at Flora, who was just finishing her orange juice. 'Can I just ask you what you'll be doing with the money?'

Ms Gunton almost spluttered on her cigarette. 'That's all spent ten times over already. Debts,' she said. 'But it's a help, that's for sure. Whoever that girl is, we could do with more of her in this world. I only wish she'd stopped long enough for me to thank her.'

'Daddy, I smell horrible,' Flora said, her little nose wrinkling in disgust as they left Ms Gunton's flat.

'This whole place smells. Come on,' he said, taking her hand. 'Let's get out of here.'

Tom led the way quickly down the stairs and back out to where he'd parked the car. A group of boys were kicking a football nearby and Tom did his best not to glance round his car to check if they'd helped themselves to any spare parts.

'A yellow Volkswagen Beetle,' he said as they got back in. 'At least that's fairly conspicuous but how are we going to find her?'

'The radio was fun. We could go back there,' Flora suggested.

'But that was only any use when we knew where she was – it was local radio, you see, but we don't know where she's gone. She could be anywhere by now.'

Flora frowned. Tom frowned too. And then he had an idea.

Grabbing a pad and pen from the glove compartment, he wrote the following words which he planned to use as his next headline:

Where's Molly? Can you help find her?

Chapter Eighteen

Carolyn gasped and then burst into hysterical laughter, which wasn't a good idea because Marty came rushing through to the bedroom.

'What's going on?' he glowered, dark-eyed, from the doorway.

Carolyn glowered back at him. 'Marty, I'm talking to Molly – this is a private conversation!'

He hovered for a moment as if he hadn't heard her.

'We're not talking about *you*, if that's what you're worried about,' she added.

His forehead furrowed in consternation. 'Well, don't be long. We'll be wanting some tea on soon,' he said before pulling the door behind him.

'Gosh,' Carolyn sighed into the phone, 'your brother is a real master at pushing his luck.'

Molly giggled. 'You don't need to tell me that.'

'Anyway,' Carolyn whispered excitedly. 'You were joking, right? This is some kind of April Fool, only in July, isn't it? You haven't really—'

'Won the lottery?' Molly interrupted. 'I jolly well have.'

'No!'

'Caro, listen, you must *swear* not to tell anyone. *Any*one!'

'Why? What are you up to? How much have you won? Where are you?'

'Hang on!' Molly laughed. 'I'm in Bradford. I'm not sure where I'm going next. I'm just concentrating on having fun – spending a little money if you know what I mean.'

Carolyn gasped again. 'Then it *was* you who gave that money to the farmer?'

'How do you know about that?'

'Moll, I told you – that reporter's on to you. It was in *Vive!* today.'

'*Vive!* I'm in *Vive!*?'

'Well, he obviously didn't know your name in this report but he's got you now and I think he's following you. He was asking all sorts of things about you. He had that sharp, hunting look about him that those guys have. You know? Like he knew he was on to a good story.'

There was a moment's silence.

'So come on – how much did you win? And what are you up to?'

Molly laughed, and it sounded like pieces of rainbow falling from a clear sky. 'It was quite a lot. Just over four million.'

'*Jeeeeeeeee-pers!* You're *kidding*!'

'No. And that's why you must promise me you mustn't breathe a word, Caro.'

'You've not told anyone?'

'*No.* No *way*! You know what the Bailey men are like. I wouldn't have a penny left if they got wind of it – you know that.'

'I suppose you're right.'

'But don't worry,' Molly added, 'I *am* being sensible about this. I've put a goodly sum away for everyone; enough to keep us all comfortable, but I don't see the point of excess, really I don't.'

'But you don't want anyone to know about that?'

'Definitely not. Not until I've got rid of it.'

'Moll,' Carolyn interrupted, 'has this got something to do with your mother?'

There was a pause at Molly's end of the phone. 'Money does strange things to people.'

'I know,' Carolyn said. 'So what are you going to do?'

Molly laughed again. 'I'm going to have a little bit of fun.'

Tom and Flora had left the Moor View flats with no particular direction in mind. They were Molly-less. There was no way of knowing where she was until he got some feedback from the next day's plea in *Vive!*.

Pulling into a pizza parlour car park, he got his map out and opened it.

'OK,' he said, motioning to Flora to pay attention. 'She started off in the Eden Valley, here, just east of Carlisle. Then we caught up with her here, in Swaledale and today she was here, in Bradford.'

Flora nodded.

'There's a definite route emerging, isn't there?'

Flora's eyes widened. 'Is there?'

'Look,' Tom said, his finger tracing Molly's route from Carlisle through Swaledale towards Bradford. 'South. She's heading south, isn't she?'

'So far,' Flora said. 'But she might go over there,' she said, pointing to the east.

'What, to Hull?'

'She might.'

Tom frowned. 'It's possible, but if she keeps on heading in the same direction, then I reckon the next place we'll catch up with her will be somewhere around Sheffield.'

'What's in Sheffield?' Flora asked.

'I have absolutely no idea but I think we're about to find out.'

When Carolyn put the phone down, she gave herself a few minutes to compose herself. If she went back through to the living room straight away, she just knew that her excitement would spill out in front of the Bailey clan and that wouldn't be doing Molly any favours. Oh no. But my goodness, it was so tempting to say something.

She could just imagine the look on Old Bailey's face if he knew his little granddaughter was out throwing money as well as caution to the wind. His very own granddaughter, for whom he'd bought a piggy bank when she was just five. Marty had told her the story of how Molly had dared to ask for a ballerina's tutu and had been given a piggy bank instead. It wasn't as if it was a pretty pink piggy bank either. It was a fat, ugly, grey one that looked more like an army vehicle than a pig, and which would have taken an eternity to fill if Molly hadn't dropped it on the quarry-tiled kitchen floor before she reached her sixth birthday. But that hadn't mattered; Old Bailey had replaced it on her next birthday. Carolyn smiled as she tried to imagine Molly's face when she'd unwrapped the present.

Walking across the room, she picked up the photo of Molly and Marty on the little chest of drawers by the window. It was one of the few photos in the room that had merited a frame. It must have been taken close to Molly's piggy bank birthday because she didn't look much older than five or six. A head full of dark, rebellious curls and a naughty twinkle to her eyes, that was Molly. It was as if she could see ahead to her lottery winning. And Marty beside her: beautiful and brooding. How was it that brother and sister could be so different? Most people had optimism and pessimism in fairly equal parts, didn't they? But with Molly and Marty, it was as if all the optimism had been tipped into Molly and the pessimism poured into Marty. Perhaps that was why Molly didn't want Marty to know about her spending spree. She knew what his response would be.

Money does strange things to people. Carolyn agreed with Molly, but was giving it all away stranger than wanting to lock it away in bank accounts? Tom Mackenzie obviously thought so. There weren't many stories centred around people who won the lottery and put all the money into tidy little bank accounts, were there? There was no fun in that.

Carolyn looked out of the window onto the back of the terraced houses opposite. She'd never known anyone who'd won the lottery before. Fancy her own sister-in-law now scooping the top prize. Excitement churned around in her stomach at the mere thought. What on earth must Molly be feeling, she wondered, and how had she kept it a secret for so long? Carolyn just knew that she'd be blurting it out to everyone if she won, but she mustn't do that with Molly's news. Absolute discretion was what was required here; that's what she'd promised Molly.

Gathering herself together, and bidding her smile goodbye, she walked back through to the living room.

'You were a long time,' Marty said.

'Yes. Just catching up with Molly.'

'Any news?'

Carolyn's bright eyes widened and she felt the beginnings of a giggle wiggling inside her. 'Er – no – not really. Just gossiping.'

Marty nodded.

'Isn't anybody hungry yet?' Old Bailey barked from his winged chair.

'Funny you should say that,' Carolyn said with unusual cheer, 'because I was just going to start tea.' And she tripped into the kitchen, pushing the door behind her just as the tears of laughter began to run down her face.

Chapter Nineteen

Tom loved early morning silence. There was something about the stillness of a morning that wasn't quite the same as any other time of day. Evenings never quite worked their magic for him because, prior to leaving his job, he was normally shattered with boredom by then, but morning had a stillness full of promise. Mornings were even more beautiful now that he was self-employed and didn't have to report in to anyone and he was particularly enjoying the presence of his mate's laptop. He'd sneak out of bed whilst Flora still slumbered, and place the portable on his thighs, running his hand across the lid, smooth and perfect as a sea-washed pebble, before opening it up and letting his fingers tap lightly over the keyboard. The lightness of touch was almost mesmeric and, twice now, he'd found himself startled out of his writing reverie by Flora bidding him good morning.

At home, he'd sometimes get up early to practise a few songs on his guitars. When he'd first moved into his house, after the split with Anise, he hadn't realised how thin his walls were until he'd had his ear bent by the mean old lady next door who didn't appreciate being woken at half past six to the strains of 'Hound Dog'. So he'd taken to playing in the bathroom as it was the only room with no adjacent walls. It was a bit odd strumming a guitar on the toilet but the acoustics were good.

Funnily enough, he wasn't missing his early morning strumming session, not with the laptop at his disposal. The words were flying out of his mind straight onto the screen; work was fast becoming something enjoyable.

By the time Flora woke up, he'd got a few hundred words down. It probably wasn't anything he'd use in his forthcoming articles but he was trying to work things out in his mind about Molly, and she was making a very interesting subject. What was her motivation? Why would anyone in their right mind want to give away so much money? It didn't make any sense to Tom. Nobody was really that selfless, were they? Not in this day and age. If Molly was like other women Tom had met, she *had* to have an ulterior motive for being so generous, and what he had to do was find out what that was.

Leaving the hotel later that morning, Tom and Flora wrinkled their noses.

'I don't like it here,' Flora said. 'Can't we go back to Swaledale?'

'There's no story there now.'

'Does that mean we have to stay here?'

'Until I get some feedback from today's article. I've put out a plea for help from the readers – hoping they'll spot Molly's yellow car and let me know where she is,' Tom explained. 'Come on,' he said, taking her hand. 'Let's go and get a paper.'

Five minutes later, Tom had a great fat smile on his face. Not only had he managed to leapfrog to page five but the editor had gone for his idea of making a public plea as to the whereabouts of Molly, printing his email address at the end of the article as so many reporters did nowadays.

His Monday report had been a vague, impersonal story – interesting, yes, but there was nothing the public could sink their teeth into. Now, Tom had given them a name, a focus and, in return, he was hoping they'd be able to help him. All he had to do now was sit back and keep his fingers crossed.

When Molly had ended her call to Carolyn, she'd visited the nearest newsagent's and bought a copy of *Vive!*. It was all very vague, she'd thought. There was nothing linking the story to her, even if Marty, Magnus and Old Bailey did stumble across it. But that couldn't be said of the article on page five of Tuesday's edition. Molly's eyes were out on stalks.

'Bloody hell!' she swore beside the supermarket newspaper stand. It was all there in black and white. Whitton Castle. Lord Henry Hewson. Moor View flats. Yellow gerbera.

He knew who she was and what she'd been up to. He'd found out, and it could only have come from Lord Henry. Molly sighed as she read the words again.

'Bare legs up to her armpits and a bosom to die for.'

She rolled her eyes to the heavens. How could he have said that? How could he have done that to her? He'd seemed such a sweet man. But then something occurred to Molly. Maybe he was still a sweet man and that it was this reporter, this Tom Mackenzie, who was the villain here. Reporters were notorious at getting the worst out of people, and this peeping Tom had definitely done that. He'd probably bribed him with money, and Molly knew Lord Henry could little afford to turn it down. But why did this reporter insist on dwelling on what she looked like? As if that had anything to do with her mission. It was just tabloid titillation, and she could murder him for it!

She read the rest of the article.

'"*I heard the letter box go and when I saw what was in the envelope I thought I'd have a look around. Thought there'd been some mistake,*" Ms Gunton said. *And, indeed, it begs the question why somebody would leave five hundred pounds to a complete stranger. Is this the act of somebody desperately seeking attention?*'

Molly's mouth dropped open. He'd never met her before and yet he was making all these assumptions and daring to put it all down in print for the nation to read. How *dare* he do that? And what was Carolyn going to make of it all? It was one thing having a girly gossip about hot lovers, but quite another to have your private life splashed across the tabloids before you got a chance to explain things yourself.

Molly's eyes stung with tears of frustration. She wanted to find this man and punch him but would that actually achieve anything? Wouldn't she be better running away from him? And what was all this about him asking for people to contact him as to her whereabouts? He'd even found out what car she drove, and that she had a dog! Molly shook her head in anger. How dare he drag Fizz into this ugly business?

For a moment, she stared at the accompanying photograph of the reporter.

'I hate you, Tom Mackenzie,' she said but, even as she said the words, she couldn't help admitting that there was something about the face that was strangely likeable. He looked almost handsome but how was that possible? He was the lowest of the low and deserved nothing but scorn.

Paying for the newspaper at the checkout, together with a sandwich and a tin of dog food, she left the supermarket, her fingers grasped angrily round her copy of *Vive!*.

Getting into the car and slamming the door, she growled unhappily at Fizz. He looked up at her, his eyes so dark under the whiteness of his fur. How sweet he looked. She ruffled his fur and, as he closed his eyes in pure contentment, she tickled his chin. She was starting to calm down a bit and put it down to pet therapy.

'I'm going to rise above this,' Molly told a bemused Fizz. 'He's not going to have the pleasure of ruffling *my* feathers. Oh no!'

She turned the ignition and revved the engine. Then, cursing loudly, she crunched her gears and drove out of the car park.

No, her feathers weren't ruffled at all.

Tom waited until eleven o'clock before checking his email, his face creasing with a smile as no less than eight messages downloaded.

'Wow!' Flora smiled.

'Let's not get too excited,' Tom said, 'there are a lot of cranks out there.'

Sure enough, the first two messages were from idiots.

I think your articles stink! Can't you leave the poor girl alone? the first one read.

Tom opened the second one. *Have you ever considered treading the path to spiritual enlightenment?* He shook his head and deleted them before opening message number three, reading it to himself quietly. Then message number four, five, six, seven and eight.

M1 south of Wakefield.

A61 at Whitley, south of Chapeltown.

A57 towards Ladybower Reservoir.

Flora was getting impatient. 'What do they say, Dad?'

'I was right, Flo!' Tom grinned. 'She's in Derbyshire.'

Chapter Twenty

It was such a relief to venture into the Peak District after getting lost in the urban sprawl of Sheffield. It was yet another area of the country Tom knew little about but he liked what he saw: hills in green and bronze, dotted with copses and sheep; stone cottages and riverside pubs, and numerous walkers thudding through the fields in tank-sized boots. The only thing that puzzled Tom was what on earth Molly was doing here. There weren't any high-rise flats so where was she planning to unload her money? Perhaps she was having a break or maybe she was looking to buy a mansion. Tom got excited at the idea. He hadn't thought about that yet but maybe Molly wasn't so selfless after all?

They stopped at the next village store and filled a basket with bread rolls, crisps, apples, chocolate, tissues and the local paper.

'OK, Flo. I'm promoting you to head researcher,' Tom said. 'Molly must have got here some time yesterday and I want you to look through that paper and tell me if you see any stories involving money. Now it could be anywhere in the paper: a full-page story or just a few lines tucked away somewhere, but I want you to read out anything to do with money, OK?'

'All right,' Flora said, opening the paper as they walked back to the car.

'Anything?' Tom asked after a few minutes.

'There's a pensioner who sold some antiques and made over fifteen thousand pounds.'

'Doesn't count,' Tom said.

Flora turned the page. 'A man has got three thousand pounds.'

'Go on. Did he find it anywhere?'

Flora's mouth set in a straight line across her face as she struggled to read the rest of the piece. 'It says—'

'What?' Tom asked, beginning to sound anxious.

'I can't read it.'

Tom took the paper from Flora and scanned it. 'Oh,' he said at length.

'Isn't it the person we're looking for?'

He shook his head. 'No. This man won his money through a court case.'

'And that doesn't count?'

'No. What we're looking for is someone who *finds* money. Or maybe is *given* money – quite unexpectedly,' he said, handing the paper back before opening a bag of crisps.

'A woman found an envelope stuffed with money on her doormat.'

'Read that one out in full.'

'*Widow, Mabel Spriggs, of Castleton, woke up to find an envelope stuffed with fifty-pound notes on her doormat yesterday morning. "I couldn't believe it," the eighty-four-year-old said. "I'd just been talking about what a struggle I was having the day before and then this happens!"*'

Tom's jaw slackened and his hand paused on its way into the crisp bag. 'That's our Molly,' he said excitedly. 'I'm sure of it.'

Just then, his mobile phone went. Stuffing the crisps onto Flora's lap he searched the back seat, which had long been lost under a layer of clothes that needed to find a launderette.

'Hello. Tom Mackenzie,' he said after finding the phone under an old sock.

'Tom, you old devil!'

'Nick!'

'Where the hell are you?'

'Derbyshire.'

'Well, get your arse over to Manchester. I've just had Susanna Lewis's personal assistant on the phone. She's been following your story and wants to do a piece with you for her show.'

'Susanna Lewis?' Tom said, a fleeting image of the buxom blonde filling his brain.

'You jammy git, you!'

'Blimey!'

'But don't go getting too excited. You'll be sandwiched between a couple of other guests and a phone-in, but this will really get your name out there.'

Tom could hardly speak for the shock, Susanna Lewis's cleavage blocking any train of coherent thought.

'You still there, mate?'

'Y-yes!'

'Just don't forget to give *Vive!* a plug for us. This could secure you a permanent place on the old rag if you play your cards right.'

* * *

Carolyn had wondered why Marty had bought her flowers. They weren't supermarket flowers either, but florist-bought, wrapped in red tissue paper with a swirl of silver ribbon.

'I just wanted to say I'm sorry for the last few days,' he'd whispered, kissing her neck delicately in a way that always set her skin on fire.

And then he'd dropped the bomb. 'I told Dad we'd go round Granddad's today. Dad wants a hand with some odd jobs round the place.'

Carolyn had stared at him. 'Marty – this is supposed to be our holiday. I thought—'

'It's only for a few hours,' Marty had interrupted quickly. 'Then we can go out this evening – have a nice meal somewhere.'

Carolyn's eyebrows had shot up in surprise. Marty never took her out to eat. 'Just think of the amount of shopping you can get for the same price,' he'd say.

'Do you mean it?' Carolyn had said.

'Promise,' he'd said. 'It'll be the real start of our holiday.' With that, he'd kissed her neck in that oh-so-tender place again.

So two hours later she found herself at Old Bailey's once again, cheap washing-up suds fizzing into nothing on her hands as she worked her way through a mountain range of dishes. As usual, Old Bailey hadn't done any washing-up since her last visit. He'd simply let it fester in assorted heaps around the kitchen: a teetering tower of teacups here, a precarious pile of plates there. Carolyn wouldn't have minded at all if she ever got a thank you, but thank yous were as rare as smiles in the Bailey household. The living room was one collective frown today and Carolyn hadn't any desire to be a part of it.

She'd hidden herself away in the kitchen for as long as she could, making friends with every dirty plate and cup; washing, drying and stacking in a vain attempt to make the time pass quickly.

She ambled through to the back bedroom and said hello to the family of photographs. She fluffed her hair up in the bathroom and was just about to tell Marty that she was going to walk to the local shops when she heard the strangest of cries. Momentarily forgetting her latest idea for an outrageously short haircut, she ran through to the living room.

'Marty? What is it?' she asked, seeing her husband on the edge of his seat, his eyes twice their normal size, a copy of *Vive!* clutched in his hands.

Carolyn felt a cold chill shake its way down her spine. Who had brought a copy of *Vive!* into the house again?

'Marty? What is it?' she asked, dreading to think what he'd found in the paper and hoping it had something to do with inflation or shares dropping rather than his sister's antics. 'What's the matter?'

'Molly!' he said, pointing at the paper. '*Molly!*'

Chapter Twenty-One

Molly had the strangest feeling that someone was calling her name, which was really rather absurd because she was sat on the side of Mam Tor with nothing around her but grass and sky. She put it down to exhaustion because she'd had a busy day.

She couldn't really say why she'd chosen to visit Derbyshire other than her love of open spaces, but it had certainly kept her occupied: widows, old people's homes, a church raising funds for a new roof, and a fete raising money for a local animal rescue centre – it was all there ready for her and her money.

Although Molly had never had so much fun in her life, there was a little part of her that wanted to return home, especially now that The Bloom Room actually belonged to her. She missed the quietness of the flowers and the golden afternoons when Mrs Purdie would call. Molly smiled as she remembered her dear customer. One of the first things she'd done before leaving on her trip was to set up a weekly delivery of flowers to the old lady, arranged via her florist friend.

The thing that amazed Molly the most was the pleasure a little bit of money gave people. It was the grease that lubricated life but it could also so easily become the spanner in the works.

Molly wondered if, perhaps, she'd kept a little too much for herself. The last thing she wanted was to become a Bailey. It was strange to think of the money she'd put away just sitting earning interest: all that money accumulating without her having to lift a finger. She'd never earned any decent interest before: her barren bank accounts had never yielded more than a few pounds each year. Her life as an earner was a constant embarrassment. Her brother, who'd once helped her to fill in her tax return, had been flabbergasted.

'Is this it?' he'd said in horrified disbelief. 'Are you absolutely *sure* that's a whole year's worth?'

Molly nodded. 'Quite sure. My maths isn't the best in the world but the figures are so small that they were simple enough to add up.'

'How the hell are you managing?'

'Bank loan.'

Marty's eyebrows rose. To him, the word *loan* was up there with *debt* and *bankruptcy* as things that would never enter his own realm.

'I know what you're thinking, but things really are improving,' Molly said. 'Look – I've worked it out – I'm up by three per cent on last year.'

Marty didn't look impressed. 'This isn't good, Moll. You need a serious injection of money into this place if you're to survive.'

'What do you suggest I do? Go out and apply for a lottery grant?'

Molly laughed as she remembered mentioning the word *lottery* but quickly stopped as she thought of how Marty would react if he ever found out. No, he mustn't ever know, she thought. Briefly, she wondered if she'd made a mistake telling Carolyn but she'd trust her with her life. She wouldn't let on. The only way Marty could possibly find out was if he read *Vive!*.

Molly frowned as she thought of the reporter again. Tom Mackenzie. Peeping Tom. He had the power to ruin everything for her and the thought made her blood boil. But the likelihood of Marty picking up a copy of *Vive!* was somewhat remote. He was a bit of a snob when it came to newspapers and there just weren't enough financial pages in that rag to tempt him to buy it.

Molly flopped back on the grassy hill, her hand resting on Fizz, who was panting after their walk. Life was good, she thought and, at least for the moment, nobody knew where she was or what she was doing.

'It's not possible,' Magnus said, a copy of *Vive!* shaking in his hands. 'I was just talking to her – yesterday – she would have said something.'

'She's said nothing to me, that's for sure,' Marty said.

'But how did she get so much money all of a sudden?' Magnus asked, his face as dark as December.

Marty scowled at the report again. 'It just says they think she's a lottery winner.'

'But *how much*?'

'It doesn't say, Dad!' Marty said, becoming impatient. 'Nobody seems to know.'

'It's that bloody Percy woman!' Old Bailey intoned, his face turning puce as he grabbed the newspaper from his grandson and read it in disbelief. 'She's to blame. Bad influence on this family – right from the start.'

'Dad,' Magnus said, 'you can't keep blaming her.'

'Why not, eh? You tell me why not!' he barked from the winged chair, heavy jowls shaking in anger.

Magnus ran a hand through his hair and shook his head.

It was at that point that Marty turned to Carolyn. 'You know something about this, don't you?' he said, his voice sounding bruised, as if instantly suspecting that she'd betrayed him.

'Wh-what do you mean?'

'She rang – yesterday.'

'I told you, Marty, we were just chatting.'

'But she *must* have said something!' Marty said in exasperation. 'Look!' He picked up the copy of *Vive!* and waved it under Carolyn's nose. 'It's in the paper, for God's sake.' And then he paused. 'Hang on a minute. Wasn't that man who visited a reporter? Caro?'

She nodded.

Marty opened the paper with clumsy hands. 'Tom Mackenzie? The same man? What does he know that we don't? Carolyn? What did he say to you?'

'Nothing! He said nothing!'

'Then why did he visit?'

'I don't know – he'd heard a rumour or something. I don't remember. I had other things on my mind that day,' she said, glaring at her husband lest he should have forgotten.

'This just doesn't make any sense. Why wouldn't she tell us?' Marty asked angrily.

Carolyn was fast becoming angry herself. They just had to

take a closer look at themselves to see why Molly wouldn't want to confide in them but they wouldn't think to do that. Sometimes, she wanted to grab hold of them all and shake them until they saw sense. Instead she stood spectator-like, as the scene escalated out of control before her.

'This is so like Molly – selfish, headstrong—'

Old Bailey interrupted Marty from his winged chair. 'I don't understand what's going on!' His bony hand extended and he grabbed the newspaper for a second time.

'We're trying to find out, Granddad.'

'Well get a bloody move on before she spends all this money.'

Marty's eyes widened at his words. 'You're right! We've got to get a move on. We've got to go after her,' he said, looking round the room excitedly as if he was already mentally packing.

'You can't be serious, Marty!' Carolyn said, fear filling her body.

'I'm dead serious,' Marty said. 'We've got to find her. We've got to put a stop to all this nonsense.'

Carolyn knew she couldn't let this happen; she had to try and make Marty see sense. 'Wait!' she said. 'Just think for a moment. If Molly has won this money and she hasn't told you, it's for a reason, and there's absolutely no point in you trying to find her because she doesn't want to be found.'

Marty's eyes narrowed. 'You do know something about this, don't you?'

'I've told you, I don't.'

'Then why did she ring you yesterday?'

Carolyn sighed. 'We were just talking – like we normally do.'

'But she *must* have said something to you!'

'Honestly, Marty, she didn't,' Carolyn said, swallowing quickly. As much as she hated lying to her husband, seeing his reaction to this firmly placed her on Molly's side.

'There's something you're not telling us, and that's why we've got to get a move on. We've got to find her before she does something really stupid,' Marty said.

'I'm coming with you!' Old Bailey shouted, and he was on his feet in a split second. 'Where's my scarf?'

'Granddad, it's the middle of August – you won't need your scarf. Anyway, just hang on a minute,' Marty said, his face scowling in deep thought. 'It's getting a bit late now. By the time we pack, we won't get very far and then we'll have to shell out for an overnighter.'

Magnus and Old Bailey nodded their heads in agreement.

'Far better to start fresh in the morning.'

Carolyn rolled her eyes. 'This is *ridiculous*. It doesn't matter what she's doing or where she's doing it. She isn't answerable to you.'

But it was no use; nobody was listening to her. The three Bailey men were poring over the newspaper again.

'Moor View flats – Bradford!' Magnus shouted. 'Bloody hell – she's been back to Bradford and she didn't tell me!'

'Five *hundred* pounds to each flat!' Marty said.

'That bloody Percy woman!' Old Bailey said, shaking a fist at *Vive!*. 'Let me get my scarf. We'll leave first thing in the morning.'

Chapter Twenty-Two

Tom could feel beads of sweat breaking out on his forehead as the make-up girl hovered over him with a damp sponge the colour of mud.

'Is that entirely necessary?' he asked.

'You don't want to appear all blotchy and shiny on camera, do you?' the girl said, running the brown sponge over his cheeks and squashing it into his nose as if she meant to remove it. 'Sit still, please,' she said in a voice like ice. 'I've got Nicole and Juliette to do yet. You're not the only celebrity on tonight, you know.'

'N-Nicole?' Tom said, his voice cracking in anticipation. It couldn't be, could it? He couldn't even begin to hope that it might be.

'Ms Kidman is in the next dressing room, and I don't want to keep her waiting.'

'N-Nicole Kidman!'

'Don't go getting any ideas about disturbing her. She's pretty down to earth but she still likes her privacy.' The make-up artist slammed his drooping mouth shut before he drooled down the chin that she'd just got perfect.

'And don't go bothering Juliette either.'

'J-Juliette?' Tom was palpitating again.

'Juliette Binoche.' The make-up artist sighed. 'Blimey. I would've thought a reporter like you would've done his homework before coming on a show with Nicole Kidman and Juliette Binoche!'

'Done my homework!' Tom said. His eyes glazed over. He wasn't worried about having done his homework. He was more concerned that his deodorant was going to hold out when faced with two modern-day movie paragons.

'Of course, I've done everyone in my time,' the make-up artist smirked, her face bloated with smugness. 'And I can tell you this for nothing – there's no such thing as a natural beauty. You wouldn't believe what some of these so-called sex symbols look like before I've dealt with them!'

But Tom wasn't listening. Nicole Kidman and Juliette Binoche were down the hall. They were in the same building. He could run into them at any moment, in fact, he probably would. What would he say? What could he possibly say to the women of his dreams?

'Hey!' the make-up artist scolded. 'Do you mind not perspiring quite so much? You're sweating my foundation off.'

Tom glared at her but, before he could think of a fitting reprimand, there was a gentle knock on the door.

'Come in!' the make-up artist yelled.

'Hi!' A friendly voice floated in from the corridor and a red-haired beauty gazed in at Tom. 'I just wanted to say good luck. You're Tom, aren't you?'

Tom nodded, his knees weak from the gorgeous

Australian accent even though he was sitting down.

'Thank you, N-Nicole.'

'Interviews always make me nervous,' she confessed, stepping into the room, her black dress revealing a good deal of honeyed thigh. 'You're very brave to go first,' she said with a silvery giggle that made Tom's flesh goosebump all over.

'I am?'

'Oh, yes! You have to warm the audience up, you know.'

'I hadn't thought about that,' Tom said, feeling his forehead was now doing a rather good impression of Niagara Falls.

'But you'll be fine, I'm sure.'

'Nicole!' Another female voice sounded outside Tom's dressing room and, seconds later, a dark-haired beauty peeped into his room. 'Gosh! It's Tom Mackenzie, isn't it? I had no idea you were going to be on the show tonight!' a breathless Juliette Binoche announced, her French accent setting his heart racing.

'I know,' Nicole said, 'it's so exciting, isn't it! He's first, too.'

'Oooooo! You can warm the chair up for me, can't you!' Juliette smiled, winking a bright eye at him.

'Juliette and I were just wondering who else was on tonight. She thought it was going to be some boring musician but we're so glad it's you.'

'You are?' Tom gazed at Nicole and immediately felt his heart accelerate into a speed that couldn't possibly be considered healthy.

'Well, ye-es!' she smiled, her eyes sparkling. 'We'd much rather have a hard-working reporter than some vain musician.'

'But I thought actresses hated reporters.'

'Think again!' Nicole said, gliding further into the room and sliding a manicured hand onto his shoulder.

Any minute now, he thought, and he was going to hyperventilate.

'You've got it all wrong,' Juliette said, placing a hand on his other shoulder, smiling her bewitching smile at him.

'Mr Mackenzie – it's time.' The make-up artist, who'd been happily forgotten since the arrival of the delectable duo, made her presence felt again as she aimed a jet of hairspray at him in a last attempt to get his look just right.

'Good luck!' Juliette smiled.

'Knock 'em dead, gorgeous!' Nicole laughed.

'Th-thanks!' Tom said, getting up and almost tripping over his own feet at the sight of his favourite actresses blowing kisses at him.

And, suddenly, he was out there: in front of the audience, in front of the cameras, in front of respected interviewer of the stars, Andre Levinson. He didn't even notice the deafening applause until he sat down, his face frozen in terror.

'It isn't often,' Levinson began, 'that we find a reporter more famous than the story he's chasing, but this would seem to be the case with you,' he said, giving Tom an encouraging smile. 'Have you found the media interest a little strange – as a member of the press, I mean?'

Tom's senses were so swamped that he wasn't quite sure he'd heard the question. Visions of Nicole Kidman's honeyed thigh and Juliette Binoche's smile refused to leave his mind's eye.

'Is it not rather odd being on the receiving end of the press's interest?' Levinson prodded again.

'*Yes!*' Tom blurted out, feeling more beads of perspiration battling through the make-up. 'It is,' he said, feeling himself floundering helplessly. 'After years of chasing other people, it is a little surreal to be on the front page of the nationals yourself.' There, he thought, he was pulling through. He was going to be just fine.

'So how does it feel to be a heart-throb?' Levinson asked with a light smile.

Tom grinned. 'Well, what can I say? I don't think you can really take that kind of adoration seriously, can you?'

'Now,' Levinson said, leaning forward slightly in his chair and steepling his fingers, 'a little bird told me that you're not only a national heart-throb and a great reporter but something of a virtuoso with the guitar?'

Tom felt himself blushing. 'Well, one doesn't like to boast...'

'I'm sure our audience would be delighted to hear you,' Levinson smiled, motioning to an awaiting band ready to take up the music. There was a ripple of applause, a few women even screamed.

Tom looked at Levinson who was clapping and nodding towards the stage. Well, Tom thought, there was no point in denying fate, was there, and, with the ease of a superstar, he walked towards the stage.

The studio lights dimmed and he found himself standing in a cool blue light, his fingers strumming, his throat huskily finding the notes he'd rehearsed so often in the shower. It was a perfect moment and he lost himself to it completely until his three and a half minutes of wonderment was up.

And then something truly amazing happened. The audience screamed. Tom Mackenzie was a hit! And, from the hysteria of the women in the audience, he was going to become a huge star. Offstage, he could hear phones ringing. Producers, record companies, even Chris Isaak – they all wanted him. The phones wouldn't stop. Ringing. Ringing. Ringing...

'Da-aaaa-ad!'

Tom woke, his heart thudding wildly, his breath coming short and sharp. Where was he? What was going on? What had happened to the audience? To Nicole? To Juliette? Where was his guitar?

And then he saw it: sitting on the floor at the end of the bed – where he'd left it the night before.

'*Dad!*' Flora shouted. 'Your alarm's been going for ages! And you were singing in your sleep again! It was terrible! You never sing in tune in your sleep.'

Tom rubbed his eyes at his rude awakening. God almighty. He wasn't on *Levinson* at all. It was Wednesday morning, and he'd woken up in a cheap bed and breakfast on the outskirts of Manchester and, what was even worse, he knew that he wasn't going to be interviewed on *Levinson*. He wasn't going to meet Nicole Kidman or Juliette Binoche, he wasn't going to be asked to sing, and he wasn't going to be discovered.

He was going to be interviewed, all right, but it was on *Susanna*: a chat show which was indistinguishable from all the other chat shows plaguing daytime TV. It aired at two in the afternoon and was notorious for having row upon row of dirty old men leering down the young presenter's blouse.

'Daddy?' Flora interrupted.

'Yes?'

'Do you think anyone famous will be on *Susanna*?'

'No,' Tom said. 'I bloody well don't,' he added under his breath as he headed into the bathroom for a shave.

*   *   *

Carolyn could think of no worse fate than spending her summer holidays trapped in a car with Marty, Magnus and Old Bailey.

'You should've turned left there,' Old Bailey barked from the back seat. 'It's quicker by half a mile.'

'Do *you* want to drive, Granddad?'

Old Bailey harrumphed. 'I'm only saying, if you want to save on petrol—'

'Granddad!'

'I'm only saying.'

Carolyn sighed and stared out of the window at the landscape vanishing fast behind them as Marty stepped on it. They were only twenty miles down the M6 from Carlisle and, already, it was mutiny in the Mini. She hadn't wanted to come on the trip at all but neither had she wanted to stay at home. Firstly, she'd decided that if she stayed close to Marty she could keep Molly informed of his every move. Now that Molly had a mobile phone, it would be easy to keep in touch with her and make sure that she was one step ahead of the Bailey men. Secondly, she hadn't wanted to stay at home alone after what had happened that morning.

Marty had been haranguing her about leaving early and had almost hammered the bathroom door down.

'I'll be out in a minute,' Carolyn had called back. One minute. Yes – that was all she needed – one minute of quiet pacing, of running her hands through her hair and of picking the browned ends off the spider plant.

One minute; that was enough. Enough for a little blue line to change her life.

She was pregnant.

Chapter Twenty-Three

Molly hesitated at the junction, her indicator knocking quietly. Which way? Left or right? For a moment, she gazed at the road in between the two signs but she knew she couldn't very well drive down it because it was a private driveway. Cedar Lodge, it said. Children's Home. Private drive.

Private. Molly hated that word. She always wanted to rebel whenever she saw it. What right did people have to hide behind that word? And what exactly were they hiding?

Molly switched her indicator off, driving straight across the junction and along the private driveway through an avenue of fine chestnut trees and before she knew it found herself at the end of the driveway and was staring at a very ugly building. Cedar Lodge was a cold, drab-looking Victorian house with tall dark windows and a door like a cavernous mouth. Molly shivered. It looked damp as well as drab, she thought. It also looked rather empty.

Parking her car on a gravel driveway overrun with weeds, she decided to go in. The door was open and led into a long black and white tiled hallway with coat hooks stacked with mountains of clothes and shoes and boots all over the place. It was cold, despite the warmth of the day, and there wasn't a single child around.

'Hello?' Molly tried, her voice echoing up the stairwell. There didn't seem to be anyone there. Funny that the front door should be open, Molly thought. People were just so trusting.

There was a large room to the left of the hallway, and Molly stuck her head round the door. It was empty apart from a huge box of toys in the centre of the room and a couple of scruffy sofas. Kneeling down on the floor, Molly rifled through the box. There were three limbless dolls, a couple of stained teddies and a few board games which looked tatty and tired. Not an inspiring lot if you were trapped indoors for the day.

'Can I help you?' a woman called from the doorway.

Molly turned around, startled, and was faced with what looked like an army sergeant in an apron. 'I'm sorry,' she said quickly. 'I didn't mean to pry. I called, but there was no answer.'

'I was upstairs,' the woman said, her brows hovering low and suspicious over her steel-rimmed glasses. 'What is it you wanted?'

Molly stood up to full height. 'I wanted to enquire how to make a donation.'

'I see,' the woman said, her voice softening a fraction. 'What was it? Old toys...?'

'Er, no. I can see you've got quite a few of those.'

'Yes,' the woman said, her lips thin and firm. 'People don't tend to give things away until they're good and used up.'

Molly smiled. 'I was thinking of some new toys, actually – brand new.'

The woman looked puzzled.

'Would you like to go shopping with me?' Molly asked.

Once again, the woman frowned, and then a slow smile began to spread across her face as she nodded. 'I'll just get my handbag,' she said.

Susanna Lewis's cleavage was showed off to great advantage by the low-cut black jacket she was wearing. Surely, Tom thought, it should come with a fifteen certificate? It certainly shouldn't have been on daytime television.

After a brief session in make-up, which wasn't half as bad as that of his dream sequence, he was led out into the studio. The audience wasn't quite as large as Levinson's, and was stuffed with old people, but it would have to do. The polite applause came to an abrupt end as he sat down on the famous flower-festooned sofa in Susanna's cottage-style set where everything was a riot of chintz. There were flowers in every conceivable size and colour, candles and glasses in rich reds and gaudy greens and, at the back of the set, a hideously large stained-glass window featuring Susanna herself. Tom was beginning to think that the make-up girl should have provided him with very dark sunglasses.

Susanna began the interview by holding up a couple of copies of *Vive!*, which Tom thought wouldn't do him any harm at all, and filled the audience in on the story so far, saying how there weren't enough 'heroes and heroines' in the country.

'But it seems to me that you might actually have found one,' she said, leaning forward slightly in a cutely conspiratorial way.

'Well,' Tom began, feeling the first beads of perspiration breaking through his make-up, 'I'm not so sure. They say there's no such thing as a selfless act – that we only ever give in the hope of receiving something ourselves, and I have a feeling that this Molly Bailey might be some sort of attention seeker.'

'Really?' Susanna's pale eyebrows rose into beautiful arches.

'Yes. I mean, don't you think it's a strange thing to do: give money away? I feel that it's not so much a selfless act as a way of getting attention.'

'So all Molly Bailey is wanting is media publicity?'

'That's what I believe,' Tom said.

'You were the first reporter on this story, and I think it's going to be just huge,' Susanna began, uncrossing and crossing her legs, 'but how do you feel now that the other tabloids are chasing the same story?'

Tom grimaced. He'd been warned that this would happen: that all his hard work would be stolen and reinterpreted by others. 'That's the way of the world, I'm afraid. I'm obviously thrilled that I was the one that discovered Molly's story, and I'm sure that my readers will be loyal and follow its progress through my column in *Vive!*,' he said.

Susanna asked a few more questions and they discussed the possible reasons for Molly's sudden wealth and her desire to give it all away. And then it was all over. Tom just managed to make a final plea.

'Don't forget, any sightings of Molly can be reported to me via my email address, which is printed in the paper, and I've just been told by *Vive!* that they're giving away book vouchers for legitimate leads.'

The audience applauded and Susanna shook his hand before turning round to introduce the next guest.

'Her name is Dr Ingrid Hoffman and it's her belief that, in today's current climate, *sex* should be a separate GCSE subject in our schools. So please give her a warm welcome as we go over to Susanna's Study for the educational section of the programme.'

Tom was off the hook and was led out of the studio. It had all passed so quickly. Perhaps he should have mentioned his talent as a musician. Maybe he'd lost his big chance. He was just about to mention it to someone backstage when he caught sight of Flora.

'How was it?' he asked, knowing she'd been watching it in the green room.

She winced. 'Daddy, you were so mean about Molly.'

'What do you mean, *mean*?'

'You don't even know her but you said all those mean things about her.'

'What are you getting so worked up about? This woman's story is paying our bills at the moment.'

Flora frowned deeply and looked down at the floor.

'I'm sorry if you don't agree with what I'm doing but I can't really stop now, can I? You heard Susanna – this story's going to be huge.' He took Flora's hand and they left the studio. 'We've both got a big stake in this, whether we like it or not.'

'I'm not sure I like it,' she said.

Tom sighed. He didn't liked being reprimanded by his own daughter; it cut him to the quick, but what was he to do? Listen to the moral rantings of a ten-year-old or follow his journalistic instincts and milk his story for all it was worth? Anyway, it was too late to do anything about it now: not only had he spoken his mind on national television but, seconds before he'd gone on air, he'd emailed his latest piece for *Vive!* saying as much as he had on *Susanna*.

They left the studios and Tom opened the car door for Flora who got in without saying a single word to him.

It wasn't until they were on the motorway that he realised his face was still covered in thick orange make-up.

The toy department was irresistible. Molly dived in, her eyes bright as she examined the wealth on display. Mrs Steele, the housekeeper, had told her that the ages of the children at Cedar Lodge ranged from eight to fourteen so, whilst they could have a ball choosing soft and cuddly companions, they should also think about something a little more grown-up for the teenagers – perhaps computer games.

'How many children are there at the home?' Molly asked.

'Twenty-three,' Mrs Steele said.

'Most of our girls prefer them to clothes,' Mrs Steele went on, rolling her eyes. 'Only problem is, the computer is so old and slow—'

'That's not a problem,' Molly said. 'We'll replace that whilst we're at it. We'll get two. Three!'

Mrs Steele's eyes were out on stalks. 'Really?'

'Yes. Come on,' Molly said, 'let's get to work.'

Molly hadn't had so much fun for a long time and, judging by Mrs Steele's flushed cheeks and broad smile, neither had she. Bag after bag was filled with toys before they headed to the computer department and chose a selection of games. Molly ordered the three computers to be delivered to Cedar Lodge and then, arms weighed down, they headed back to Molly's car.

'Careful not to squash Fizz!' Molly warned as they crammed the bags, which wouldn't fit into the boot, onto the back seat. 'Will you be OK to sit here for a moment?'

'I think so. Why?'

'I'm just going to nip back and get something. I won't be long.'

And she wasn't. When she got back to the car, she presented a handful of wallets stuffed with gift vouchers: one for each child in Cedar Lodge.

'I used to hate it when adults bought me clothes,' she explained.

Mrs Steele's mouth dropped open. 'But this is too much!'

'I don't think so. What are a few gifts? They haven't got parents to give them any.'

Mrs Steele nodded. 'You know, it's always puzzled me, but it's not very often that we get a child who wants to find their birth parent. They seem to realise that they're at Cedar Lodge because things were difficult, and they don't ask questions.'

They don't ask questions, Molly thought. But *she* had, all the time. Why had their mother left them? Had she simply woken up one day and stopped loving them? Had she and Marty done something to upset her? No. Molly may have thought those things to begin with but the slow realisation of what a nightmare it must have been to live with their father had dawned upon her.

Mrs Steele chuckled suddenly, pulling Molly out of her dark thoughts. 'We once had an incident when one of our girls, Alexis, tried to find her birth mother. She even went as far as contacting a private detective. I think she'd just got a bit carried away after watching the repeats of *Moonlighting* on Sky.'

'But private detectives cost a fortune!' Molly said.

'Yes,' Mrs Steele agreed. 'I don't think Alexis had thought

that far ahead.' She laughed. 'I'll never forget picking up that envelope from the Marie Celeste Detective Agency.'

'*Marie Celeste*?'

'Yes! It's quite reputable. One of the best, I hear. The man who runs it is rather eccentric, though. He turned up one afternoon not realising that Cedar Lodge was a children's home and that the letter had been written by a fourteen-year-old. Anyway, she forgot about it all when Johnny arrived.'

'Johnny?'

'The Cedar Lodge stud.'

'Ah!'

'Turn left here,' Mrs Steele said as they left the suburbs behind them and ploughed on into the countryside, 'and then straight along until you see the line of trees.'

It was a bit of a rugby scrum getting through the doors with eighteen bags of shopping but they just about managed it. Mrs Steele collapsed into an armchair whilst Molly arranged the bags so that the contents wouldn't spill out all over the front room carpet.

'I can't tell you how much I've enjoyed today,' she sighed. 'I don't often get away from Cedar Lodge.'

Molly smiled up from her home on the floor. 'I'm so glad you came. I don't think I could've managed without you.'

Mrs Steele's eyes narrowed a fraction behind her glasses. 'Oh, I'm sure you would've managed. You look like the kind of girl who manages everything *perfectly*.'

Molly held her gaze for a moment, knowing that something was coming next but not quite sure what it was.

'Can I ask you what made you do this today?' Mrs Steele asked.

Molly smiled. She knew the question had been on the tip of

her tongue all day. 'Let's just say that there's a part of me that understands how these children must feel.'

Mrs Steele nodded. 'Have you time for a cup of tea? The children won't be back for another hour or so. It's not often they get a day out, bless them, but it would be a shame if you missed them.'

'No, thanks. I'm afraid I've got to hit the road.'

Mrs Steele frowned. 'But they'd love to meet you.'

'Be sure and say hello for me, won't you?' Molly said, fishing her car keys out of her jacket pocket. 'I'm really sorry I can't stay.'

'You're going right now?'

Molly nodded. 'I'm afraid so.'

'I don't know how to thank you.'

'You don't have to. I didn't do it so that I could be thanked.'

Mrs Steele crossed the room and surprised Molly by wrapping her arms around her. 'You're an angel,' she whispered, and then pulled away quickly and hurried through to the kitchen.

Leaving the house and cranking up Old Faithful, Molly took a last look at the old Victorian building. She'd have to ring a builder and decorator before she left the area if she was really to be of help to Cedar Lodge but that was easy enough to arrange with a couple of phone calls. She'd also make sure that Mrs Steele received the biggest bunch of flowers the very next day for being such a dear and it would, of course, include half a dozen yellow gerbera.

But there was another phone call she had to make: to the Marie Celeste Detective Agency. At school, she'd been known as 'no-mummy Molly' but it had never occurred to her to try and find her mother. Until now.

Chapter Twenty-Four

Carolyn watched as Marty crossed the road back towards the car, shaking his head. It didn't look good. She sighed. They'd already tried at least half a dozen bed and breakfasts in the area, and all with the same message: no vacancies. But what could they expect during high season? It wasn't as if they'd done anything rational like booking ahead or anything.

Getting into the car, Marty started the ignition. 'They've only got two doubles left,' he said.

'How much?' Old Bailey barked from the back seat.

'Thirty-five per person per night.'

Old Bailey shook his head. 'It's a bloody rip-off but it's the cheapest so far.'

'But they've only got doubles left, Granddad. I've just said.'

'So? I can share with Magnus,' Old Bailey harrumphed.

Marty turned the ignition off and screwed up his face in alarm. 'Share? With Father?'

'Come on, let's get in there before someone else books it,' Old Bailey said, winding his scarf around his neck before opening the car door and making for the boot.

'Marty?' Carolyn said as Magnus got out of the car in resignation of the night ahead.

'What?'

'Isn't it just a little bit early to be checking in for the night?'

'Five o'clock? You know what Granddad's like – he's a creature of habit. Five o'clock is time for a drink and a snooze before teatime.'

Carolyn grimaced. Although she felt she could sleep too after being squashed in a car all day with the Bailey men, she didn't fancy being trapped in a bed and breakfast with them.

'Can we go out later? See a bit of the Peak District before it gets dark?'

'I'm shattered, Caro. I feel as if I've been driving all day.'

'OK,' she said, resigning herself to an evening with her book.

'We'll see,' he said, obviously feeling bad, which, in turn, made her feel bad. He looked absolutely drained; his face that peculiar white that comes from hours of concentrating on traffic.

'No,' she said, 'don't worry.' And then she thought of something. She had something to do; something she hadn't been able to do all day with so many pairs of beady eyes on her: ring Molly.

The Marie Celeste Detective Agency might have had the best reputation in the Greater Manchester area but it was nothing more than a single office behind a tatty launderette which looked as if it could do with a good wash itself. It had also been incredibly difficult to find. Molly felt sure she was going to be late for her five o'clock appointment but perhaps that had been half of the test. If clients could find the agency, it would prove that they had some wits about them and might have actually tried to find their particular missing person.

Taking a deep breath, Molly pressed an intercom to the side of an enormous shiny black door and was buzzed through to be greeted by a dark entrance hall. It took a couple of seconds for her eyes to adjust, but when they did she saw a plaque on the wall that pointed the way to an office door. Molly walked forward, Fizz trotting alongside her, and knocked.

'Come in!' a husky voice sounded from the other side.

Molly opened the door and stepped inside. The room, like the hallway, was dark despite the large window at the back of the room but, as it overlooked other buildings over a narrow alleyway, it wasn't that surprising that there wasn't much room for light.

'Mrs Bailey?' the owner of the husky voice enquired.

'Miss. Molly.'

'Miss Molly?' he said, making her sound like a character from *Gone with the Wind*.

'Just Molly.'

'Molly.'

'Yes. And Fizz the dog.'

'I'm Malcolm McCleod,' he said, acknowledging Fizz with a nod.

Molly extended her hand and, resting his cigarette on the side of an overflowing ashtray, he shook it. She'd half expected him to get up from his chair but he remained seated.

'Please, sit down,' he said, motioning to a cracked leather chair.

'Thank you,' Molly said as she sat down, Fizz flopping down beside her.

'Now, let me find your notes,' he said, sifting through some papers on his desk. 'They're here somewhere. I thought they were...' He tutted, losing himself in an avalanche of paper.

Molly glanced around the room but it wasn't very easy to see anything with the lack of light and the smoke which filled it with an ugly fog, so she turned her attention to Malcolm McCleod instead. He had tight red curly hair and was wearing a hideous tartan shirt, making him look as if he was about to play a round of golf and do the Highland fling at the same time.

'Ah! Here we are,' McCleod declared at last. 'Cynthia Bailey, née Percy.'

'That's right.'

'Your mother.'

'Yes.'

'Why do you want to find her?'

Molly's eyes widened in surprise. 'Why? She's my mother.'

'I know, but I must know if this is to be an amicable reunion.'

'You mean you won't help me if I'm out to kill her or something?'

McCleod cleared his throat. 'That's right.'

'Do you get many clients who want to commit murder, then?'

It was McCleod's turn to give a wide-eyed stare. 'We've had one or two incidents in the past, yes, which is why I'm asking you this now.'

Molly felt the beginnings of a small smile. 'No, I don't want to kill my mother.'

McCleod squinted at her across the table. 'Good. Then I should be able to help you.'

'Thank you.'

'So when was the last time you saw your mother?'

Molly's mouth dropped open a fraction. When was the last time she'd seen her? It was so long ago.

'When I was eleven. Sixteen years ago.'

'And you've not kept in touch?'

Molly shook her head, her dark curls knocking against the side of her face.

'Did she leave a note? Did she phone?'

'No. She only left a cardigan.'

'A cardigan?'

'Yes. I don't think that's very important though. To you, I mean.' But it was important to Molly. Her mother's baggy woollen cardigan known as the cardigan of many colours. It was a collection of squares she used to knit whilst watching television, which she'd then joined together into a ginormous patchwork cardigan. When she and her brother were small, they could get lost in it for days.

'You don't think the cardigan is relevant?'

'No,' Molly said. 'I think it was just meant as a token of comfort or something.'

'So why did she leave?'

Molly sighed. 'I think she just got tired of my father.'

'Were there marital problems?'

'More monetary problems, I think. She liked to spend money and he didn't. It sounds silly but he was a constant nightmare.' Molly watched as McCleod made some spidery notes with a black fountain pen.

'And do you think she wants to be found? Have you planned what it is you'll say when you find her?'

'Gracious!' Molly exclaimed. 'I haven't, no.'

'Well, you should. Start thinking about that now. We've

been known to find people very quickly and it's advisable that you're prepared.'

'We? You mean, you don't do all the work yourself?'

McCleod smiled a strange smile and then pushed himself away from the desk. It was then that Molly saw he was in the biggest, brightest wheelchair she'd ever seen.

'Legs,' he said.

Molly frowned. 'What?'

'Legs – he's my sidekick – ha!' He laughed at his own joke. 'He does all the hoofing. I'm mostly office-based now, thank God. The brains behind the desk.'

'I see.'

'You're surprised.'

'No!'

'Trust me. Legs is the best guy for the job. You can trust him with your life. Or your mother, at the very least.'

'So what's the next step?'

'Give me your mobile phone number.'

Molly did as she was told. 'And what do I do?'

'Keep in an area where your mobile phone works. We'll get in touch if we have any news.'

Molly nodded. So that put paid to her trip into the Welsh mountains, then.

'And you don't need anything else from me?'

'Did you bring the photo?'

'Oh, yes,' Molly said, digging in her pocket and bringing out a tiny photo she'd carried around with her for sixteen years. She handed it over.

'Thank you,' he said, examining the photo closely. 'You look just like her.'

Molly gave a little smile. 'I guess that's normal.'

'But she won't look like this now, will she?'

'I guess not.'

'And that's something else you should prepare yourself for.'

When Molly left the Marie Celeste office, her eyes blinked at the harsh light outside.

What had McCleod said? *Keep in an area where your mobile works.* Molly patted her pocket, not even sure if the phone was switched on. She took it out and looked at it. No, it was definitely on.

Suddenly, it began to ring.

'Hello?'

'Molly! *Thank goodness.*'

'Caro? What's the matter?'

'It's the Bailey boys, Moll. They're on to you.'

'What do you mean?'

'We're in Derbyshire. They're trying to catch up with you. They know about the money, Moll.'

'What? *How?*'

'They got hold of a copy of *Vive!.*'

'You're joking!'

'I'm afraid not. They've been following that reporter, Tom Mackenzie.'

Molly bit her lip to prevent herself from swearing. So, she'd been found out, had she? The Baileys were on to her, were they?

'Caro?' she said. 'Are you with me on this?'

'Of *course* I am. That's why I'm ringing.'

'OK,' Molly said, 'here's what I want you to do.'

Chapter Twenty-Five

Since the disagreement over Tom's *Susanna* interview, Flora hadn't uttered a single word to her father. Instead, they'd driven in stony silence, their faces etched with fury. God, he thought, she was so like him sometimes that it was frightening but, he supposed, he'd rather have it that way than her taking after her mother. He couldn't think of anything worse than being trapped in the car for the duration of the summer with a mini-Anise. But, what was even more frightening was that Flora really did have a point. What if he'd taken the wrong angle on his story and this Molly Bailey was just a genuine do-gooder? He shuddered at the phrase. He was sure that nice people and good deeds didn't sell as many papers – there *had* to be another angle if he was to make his story the biggest this summer.

For a moment, he thought about his victim. What was she really like? He only had that photograph he'd found of her on the Internet the day before, winning some florists' award, and the rare physical description with which to try and pin her down. He brought to mind Lord Henry's ardent observation

of her: *bare legs up to her armpits and a bosom to die for.*
Tom grinned. Then there'd been the *big, black, bouncy curls
like I've never seen before.* Yes, this Molly Bailey sounded as
if she might be a real corker. In fact, she sounded rather like
the kind of woman Tom himself went for.

Realising that he'd best find somewhere to park so he could
check his email for any potential Molly sightings, he pulled off
the main road and headed into a sleepy village. There was no
telling what Molly might have been up to or where she might
have headed since he'd gone to Manchester for his television
appearance.

Parking on a quiet street, he unclipped his seat belt.

'Can I go and get some sweets?' Flora asked. Tom looked
up in surprise. It was the first thing she'd said in ages.

'Where?'

'There's a shop over there,' she said, her voice subdued and
sulky.

Tom looked across the road at the village shop. 'OK,' he
said, 'but don't be long, and, here,' he added, handing over a
five-pound note, 'buy us a copy of all the tabloids.'

'*Vive!* too?'

'Of course.'

He watched as she looked both ways before crossing the
road, and then he sighed. He hated it, really hated it, when
they fought. It always seemed such a huge waste of energy:
energy they should be spending in having fun and making the
most of their summer together. It wasn't often that he got to
see so much of her. He really shouldn't be wasting time
fighting with her.

As Flora disappeared into the shop, Tom turned his
attention to the laptop and watched in amazement as it

downloaded his emails. Thirty-two in total. Wow! He was becoming popular. He opened them up, one by one, and a huge smile soon filled his face. He had fans! Real-life fans from all corners of the country. He'd been expecting some up-to-date sightings of Molly but most of the emails were about his very recent appearance on *Susanna*.

Hi there, Tom. Fancy tracking me down? Rebecca Collins from Bristol had written, signing off with six kisses and attaching a photo. Tom opened it, his eyes widening at the voluptuous redhead that greeted him. Not bad, not bad.

He opened the next message. *I didn't notice a wedding ring on TV, so thought I'd drop you a line*, Faye Asher had written in a dark-red font. Tom could feel his face heating up as he trawled through the messages. He'd never had so much attention before.

For a brief moment, he flirted with the idea of replying to red-haired Rebecca from Bristol. How far away was Bristol? He quickly got the road atlas out and realised that it was quite a stretch. Still, if Molly headed down that way, what harm would a quick hello do? He felt as if he deserved some fun.

'I've got them,' Flora said, opening the back door of the car and interrupting her father's thoughts of extra-curricular research in the West Country.

'Thanks,' Tom said, quickly flicking through *Vive!* to check that his stuff was still being prominently displayed.

'It's on page three,' Flora said.

Tom grinned. 'Is it?'

Flora nodded. 'Yes.'

'And what did you think of it?'

''Sokay,' she said, reaching into a white paper bag for a strawberry bonbon. 'But I still think you're mean to Molly.'

'You don't even know her,' Tom pointed out.

'Doesn't mean you can say horrid things about people just because you don't know them.'

Tom swallowed hard. He was torn between clouting her and hugging her and, remembering his resolve not to waste any more energy in fighting with her, he grabbed hold of her and planted a fat kiss on her cheek, which was swollen with the undissolved bonbon.

'You're right,' he said. 'You're Daddy's little philosopher, aren't you? To keep me on the straight and narrow.'

'Aw! Daddy!' she yelped, pushing him away before he could kiss her again.

'Just keep an eye on me, won't you?' he said, brushing a strand of her fair hair out of her eyes.

'Daddy,' she said, looking up at him with wide eyes.

'Yes?' he said, loving how adult she could sound.

'You've still got your make-up on.'

It had been easy for Carolyn to slip out of the bed and breakfast. She'd told Marty she was just popping down to the local convenience store for some moisturiser and he hadn't asked any questions. As soon as she was out of the B & B, she rang Molly from her mobile.

And that's when Molly had asked her. Carolyn still couldn't quite believe it: her and Molly in cahoots: the Bailey women against the Bailey men. It was naughty, it was exciting, and it was really rather stupid.

Carolyn sighed as she sat down in an old Lloyd Loom chair in their rather tatty, chintzy room. Marty was sprawled out on the bed, snoring sonorously. She bit her lip as she watched him. What if he was to find out? First, she'd lied to him about knowing Molly had won the lottery, and now she was going to hide Molly's whereabouts from him whilst feeding him duff information. Was Molly sure she was doing the right thing? Carolyn had warned her about Tom Mackenzie's column in *Vive!* and how he had the whole nation looking out for her.

'Shouldn't you think about trading Old Faithful in?' she'd suggested.

'There's absolutely *no way* I'm parting with my car over this. Why should I? Anyway, Caro, don't worry. He can't possibly predict where I'm going next or what I'm going to do. He's always going to be one step behind me.'

But Carolyn wasn't so sure. Tom Mackenzie was a smart guy with a moneymaking agenda, and that spelt trouble. As for Carolyn, was she really up to blatantly lying to her husband? She watched him as he slept, blissfully ignorant of the plan that she and her sister-in-law were hatching.

'It's dead simple,' Molly had said. 'All you have to say is that you've gained my confidence and I've confided in you.'

'And you think he'll believe that?'

'He'll *want* to believe it, Caro, and that's the main thing.'

But *would* he? As he stirred in his sleep, Carolyn became more and more nervous. She hadn't even told him about her pregnancy yet; there just hadn't been a good time. The only moment they'd had to themselves all day had been after lunch when Magnus and Old Bailey had gone to the Gents', but Carolyn hadn't felt like breaking the most important news of her life in a Little Chef car park.

As Marty slept on, she became more and more paranoid. What if he didn't want this baby? When they'd got engaged, they'd sat down and written a long list of what they'd both wanted out of life. Well, Marty had written it; Carolyn had just watched in amazement. Did people really make life-changing decisions with lists?

'I'd like to have pets,' she'd suggested. 'Would you?'

Marty had shaken his head. 'No. Too many allergies are caused by pets.'

'What about children?' she'd said hesitantly after a few minutes' silence.

Marty had blushed. 'All in good time,' he'd said in a very subdued voice.

All in good time, but was *now* a good time? Carolyn wasn't sure. With all this Molly and *Vive!* business, she might have to wait before she broke the news to him.

Picking up Marty's discarded copy of *Vive!*, Carolyn thumbed through it until she came to Tom Mackenzie's column. The cheek of the man, coming to her house thinking she'd help him to ensnare her own sister-in-law! And now making a plea to the nation for sightings of Molly. Was there no limit to the depths this man would plunge in order to make a few quid? He'd even published a photograph of Molly winning her much treasured florists' award a few years ago.

Carolyn started as she thought of something. No, it couldn't possibly work. Could it? She threw the paper back onto the bed and quickly found a pen and some paper.

Just off for a quick walk. Love, C, she wrote, placing the note on Marty's bedside table. Then, picking up her handbag, she left the room, sneaking down the stairs and out of the front door before anyone could notice she'd gone. Reaching into her handbag, she found her mobile again and the little fawn card she'd been given. She shook her head. Either she was completely mad or her hormones were getting the better of her already, but her hammering heart told her that she could just be on to something.

'Hello? Tom Mackenzie?' she said a few seconds later. 'It's Carolyn Bailey here – Molly Bailey's sister-in-law. Look, I have some information you might be able to use.'

It was late Thursday evening and Molly had quite a few miles under her belt. She didn't know why she hadn't thought of it herself, and couldn't quite believe that it had been Carolyn who'd come up with the idea. It was a stroke of sheer sister-in-law genius from the old sparky Caro – the girl Molly hadn't seen for such a long a time.

Molly smiled as she remembered Carolyn's excited phone call.

'I've got his phone number right here, Moll. He asked me to give him a call if I found anything out. So, what do you suggest I find out about you?' There'd been a definite playfulness in her voice and it had made Molly laugh.

The beauty of this plan had been that, whether or not Marty believed that Carolyn knew where Molly was, he'd believe it once he read it in *Vive!*. The only thing to worry about was the public sightings. That could seriously confuse things. Still, she wasn't the only yellow Beetle on the road, was she? Anyway, it would probably get him off the scent for the next couple of days.

From Derbyshire, Molly had dipped in and out of several counties, depositing an awful lot of money and endless yellow flowers. Now, winding her way through the golden villages of the Cotswolds, she was screaming for a good meal.

She'd passed several candidates for pubs: there was The George Inn, which looked extremely upmarket for the middle of nowhere; she'd be way too conspicuous there in her great silver boots. There was the tiny Dog and Gun, but that would probably be full of farmers. No, she wanted something nice and ordinary; somewhere she could relax, have something to eat and leave without anyone noticing her.

Finally she chose The Swan, parking her car at the side of the road and making sure Fizz had a drink before she took her own fill. The pub looked like a setting from a Grimm's fairy story, emerging as it did from a small forest of trees. The honey-coloured stone was worn and weather-beaten, and there was moss growing on the roof. It looked more like a private residence than a pub and that made it all the more inviting.

It looked quiet from the outside but as soon as Molly opened the double doors a wall of noise hit her. She looked round in surprise and noticed that the pub was chock-full of tiny men. It was the most bizarre thing she'd ever seen. Molly, who'd always thought her five-foot two was tiny, felt positively Amazonian in comparison, wearing her favourite silver boots with the three-inch heels.

Walking to the bar through an avenue of low wolf whistles, Molly tried hard not to smile. Even though she wanted to let her hair down, she knew she had to be on her guard. After all, she had over two and a half thousand pounds in her handbag, and it wouldn't be a good idea to start flirting with someone who might take advantage of her: moneywise or otherwise.

Ordering a meal and a drink and snack, she sat on a bar stool. It was high but it was bliss to be able to stretch her legs out after a day behind the wheel. She sipped at her white wine and opened her bag of crisps. It didn't matter how much money you had in your bank account, it was still hard to beat a glass of white and a bag of salt and vinegar.

'What's a nice girl like you doing in a place like this?' a deep Irish voice asked from behind.

Molly rolled her eyes at the cliché. She usually managed at least half a drink whenever she dared to go out before men tried to pick her up. This guy obviously didn't trust the competition. Turning round, she saw the tiniest man she'd ever laid eyes on. How come somebody so small had such a deep voice? she wondered. His voice had been that of a six-foot six rugby player yet he barely came up to her shoulders, and that was when she was sitting down.

'Hi,' he smiled a cheeky smile. 'I'm Declan,' he said, holding a hand out for her to shake. Molly hesitated for a moment, wondering if she should shake it or snub him, but snubbing was little fun so she took the easier option of shaking.

'Molly,' she said.

'Pretty,' he replied, the low light of the pub making his eyes glint. 'I'm a jockey,' he added.

Molly's eyebrows rose. 'Oh?'

'In case you were wondering.'

'I wasn't.'

'I'm here with me mates. We're all jockeys in case you wondered why we're so vertically challenged.'

'I wasn't,' Molly said.

'Ah, come on! I bet you were.'

There was such an irresistible twinkle in his eyes that it was impossible for Molly not to smile. 'OK then, I was, but only because it's such an unusual sight.'

'We're nothing if not unusual,' he said, winking. 'Now, let me get you another drink.'

'I've not finished this one yet,' Molly said, realising that, now the preliminaries were over, he was trying to move on to the serious business of getting her tipsy.

'Ah! You'll be wanting a second in no time, won't you?' Again, his eyes twinkled.

Molly thought of the meal she was about to have and the choice to either sit in the corner of the pub on her own, watching everybody around her having fun, or to take a chance and have a bit of fun herself.

'I'll have another white wine, then,' she said, her eyes twinkling right back at his.

'Bloody wild goose chase,' Tom muttered as he flung his body under the shower, which dribbled over his body like a baby. It had been a long and uncomfortable drive south before heading into Wales, and he was almost sure it was all in vain. He'd received two emails of sightings of Molly around the Cotswolds but Carolyn Bailey had informed him that she was now in Wales.

'She told me she was heading to Rhosllanerchrugog but then she's planning to go to Betws-y-Coed,' she'd said, even spelling the places out for him oh-so-carefully, but Tom wasn't convinced. These places were in the middle of nowhere and he had every suspicion that that was exactly where Molly wanted to place him. But were the email sightings any more reliable? There was surely more than one old-style yellow VW Beetle on the roads. It didn't automatically follow that the ones seen were Molly's.

Reaching out for a fluffy white towel, Tom stepped out of the shower. He'd have to sit down and reassess things tomorrow. He couldn't afford to lose readers at this stage of the game. Although he had quite a fan club owing to his TV appearance, that wasn't going to help him secure a good post in the long run.

Combing through his wet hair and running a hand over his two-day stubble, he determined one thing: if Molly and Carolyn Bailey were going to play dirty then he was jolly well going to play dirty too.

Food eaten and her second glass of wine long emptied, Molly gazed across the tiny table at her new friend.

'How's about another?' Declan asked, nodding at her empty glass.

Molly chewed her lip thoughtfully. 'I don't know.'

'How's about a bottle of white this time – cheaper than endless glasses?'

'Oh, don't worry about the cost. I'm getting them in.'

Declan's eyes widened happily. 'Hey! I've always wanted to find a rich woman to look after me.'

'Well, you've found one,' Molly said and then hiccuped. Perhaps she shouldn't have said that.

'Well, in that case, I'll just sit here and watch you get them in.'

Molly smiled. What harm could another glass do?

An hour later, she had her answer. She hadn't had so much to drink in one go for ages and the pub food didn't seem to be doing its job of soaking it all up.

'I don't think I should drive anywhere,' Molly slurred, suddenly realising that she should try and find somewhere to stay for the night.

'You don't have to,' Declan said. 'There's a hotel just round the corner.'

Molly nodded, trying to compute this new piece of information. 'I've got a dog.'

He gave her a quizzical look. 'Where?'

'In my car,' she explained.

'Well, I'm sure he can come too. As long as he's not a Rottweiler.'

Molly dissolved into laughter, as if his line was the funniest thing she'd ever heard. 'He's a terrier!' she said, wiping the tears away from her eyes.

Declan grinned. 'A real guard dog, then?'

'Oh, yes! So don't try any funny business or he'll have your arm off.'

'So you want to give this hotel a try?'

Molly nodded. 'Do you think they'll still have vacancies?'

'There's only one way to find out.'

'Oh!' Molly said, seeing he was following her as she made to leave. 'I don't want you going to any trouble. I'm sure I'll be able to find my way.'

'You obviously don't know the sorts of dangers there are lurking in the Cotswolds at this time of night,' Declan said in a dramatic whisper.

'You mean, *other* than you?' Molly giggled.

'Ah! Really!' he said, pushing the door open and letting Molly through first. They left the pub accompanied by a few low wolf whistles from Declan's jokey jockey chums, who were still knocking back the spirits. Molly tutted. What did they think they were up to? He was only making sure she found the hotel safely.

'Those are the most amazing boots I've ever seen,' Declan said, eyeing Molly's silver legs. 'And I bet there's a great pair of pins inside them too. Hey! Steady on there,' he added as Molly swayed towards him. He held out his hand for her to take.

Molly placed her hand in his. 'You're tiny!' she said, a little giggle bubbling from her mouth. 'Sorry! That was very rude of me.'

Declan looked at her and then leant into her face to whisper something. 'I'm not that tiny, you know.'

After grabbing a small overnight bag and putting Fizz on his lead, they found the hotel and were given a room on the first floor.

Molly flopped down onto the bed in relief. It was soft and saggy: perfect for a quick doze. But she couldn't fall asleep yet, could she? That would be very rude after he'd walked her from the pub.

Through a wine-warmed fog, she watched as Declan unbuttoned his shirt. He was small, but perfectly formed. There wasn't an ounce of fat on him and his chest was smooth and tanned. He was lovely and, all of a sudden, he was very close.

'Has anyone ever told you you've got the most beautiful eyes?' he whispered, his breath spirit-scented.

'Has anyone ever told you that you come out with the most awful clichés?' Molly whispered back, swallowing a giggle.

'As a matter of fact, no, they haven't.' With that, he kissed her. Molly closed her eyes. Well, there was no harm in a kiss, was there?

* * *

The next morning, Molly woke, her eyes seeming to spiral like Ka's in *The Jungle Book*. Sitting up slowly and pushing her dark curls out of her face, Molly took the measure of the night before. She hadn't intended to sleep with him. Not after the Lord Henry fiasco, but it had just sort of happened. Not that it had been an unpleasant experience – far from it. Declan had shown his riding technique off to fantastic effect and they'd completed at least a couple of Grand Nationals together. But she knew that it hadn't been the wisest of things to do in the circumstances. She didn't know anything about this man. She could have had her throat slit. She could have been robbed.

'*Oh my God!*' Molly suddenly shouted, looking round her room for her handbag and finding it on the floor by Fizz. She opened it up, her heart beating madly.

It was gone.

Of course it was gone. What had she expected? Two and a half thousand pounds. That was the most expensive night she'd ever had, and she had nothing to show for it but a nasty love bite at the base of her throat.

'Fizz! You really aren't a guard dog, are you?' she said, her eyes crinkling in consternation. He looked up at her with blissful ignorance. 'You know that was for the animal home we passed, don't you? To help homeless dogs, like you once were.' Molly groaned. 'Two and a half grand,' she said, shaking her head in disbelief. 'And I bet he doesn't even need it.'

Chapter Twenty-Seven

Molly left the hotel, her forehead furrowed like a newly ploughed field. She just couldn't believe that Declan could do something like that to her. How could he? And just after they'd...

She shook her head. She didn't want to think about it. He wasn't worth the head room.

'Bastard,' she cursed, kicking a stone into the hedgerow and causing a pensioner to turn round and glare at her.

'Sorry,' Molly mumbled in embarrassment, 'but you know what men are like?'

The woman's gaze lingered a moment and then she nodded. '*Bastards!*' she said with such vehemence that Molly almost tripped over her own feet. No, she wasn't the only woman to have been screwed and screwed over by a man, was she? They got everywhere, did men. They sought you out and used and abused you. No wonder Molly had stayed so resolutely single. Dogs were far more trustworthy companions.

'Come on, darling,' she said, giving Fizz's head a ruffle, 'let's get you some breakfast.'

Walking back towards The Swan where she'd left the car overnight, Molly wondered if she should hang around for a while on the off chance that Dodgy Declan might make an appearance, and demand that he returned her money. But at what cost? There'd only be an ugly scene and she didn't want to make herself conspicuous, particularly where money was concerned. It was best to try and forget about it, no matter how mad it made her. Anyway, as she turned the last corner towards the pub, she realised that the stolen money was the least of her problems.

Her car had disappeared.

'*Wales?*' Old Bailey barked over his cooked breakfast, puncturing his egg yolk with an angry fork.

'That's what this reporter is saying, although why Molly would go to Wales is beyond me,' Marty said, shaking his head as he took a bite out of his fried bread.

'Why would she go to *any* of these places?' Magnus asked. 'I don't understand it. What *does* she think she's doing?'

'Enjoying herself?' Carolyn piped from the end of the table.

Three pairs of stern eyes turned and glared at her. Carolyn tried not to swallow her mouthful of tea down the wrong way.

'Enjoying herself with *our* money!' Old Bailey said, teeth smeared with egg yolk.

'How's it *your* money?' Carolyn dared to ask.

Old Bailey blinked a rheumy eye at her. 'Who do you think raised the girl? Who fed and clothed her and saw her through college?' He gave a dramatic pause before answering his own question. '*We* did!'

Carolyn stared at him as if to say *so what*? But she knew what he was getting at. In some families, gratitude had no expiry date, and this was such a family. Remembering what Molly had told her over the years, it had always been the same with the Baileys. Now, according to Old Bailey, Molly owed them, and they were out to get every penny they could before it was distributed elsewhere.

'Some people just don't know how to be grateful,' Old Bailey grumbled into his bacon rashers.

Carolyn tried to tranquillise herself with more tea. She'd have been dosing herself up with wine if it wasn't just gone nine in the morning and she wasn't pregnant.

'I've had a look at the map,' Marty said, 'and I think I've come up with a good, fast route. Now, whose turn is it to pay for petrol?' he asked, and watched in undisguised dismay as Magnus and Granville proceeded to find their respective cutlery and handkerchief worthy of prolonged examination.

After cross-questioning the landlord of The Swan as to the whereabouts of her car, Molly stormed back out into the car park.

'If you hadn't had so much wine, you might have remembered where you'd parked it!' the surly landlord yelled after her. It wasn't the reaction she'd expected from a Cotswold publican. She'd naively thought that the people in this part of the country would be as mellow as the Cotswold stone but they were far more brick-faced. Anyway, there was no doubt in Molly's mind where she'd left it, and it wasn't there now.

'Well, it's a good job I didn't leave you in Old Faithful,' Molly said, picking Fizz up and hugging his furry body to her. It was also lucky that she hadn't left any money in it too. Two and a half grand was quite enough to lose in one go.

So what had been worth stealing? It was nothing more than an old banger with a boot full of gerbera. She had to laugh at that even if she had also lost most of her clothes. Being a woman, she'd packed virtually her entire wardrobe for the trip and would have to go out and replace it all. Still, even though she objected to spending money on herself, she'd try and make the experience a fun one.

She shook her head and rolled her eyes up to the blue skies above. There was no getting round it: she'd have to buy a replacement for Old Faithful too. She couldn't continue her one-woman crusade of England on foot, that was for sure, especially with Peeping Tom and the Bailey bunch on her tail.

With a weary sigh, Molly walked back to the hotel to ring for a taxi. The girl on reception greeted her with a warm smile.

'Me again,' Molly said.

'Decided to stay another night?'

Molly returned her smile but didn't say what she really thought about her time spent in the village so far. 'No, I'm afraid not. I was wondering if you could help me?'

'Sure. What is it?'

'I don't suppose you know where the nearest Volkswagen showroom is?'

Carolyn was beginning to wish that she hadn't been guided by the Bailey men and had such a hearty breakfast.

'It's all included in the price, so I'm having the works,' Old Bailey had said earlier that morning, and Carolyn had followed his lead but, as Marty navigated the back roads into Wales at breakneck speed, Carolyn thought she was going to throw up right there in the car. They'd already stopped twice and she could see that the Bailey men were going to hold her personally responsible if they missed Molly, but she couldn't help it; she felt dreadful.

'Marty,' she said in a low voice as he took a hairpin bend at thirty miles an hour.

'What?' he said, his voice a deep growl.

'Can you *please* slow down?'

He took his eyes off the road for a second. 'You OK?'

'No!'

'Carsick? You've never been carsick before.'

'Well, I am now! So bloody slow down.'

Marty flinched at her expletive. 'Caro!'

'Slow *down*!'

Marty hit the brake and everybody jerked forward a foot.

'What's going on?' Old Bailey yelled from the back. 'Why have we stopped?'

'We haven't stopped. We're just slowing down. Caro's not feeling so good,' Marty explained.

'Wind a window down,' Magnus said.

'Have a rich tea biscuit,' Old Bailey suggested, digging into a voluminous pocket and procuring a crumpled packet which he shoved under Carolyn's nose.

'No, thank you,' she said, her nose wrinkling in disgust. They smelt of mothballs.

'Not up the duff, are you?' Old Bailey harrumphed.

Carolyn felt herself blushing and quickly glanced at Marty to see his reaction.

'Granddad! For goodness' sake! She's just a little carsick, that's all.'

''Cos once you start having kids, you won't have a spare penny to rub together, I can tell you that for nothing,' Old Bailey continued, undeterred. 'They absorb all your money like a dry sponge. You can wave goodbye to holidays and fancy clothes.'

'Yes, thank you, Granddad, but you've no worries on that count.'

'So you're not planning on making me a great-grandfather yet?'

Marty chuckled. 'Haven't we got enough to contend with at the moment?'

'Your granddad's right,' Magnus chipped in. 'The cost of living's going up all the time. I wouldn't like to bring up children in today's society.'

'Well, you don't have to,' Carolyn suddenly interrupted.

The car fell silent for a moment.

'Feels as though I'm *still* bringing up my children with this behaviour of Molly's,' Magnus said, half to himself.

'Nobody asked you to get involved,' Carolyn said.

'But we *are* involved,' Old Bailey grunted. 'Like it or not, when something goes awry, the whole family's involved.'

Carolyn's mouth dropped open. Had she heard him right? Had he completely forgotten about Cynthia? Old Bailey hadn't exactly rallied around after she'd walked out on Magnus, had he? According to Molly there'd been 'neither hugs nor tears' between the two men. They'd wiped Cynthia out completely as if, by walking out on Magnus, she had erased her very existence.

Carolyn bit her lip in order to prevent her from rubbing Old Bailey up the wrong way again. Anyway, she had something more pressing on her mind. The whole world had gone woozy.

'Marty,' she said.

'What?'

'Can you pull over, please? I think I'm going to be sick.'

Chapter Twenty-Eight

As the Bailey bunch crossed the border into Wales, Tom and Flora crossed back into England. Hot and annoyed, Tom didn't dare think of the time and money he'd wasted listening to the so-called *inside information* of Carolyn Bailey's. Wales had been a waste of time and he was now heading to the Cotswolds. He'd had a steady stream of email sightings of Molly and had left first thing that morning.

Flora, who seemed to be flagging with the constant upheaval, was sleeping beside him. He took a quick glance at her: lashes fluttering in deep dream time, rosy lips parted a fraction. Poor Flo, he thought. She should have been running round the garden in bare feet, or bucket and spading by the beach, not stuck in a hot car chasing a mad woman around the country. He smiled as he remembered what she'd said to him last night.

'It's all right, Daddy. At least I'll have the best *what I did in my holiday* essay when I go back to school.'

But it wasn't fair on her really, and he couldn't help feeling guilty about it.

Flora stirred and a solitary grey eye peeped open.

'Where are we?' she asked, her voice thick with sleep.

'I have no idea,' Tom said.

Flora opened both eyes and squinted, as if assessing whether it was worth her staying awake or not.

'Can we check your email?'

'Why?'

Flora shrugged. 'Something to do.'

'OK,' Tom said. 'We'll pull into the next service area.'

Ten minutes later, they parked and set up the laptop. One, two, three, four...

'Oh! Only eight today,' Flora said sounding disappointed.

'Still, not bad.' Tom opened them and blushed.

'What is it?' Flora asked.

'Nothing.'

'Let me see.'

'Flo – they're private.'

'Are you still getting soppy messages?'

Tom frowned at his daughter. 'Look, I've told you not to mention those again. It was very naughty of you to open those up last night. You shouldn't read people's private mail.'

'Oh, Daddy! Don't be so *boring*!'

Tom sighed. 'If you must know – yes – most of them do seem to be from – *bloody hell*!' Tom's blush deepened until his whole face was robin-breast red.

'What is it?' Flora's head popped round the laptop's screen.

'Don't look!'

'Why not?'

'I'm deleting it. It's obscene!'

'What's obscene mean?'

'It means you're not allowed to read it.'

'Can't you read any out to me?'

'Not yet,' Tom said, skimming through another two. 'Wait a minute,' he said at last.

'What is it?'

Tom's eyes crinkled as he smiled. 'If this lead is true, I think we might just have landed ourselves a front page.'

'Really?'

Tom nodded and pulled his mobile phone out.

'Who are you ringing?'

Tom shushed her with a finger held to his lips. 'Hello?' he said. 'Is that Declan O'Hara? I've just received your email. You say you've got a story for me?'

Molly sat at the wheel of her brand new Volkswagen Beetle, a huge grin plastered across her face. This was a dream of a car; a metallic symphony; ecstasy with an engine and, being a shade or two darker than dear Old Faithful, it looked like an enormous smile on wheels. Molly couldn't stop grinning. It was beautiful, it was brand new and it was all hers. She'd never owned anything so new or so expensive before and the novelty of it made her body charge with excitement. She'd spent the whole morning spending money and her new, as yet nameless car was chock-full of clothes. She'd also bought a floral-festooned dog basket, two pink and silver dog bowls and all sorts of other doggie things including a very smart dog seat belt, which Fizz was wearing now. In her excitement, Molly had forgotten to buy a suitcase so the clothes were stacked in the boot and on the back seat in their shiny shopping bags.

She'd then test-driven the Beetle round the country lanes. Fizz had never had so many walks in his life as Molly insisted on parking and getting out to take photos with her new camera. She had a photo of her car in virtually every village of the Cotswolds.

Now, it was a beautiful evening, the sunshine singing through the trees, creamy clouds lacing the sky and birdsong threading through the hedgerows. There was only one thing worrying her as the day wore on: No vacancies. No vacancies. No vacancies.

Molly drove on, wondering if she and Fizz were going to have to make do with the back seat of the car, but the hand of fate pushed her on round the next corner and she slowed down as she spied a sign on a honey-coloured gatepost, half hidden by thick ivy.

She wasn't sure if it was a good idea. The board with the handwritten 'B & B' didn't exactly look official but she was tired so, trying hard not to think about Janet Leigh pulling off the highway in *Psycho*, she turned into a long driveway.

The last rays of the day's sunshine were being sucked into a navy sky but there was still enough light to see Chartlebury Court. Molly wasn't very good with her architectural history but this place was definitely old. Tudor? Elizabethan? Jacobean? She had no idea. Four storeys high, in the fantastic honeyed stone of the Cotswolds, it filled her eyes with wonder. Huge mullioned windows winked darkly in the low light of sunset, and the castellated turrets of the towers at either end of the house gave it the sort of grandeur that made Molly want to salute it.

Parking her car and leaving Fizz on the passenger seat, she went in search of the front door. It didn't take her long to find. It was about the size of the front of Molly's florist's and there was another handwritten sign in poster paint which read

Please knock very loudly. Molly bunched her fingers up into a fist and banged on the door. It didn't sound very loud to her; not like the echoey bangs in films when unsuspecting victims knock on castle doors before being consumed by a posse of sexy vampires.

Molly took a few paces back and looked up at the windows for signs of life, but there weren't any. She wondered whether to knock again but didn't think her fist was up to it, so hastened back to her car and gave her new horn a quick pip. Fizz looked up at her expectantly and Molly shook her head.

'I think we're going to have to find somewhere else,' she said, getting back into the car. She was just putting it into reverse when she saw a tiny woman in her rear-view mirror.

'Hello,' Molly began, getting out of the car again and beaming a smile. 'I'm looking for the bed and breakfast.'

The old woman, dressed from head to toe in maroon wool, with multicoloured beads clasping her throat, narrowed her eyes by way of response.

'Bed and breakfast?' the old lady croaked.

'Yes. There's a sign on the gatepost.' Molly pointed.

'Oh, God, yes,' the old lady said. 'It's such a long time since anybody actually drove by, I'd forgotten it was there. How did you find this place?'

Molly shrugged. 'By accident, really.'

'See.' The old lady held her gaze. 'Nobody comes here *but* by accident.'

'But you *do* run a bed and breakfast? I can stay here?'

At last, the old lady smiled. 'Of course you can. Follow me. And bring your dog with you.'

Molly grinned. So she'd spied Fizz.

With a shopping bag in one hand, and Fizz on a lead in the

other, she followed the old lady back towards the house and in through the door on which she'd almost cracked her knuckles.

'I know,' the old woman said, as if reading Molly's thoughts, 'I should get a bell.'

'Then why don't you?' Molly said without thinking how rude it sounded. 'Sorry,' she added quickly.

'It's all right,' the woman sighed, closing the heavy oak door behind them and watching Molly's eyes double in size as she took in the entrance hall. 'It's money. Always money.'

Molly nodded.

'By the way, it's sixty-five pounds a night.'

Molly nodded again.

'There are three rooms,' the old lady said, leading Molly up a wooden staircase. 'You can have the one that's least damp.'

Molly suppressed a giggle and tried to concentrate on her surroundings. It was the most unusual bed and breakfast she'd ever seen. There was so much wood that she felt as if she'd walked straight into the heart of a tree.

'Up this way,' the old lady said as the staircase split in two.

Molly followed, gazing open-mouthed at the portraits that lined the walls, pale faces staring out of dark backgrounds.

'Are these your ancestors?'

The old lady nodded. 'Been glaring down at me for seventy-two years.'

'You've lived here all your life?'

'No other home.'

'Who else lives here?'

'Just me.'

Molly stopped and stared at her. 'You live here *alone*? But it's so huge!'

'It might be huge but it's still home.'

Molly gave a long, low whistle. 'I only have two rooms at home.'

'Think yourself lucky.'

'Oh, I do. But it would be nice to have a little more space sometimes.'

'Try living with twelve bedrooms for a few years. You'll soon yearn for your old life.'

'But it's so beautiful,' Molly sighed, her head trying to turn in every direction at once.

'Oh, yes.' She stopped at the top of the stairs and stuck her bottom lip out in thought. 'It's lovely all right but it's bloody expensive.'

Molly smiled. She hadn't quite expected such colourful language from a woman in wool and beads.

'I'm not really the owner, you see. It's mine in as much as I can live here but I can't do anything with it other than try to keep it intact. I'm no more than a curator, really.'

Molly's eyes narrowed in puzzlement.

'Those heritage people have been badgering me for years to sell it to them and, much as I'd like to pass on the responsibility, they're not getting their thieving hands on it. Not in my lifetime.'

'You could always open it up to the public, couldn't you?' Molly suggested.

The old lady shook her head and tutted. 'I refuse to live in a single room and watch coachloads of tourists wandering around picking plaster off the walls and sneaking cuttings into their handbags.'

Molly nodded. It was obvious that the old lady had spent a great deal of thought on the subject already.

'Here we are – your room. Best room in the house. It overlooks the courtyard garden. It could be pretty if I could afford a gardener but it's all gone to ruin now.'

Molly walked into the room and straight over to the window. The sun had dipped low behind a row of trees and the courtyard was full of shadows.

'It looks quite magical,' Molly said. 'And it's such a beautiful room,' she added, nodding towards the grandiose four-poster and the forest of dark wood furniture.

'Hope you're not scared of ghosts.'

'Oh? Are there any?' Molly's eyebrows raised in momentary excitement.

'No,' the lady smiled, shaking her head from side to side. 'I don't think so. There have been stories down the decades, much the same as any house of this age: headless horsemen, grey ladies, clanking armour – all that nonsense.'

'But there aren't any really?' Molly asked, sounding somewhat disappointed.

'No. But I have heard tell of a maroon lady who frequents the landing at night.'

Molly's eyes widened.

'But you mustn't worry. It'll just be me getting up for a glass of whisky.'

Molly grinned. 'I'll try and remember.'

The old lady nodded. 'If you want to go out, use the door from the kitchen at the back of the house. There's a key under the spider plant. Come and go as you will but don't leave the door unlocked.'

'OK. Thank you,' Molly said, and watched as the old lady wandered back into the hallway.

'By the way,' she said, her hand stroking the multicoloured

choker. 'My name's Eleanora. Don't ask me why. Just call me Ellie.' Her eyes sparkled and Molly smiled.

'I'm Molly.'

'Molly? I once had a Labrador called Molly. Horrible little bitch.'

Molly grinned and watched as Eleanora shuffled down the hallway leaving a faint trace of talcum powder and old roses floating on the air behind her.

Molly crouched down and rubbed Fizz's belly. 'I rather like it here,' she told him. 'I think we might just have found the perfect hideaway.'

Chapter Twenty-Nine

Tom spent the whole of Friday night in a state of panic. Would he make the front page? Was this the breakthrough story he'd hoped for? He'd rung Nick at *Vive!* and he'd sounded suitably excited but couldn't promise him anything, so he spent the better part of Friday night pacing up and down their tiny bed and breakfast room, which really annoyed Flora because every other floorboard squeaked like a mammoth-sized mouse.

'Go to bed, Daddy!' she yelled over her duvet sounding scarily like Anise.

'All right, all right, I'm going.'

'You said that an hour ago.'

'Don't be so tetchy,' Tom said.

Flora sighed like a weary parent. 'I don't know what that means but I don't care. Just go to bed!'

Finally, he made it into bed but he hardly slept. He just kept playing his story over and over in his mind, creating headlines, imagining how it might look. This could be the moment he'd dreamt of: *his* moment.

He closed his eyes and a funny thing happened: he was

instantly back on *Susanna*. No, make that *Levinson*. He smiled to himself as he buried his head further into his pillow and got comfortable.

'It's not often that we have the same guest on the show only a month after their last interview, but our next guest is rather special,' Levinson announced. 'It's my great pleasure to welcome back, by popular demand, reporter extraordinaire, Tom Mackenzie.' There was a huge eruption of applause from the audience as Tom walked down the steps and shook hands with Levinson.

'Now, Tom, you caused quite a stir the last time you were on the show, didn't you?'

Tom smiled, a sexy A-list actor kind of smile, and got an instant whoop from a few audience members.

'Don't be modest, now,' Levinson insisted. 'The phones didn't stop all night after you sang for us. In fact, I'm rather surprised to find you're still writing for *Vive!*. I thought you would have a record deal by now.'

'It's funny you should say that,' Tom said, a boyish grin playing round his face, 'because I was signed up the very next day after your show, and my first single, "His Own Boss," will be out next week.'

'But I'm right in thinking you're still working as a reporter?' Levinson asked, stroking his chin in a thoughtful manner.

'Andre,' Tom said, leaning forward slightly, 'I felt I owed it to the nation to keep on reporting the Molly Bailey story. Some stories just have to be told.'

When Molly and Fizz ventured downstairs to the dining room on Saturday morning, Eleanora was sat in a deep winged chair with what looked like a hundred cushions supporting her.

'Morning!' Molly trilled.

'Ah! Morning!' Eleanora said, lowering her magazine and smiling at Molly.

'What are you reading?' Molly asked.

'*Hello!*'

'Really?'

Eleanora's eyes narrowed with mischief. 'Just because I live in an ancient pile doesn't mean I don't know what's going on in the world. I know all the latest celebrity gossip.'

Molly was just about to ask her what was going on this particular morning when panic rose. She'd almost forgotten. Chartlebury Court had waved its magic wand over her and she'd almost been able to forget about the outside world where people like Tom Mackenzie operated.

'You don't get *Vive!*, do you?' Molly asked hesitantly.

'Yes. I couldn't begin the day without a dose of *Vive!*. Why? Are you a fan too?'

'No,' Molly said. 'Well, yes,' she added quickly. 'I mean, do you mind if I read it first when it arrives?'

'Be my guest,' Eleanora said and then smiled. 'You *are* my guest!'

'When does it normally arrive?'

'Anytime now. You in a hurry to read your star sign?'

Molly shook her head. 'What's for breakfast?' she asked, keen to change the subject before Eleanora suspected something.

'Anything you find that hasn't gone out of date on that table,' Eleanora said, pointing behind Molly to the longest trestle table she had ever seen.

'This looks gorgeous,' Molly said, picking up a pale gold napkin embroidered with the initials *EH*. 'Are these your initials?'

Eleanora nodded. 'Eleanora Howard. As in the great Howard family. Believe it or not, I'm a distant relative of Catherine Howard's.'

Molly's eyes narrowed slightly. Her history just wasn't up to scratch.

'Henry VIII's number five.'

'Oh! *Really?*'

'Silly girl lost her head. Wouldn't catch me losing my head over a man.'

'Or me,' Molly said.

'Never have and never will,' Eleanora said emphatically and Molly nodded in agreement. 'Except for Philip Carr-Forrester,' she added by way of an afterthought. 'And Robert Benjamin.'

'There are always exceptions,' Molly agreed, remembering beautiful Andrew Fellowes from her horticultural training days.

'So you've no young man now?' Eleanora asked.

Molly could feel her face heating up like a furnace. 'No,' she said, diving into a packet of cornflakes in the hope that she'd avoid further questioning.

'Ah! Here's our young paper boy now,' Eleanora announced, peering out of the window at the young boy cycling up the driveway.

'That's OK!' Molly said, on her feet in a split second. 'I'll get it for you.'

'Thank you, dear.'

Molly left the room and walked quickly to the front door, Fizz following closely behind her in the hope that he was going to get a walk. She didn't dare look at the paper when she picked it up but folded it neatly in half and marched back to the dining room.

'You take your time with *Vive!*,' Eleanora said, 'I'm still reading this film premiere report. Well, looking at the pictures at least. Goodness, the things these celebrities wear. Look at this one! There are more holes in it than a golf course!'

Molly sat down and quickly opened the paper. Nothing on page two or three. Or four or five. Six and seven were devoid of anything by Tom Mackenzie too, as were eight and nine. Molly felt a smile warming her face. Had he lost her, then? Had Carolyn's plan worked? Or had he decided to pack his job in and admit defeat?

Breathing a huge sigh of relief, Molly closed the paper. It was then that she saw it. In letters as thick and black as midnight, the headline on the front page hit her as hard as a boxer's punch.

My Night with Millionaire Molly.

Chapter Thirty

Tom was beaming like a court jester. He was jumping up and down like a kid on springs. He was laughing like an idiot. He was everything happy that had ever existed because he'd got his front page.

This kind of behaviour *might* have been passable if he'd been in the privacy of his own home, and *might* even have been forgivable if it had been in the middle of a busy street, but it wasn't; he was in a small Cotswold newsagent's.

'Daddy! People are looking!' Flora cried, tugging at his sleeve.

'Let them look! Let them look at a front-page reporter!' he said, doing a little jig in the middle of the shop floor.

'*Daddy!*'

'Excuse me, sir!' a deep voice suddenly interrupted. 'I'm going to have to ask you to leave.'

Tom turned round and came face to face with a man no bigger than his mother, and she'd only ever been a couple of inches taller than a washing machine.

'Excuse me?'

'You're going to have to leave, sir. Take your purchases and leave, please.'

Tom stared, eyes wide in disbelief. 'Do you know who I am?'

'*Daddy!*'

'No, Flora, I think the man should know who he has in his shop.'

'I don't care if you're Elvis Presley, you're upsetting my customers and I want you to leave.'

'Upsetting your—'

'Daddy – *come on!*' Flora interrupted, grabbing him by the arm and dragging him outside.

'Flora! That was really embarrassing,' he said once they were both outside.

'You're embarrassed? What about *me*? *You* embarrassed *me!*' she shouted, her grey eyes flashing wildly.

'Get in the car, Flora. You're causing a scene,' Tom said very calmly.

Flora's mouth dropped open as if in miscomprehension. 'It's not me who's causing a scene,' she said, her voice suddenly very quiet.

'Get in the car.'

'No.'

'What?'

'I'm not getting in the car.'

'We're leaving right now so get in the car,' Tom repeated.

Flora shook her head. 'I'm staying here.'

Tom's eyebrows crashed together. 'You're staying here? On your own? In the middle of Gloucestershire?'

'I'm not going with you.'

'Why not?'

Flora glared at him. 'Because you're turning into a real big head. You're worse than Ian Evans in my class, who's always showing off his flipping swimming trophies.'

'*Flora!* Watch your language.'

'*Me* watch my language! I've been listening to your bad language non-stop.'

'Look! I'm not going to stand in the middle of the street talking about this. Get in the car.'

'No.'

'*Flora!*' For one brief moment, Tom really felt that he could have smacked her but, as he looked down, he saw an anxious ten-year-old girl, as fragile as a buttercup, and he just wanted to hug her.

'Flo,' he began again, his voice calmer now. 'I'm sorry if you haven't liked me much of late, but I've been under a lot of pressure to get this story right. If my reaction to getting a front page doesn't please you, if I swear too much and show off too much, then I'm sorry. Really, I am.'

Flora kicked one of her pink sandals against the other and chewed her lip.

'Flo? Do you accept my apology?'

Flora looked up at her father, her eyes diamond-bright as if she might be about to cry. 'OK,' she said in a tiny voice.

Tom smiled with relief. 'Come here!' he said, his arms enclosing her in a hug. 'I love you, you know,' he whispered into a perfect pink ear.

'I love you too, Daddy.'

Tom blinked hard. This was turning out to be quite an emotional day. 'Shall we get going, then?'

'OK,' she said. 'But I want you to promise not to get all silly and big-headed again. And to stop swearing too.'

'I promise!' he laughed, and they got into the car.

Leaving the village, they headed out into the countryside. They hadn't been driving for more than five minutes before Tom spoke.

'Do you know how hard it is to get a front-page story?'

'Daddy! You promised!'

'*Front page*, though, Flo! Pretty bloody good, eh?'

Flora sighed wearily and stared out of the window in resignation.

Molly scanned the front-page article quickly and quietly, her heart racing like a marathon runner's as she read Declan's account of their night together.

What Declan O'Hara didn't realise was that his pretty bedfellow was none other than Molly Bailey – England's new Robin Hood. 'I bought a copy of Vive! *the next morning and read the Molly column, and it just clicked,' he said.*

'Just clicked!' Molly said under her breath. 'Bastard.'

'She'd told me about a few of the people she'd helped recently but I thought she was just a nice person. I didn't realise that she was Molly Bailey.'

'*Lying* bastard!' Molly corrected.

'What's that?' Eleanora called from the other side of the room.

'Nothing!' Molly said quickly. 'Just talking to Fizz.'

'Has he had his breakfast?'

'Yes, thank you, he has,' Molly said and, seeing that Eleanora was still deeply involved in celebrity gossip, took the first page of the newspaper and scrunched it up into a tiny ball and stuffed it up the sleeve of her jumper. She could always blame it on Fizz if the page was missed.

'Drat it! What does this say?' Eleanora suddenly asked, pointing a long finger at the magazine caption. 'These glasses don't seem to be working anymore and the print's too small for me to read.'

Molly crossed the room and read the brief article for her, then, sitting on a footstool opposite her, said, 'How would you like to go shopping?'

Eleanora's lipsticked mouth dropped open. 'Shopping?'

'We could buy some new glasses for you, some lampshades, new cups and saucers, clothes—'

'But I can't aff—'

'I can,' Molly interrupted.

Eleanora looked baffled, her eyes narrowing with just a hint of suspicion.

'I know what you're thinking,' Molly said. 'You're thinking, what do *I* get out of this? Why should a complete stranger do a good deed for you? Am I right?' She paused and saw Eleanora's nod of affirmation. 'Please,' Molly began, 'you don't have to worry about that with me. I'm not after anything. This is simply something I do.'

'But—'

'No buts. It will be my pleasure.'

'I haven't been shopping for years,' Eleanora said.

'Well, you've got some catching up to do, haven't you?'

It was slow progress at first. Eleanora didn't even want to accept a free cup of tea from Molly.

'I won't accept charity!' she said when Molly tried to push her into a ladies' boutique.

'This isn't charity,' Molly told her. 'It's two women having a bit of fun.'

But she soon got into the swing of things and, before they knew it, they had spent four fun-filled hours in Cheltenham and came away having ordered two brand new pairs of glasses and bought two sets of china cups and saucers, a new rug for the hallway, five picture frames for homeless photos, four lampshades, a new television, and about a hundred other bits and bobs.

'Molly,' Eleanora started when they got back to the car, 'why did you just do all that for me?'

'Because I wanted to,' Molly said but she could see that Eleanora didn't look convinced. 'Let's just say that I've come into some money, and I want to share it.'

'Really?' Eleanora said. 'Ah! I see!'

'What?'

'You're like that girl in the paper.'

'What girl?'

'That girl they're calling the new Robin Hood.'

Molly panicked. She knew, didn't she? Molly had recognised that knowing look in her eyes that morning as soon as they'd started talking about *Vive!*. Eleanora had said she read all the stories and knew exactly what was going on in the world. So why hadn't she mentioned anything?

'I wouldn't believe everything you read in the papers,' Molly cautioned.

'Wouldn't you?'

'No. It's probably written by some unscrupulous journalist who's made half of the facts up.'

'Really?' Eleanora said, sounding somewhat deflated, as if the thought that newspapers might actually tell lies had never occurred to her.

'I wouldn't be the least bit surprised.'

'But can you imagine what it would be like to have a big win on the lottery like that?' Eleanora asked. 'What would you do with the money?'

'I don't know,' Molly shrugged, hoping that she wasn't blushing and giving herself away. 'What would you do?'

Eleanora gave a little chuckle. 'Chartlebury Court has done a good job of spending all my money in the past. I'm sure it could handle a few thousand more.'

Molly nodded, remembering the crumbling plaster ceiling in the dining room.

'And it would certainly stave off those heritage people for a bit longer. Don't get me wrong,' she said, 'I admire the work they do but I want to do it myself.'

Molly nodded but she could see that that would never happen, not without a large injection of funds, but it was nice that Eleanora was so determined and independent.

'How will you raise the money you need?'

There was a loud sucking of air through teeth. 'In the usual way, I expect. Open days – which I loathe. Hosting the local garden fete. Sending out begging letters to anyone who'll read them, and selling the occasional painting – though I only resort to that if there's major work needing doing. There's not much point hanging on to a painting if the roof above is letting rainwater in to damage it, is there?'

'It must be difficult for you.'

'And for my father before me. Each generation has owned a little less and had to repair a little more.'

Molly sighed and they drove in silence for a few minutes, heading out of Cheltenham and winding through the golden villages which lined the route back to Chartlebury Court.

'I suppose you'll be heading off soon?' Eleanora said. Was

it Molly's imagination, or was her voice tinged with regret?

'I was hoping to stay,' Molly said, 'but something's come up and I'm afraid I'd best be moving on.'

'Where are you heading?'

Molly smiled. 'I haven't made up my mind yet.'

Eleanora nodded. 'That's fine,' she said, her eyes misty and wistful as if she thought such indecisiveness was delicious.

After unpacking Eleanora's goods and packing the new overnight bag she'd bought herself, Molly took out the latest instalment of money she'd withdrawn from her bank accounts and placed it in a creamy envelope. She hesitated before putting the yellow gerbera inside but it just wouldn't be right not to leave her own personal calling card.

Sneaking into the kitchen, she propped the envelope against the mug tree for Eleanora to find later and then headed outside to take Fizz for a walk, breathing in the luxuriant scent of the sky-scraping hedges. It was a beautiful place. A place a person could fall in love with very easily. Molly could quite easily imagine a quiet, unobtrusive sort of life here. A life of rose pruning and chicken feeding; of mowing lawns and making jam.

Fizz pulled hard on his lead, tugging her out of her daydreams. She watched as he pushed his snowy nose into the long grass at the side of the road and came out wet with dew. He looked up at her briefly, before shoving his nose into a clump of dandelions. Molly threw her head back and gazed up into a sky so blue that it hurt her eyes. No, she really didn't want to leave but, after the Declan declaration, she'd have both her family and Tom Mackenzie seeking her out before long and she didn't intend to be caught just yet.

'Come on, sweetheart,' she said to Fizz. 'It's time we moved on.'

Chapter Thirty-One

'You have absolutely no idea where you're going, do you?' Carolyn said to Marty after he pulled into the roadside and opened his atlas.

'Well, I don't see any of you clamouring to help with directions.'

Carolyn sighed wearily and stuck her head out of the car window. It was a beautiful stretch of road overlooking a valley with a river snaking through it. She smiled as she saw a father and daughter picnicking at the side of the road. They'd spread a tartan rug out and there was all manner of things on it including a guitar. The father had his back to the road and was staring deep into the valley below, and the girl had a book in one hand and an emerald apple in the other. Would that be them in the future? she wondered, trying to imagine Marty in the role of father.

Casting him a quick glance, she saw that his expression was darker than ebony. He wasn't in a good mood. The front-page story in *Vive!* had shaken him. He'd tried to keep it hidden but Magnus had got hold of it. But at least they hadn't read it out to Old Bailey, and they hadn't talked about it either. All their concentration had been focused on finding The Swan and hoping they'd be able to find Molly from there.

Poor Molly, Carolyn thought. For the first time in years, she was having a little fun and it went and made the front page of a notorious national newspaper. Life wasn't fair, was it?

'Here we are!' Marty suddenly yelled. 'We're only about three miles away. Right, I want you all to keep your eyes open for Molly. She could be anywhere round here.'

Carolyn rolled her eyes. She was going to have to sneak a call to Molly at the earliest opportunity and see how she was and, more importantly, *where* she was.

Molly had left Chartlebury Court with a lump in her throat.

'I'll come back one day,' she'd told Eleanora. 'When I've got more time.'

'You do that,' Eleanora had said and they'd hugged as if they'd known each other all their lives and not just two days.

Molly could still feel the sting of tears as she drove away but a fiercer emotion was beginning to surface: anger. She was burning with fury at having her private life splattered across the front page by a man who didn't even know her. But what was even worse than her own madness was the fact that she knew her family would read it and judge her. She hadn't been answerable to her family since leaving home and she dreaded to think what they'd have to say on the subject of her bad behaviour with an Irish jockey. How would her father react to this? And her brother? And Old Bailey? Molly scrunched up her face in panic. No wonder her mother had left. There'd been no freedom to do *any*thing in their household. That reminded her, she hadn't had word from McCleod yet. She supposed it was early days but how long were these things meant to take?

She pulled over at a convenient spot and Fizz immediately did a little dance on the passenger seat.

'Later, sweetheart,' she said, looking down into a beautiful valley with a wide river winding through it.

She hadn't quite got the hang of programming numbers into her mobile phone yet so entered it manually from the black-edged business card he'd given her.

'McCleod,' he barked.

'Hello. Mr McCleod? It's Molly Bailey. I was just—'

'Ah! Molly! I'm glad you rang. I've just had a call from Legs.'

'You have?'

'He's got a lead on your mother. He didn't say much but he said he was heading to London. Where are you now?'

'The Cotswolds.'

'Good. That's not too far away.'

'Should I head to London?'

McCleod cleared his throat and Molly pictured him spluttering into the smoky, smoggy room. 'Not yet. Best not jump the gun. This lead may lead somewhere else. We've had that before.'

'So I just wait?'

'You need patience in this game.'

Molly nodded. 'OK,' she said. 'Thank you.' She heard him clear his throat again before he hung up.

Staring out at the view ahead, Molly tried to imagine where her mother was. What was she doing in London of all places? She might not be there now, of course, but what had taken her there in the first place? She'd always hated cities. She couldn't even bear Penrith on a Saturday afternoon, so what on earth was she doing in London?

'Cities are cages,' she'd once told Molly, her nose deep in her favourite honeysuckle, 'and people aren't meant to live in cages.'

No, Cynthia's home was the countryside with open views and room to roam. Somewhere very much like here, Molly thought. She had a feeling her mother would have approved of the Cotswolds. It had the same serenity as the Eden Valley in Cumbria.

It was funny but, even though she hadn't seen her mother since she was eleven, Molly could sometimes *feel* her. There seemed to be an invisible bond, some intangible link, which might be heartlessly explained by genetics but which Molly liked to think of as the kindred spirit. She'd felt a little of it too with Eleanora. It was strange. They weren't related, were from completely different backgrounds and different generations and yet there'd been a connection: a unique place where two souls meet for a brief time in a turbulent world.

Molly turned the ignition and pulled back out into the road before picking up some speed to make up for lost time. She was getting all emotional again and that wouldn't do. Now wasn't the time. She had to keep her head and remain in control if she was to finish the job she'd set out to do, and that meant leaving the county of Gloucestershire before anyone managed to track her down.

Taking a bend in the road a little too fast, Molly slammed on the brakes.

'*Bloody hell!*'

She couldn't believe her eyes. There, on the side of the road, was a little girl, cartwheeling to within an inch of her life.

Molly's heart thudded in her chest. What did she think she was playing at? Wasn't there anyone looking after her? She'd almost been run over.

Taking a quick look in her rear-view mirror, Molly saw a young man leaping up from a tartan rug.

'*Idiot!*' Molly yelled out of her open window. Honestly, men couldn't be trusted with anything, could they?

'*Flo!*' Tom yelled, as he heard the car brakes.

'*Daddy!*' Flora yelled back, the world settling itself again after one too many cartwheels.

'Get away from the road!' Tom dropped his guitar and grabbed Flora in a vice-like hug. 'God almighty, Flo! You nearly gave me a heart attack.'

'I couldn't tell where I was anymore,' she said, swaying slightly.

'Well, we're going to have to ban cartwheeling.' Tom gave her a big squeeze, his heart still racing in his chest, and then looked down the road. 'Shit!'

'Daddy!'

'That car!'

'It nearly ran me over.'

'It's a yellow Volkswagen Beetle.'

'Molly's car?'

'But it's a brand new one,' Tom said, squinting as it disappeared round the bend. 'Did you see the driver, Flo? Quick – think!'

'It was a woman. With dark hair, I think.'

'It could be Molly! Maybe she's got herself a new car with her money. There can't be too many yellow Beetles in the Cotswolds, can there? Not driven by dark-haired women.'

Tom was on the move, chucking the remains of the picnic into carrier bags. 'Get the rug, Flo. *Quickly!* We've got to follow her.'

Flora grabbed a corner of the rug and pulled.

'Hurry up!' Tom said, legging it back to their car. 'We've got to catch up with her.'

'Can I have a wee behind that hedge?'

'No!' Tom said, doing his seat belt up and starting the car. 'Get your belt on. Hurry up!'

'It's on!'

Tom pulled out and put his foot down. He wasn't sure where the road went and if there were any turnings or not but he'd soon find out. Could this be it at last? The chase? The confrontation? The culmination? And, if it was, how did he think it was all going to pan out? Would Molly simply pull over and let herself be interviewed? Probably not. Not after the press coverage she'd received at his hands. She'd be more likely to punch him on the nose.

'There she is!' he shouted, seeing the yellow Beetle ahead of them.

'Daddy!'

'What?'

'I think we've forgotten something,' Flora said in an anxious voice.

'What, Flo? I haven't got time for a moral debate now.'

'No! *Really* forgotten something. Isaak!'

Tom's face drained of colour. 'You're kidding!'

Flora shook her head and turned round to check the back seat. There was no Isaak there.

'Shit!' Tom cursed. 'And don't *Daddy* me!'

'I wasn't going to!' Flora objected.

Tom's face crumpled. What was he to do? In front of him, there was the woman he suspected was Molly Bailey. He couldn't prove it, of course, but the odds were fairly good. Behind him was Isaak, the beloved guitar he'd bought with his first pay cheque. After Flora, that guitar was his best friend, and it'd be impossible to replace.

'*Damn it!*' He hit the steering wheel with a hand full of choice-torn rage. Words tripped wildly through his head. Molly. Isaak. Molly. Isaak. Story. Guitar. What was more important? He could surely catch up with Molly but he might not be able to find Isaak again. If he went after Molly, he might lose her or she might not even be Molly but, if he didn't go back for Isaak, he'd lose him for ever.

With his brain overheating inside his head, the VW Beetle became smaller and smaller until it disappeared round a corner. And that's when he stepped on the brakes.

Chapter Thirty-Two

Thankfully, Isaak was still there, lying on the grass looking very sorry for himself.

'He looks so sad,' Flora said.

'Not as sad as I'd have looked if I'd lost him,' Tom said, picking him up and dusting him down with loving hands. 'Come on, Flo. Let's see if we can catch up with Molly.'

But they couldn't. Shortly after finding themselves back at the farm track in which they'd turned round in the first place, there was a three-way junction, and the yellow Volkswagen Beetle was long gone.

With a weary sigh, Tom pulled over again and got his road atlas out. He'd never done so much map reading in his life as in the last few days and his eyes felt sore from poring over the pages.

Of course, he knew Molly had been continually heading south, but did that mean she was now heading to Cornwall, Devon, Dorset or Kent or anywhere in between? He'd have to put out another appeal for help, but what did he do in the meantime? Take a chance and hit the M5 or rest up in the pleasant surroundings of the Cotswolds?

Taking the turn to the right, he soon had the distinct impression that it was taking them in the direction from which they'd just come. What was it with these Cotswold back roads?

'For goodness' sake!' Tom said, pulling over again. He felt exhausted, and in dire need of a holiday. He paused at the thought. Why not?

'What do you think, Flo? Shall we stay here until we get some reports about Molly?'

Flora beamed a smile at him and nodded enthusiastically. 'Look!' she said. 'Here's the perfect place.'

Tom followed the direction she was pointing in and his mouth fell open as he took in the oldest, crumbliest, most beautiful house he'd ever seen.

'Can we stay there?' Flora begged.

'I don't think so. It's a private house.'

'But it says bed and breakfast – look!'

Tom turned round and saw a home-made sign hiding in thick clumps of ivy. 'Good heavens! Let's give it a go, then, eh? See if we can book in for tonight – special treat!'

Driving up the gravelled drive, they parked the car.

Tom gave a long, low whistle. 'What a house! Flo, I'm not sure we can afford this. Stay here a min and I'll find out.'

Tom got out of the car and walked towards the house, rolling his sleeves up as he went. His arms were beginning to turn a wonderfully warm gold, which was a vast improvement on the chalky white he was used to.

'Oi!' a voice suddenly called out from behind him.

Tom turned round to see an old lady in maroon charging

towards him with a broom poised perilously in her hands.

'Get out of here you no-good piece of garbage!' the old lady said, her face the same scary maroon of her suit.

'Can I help you?' Tom asked hesitantly.

'No you can't! Get out of here. You'll get no answers from me so push off! Go back to London where your scum belong.'

'But I'm not from London.'

'Well, clear off my land before I do some damage with this here broom!'

'I don't understand,' Tom said. 'I only wanted a room for the night.'

The old woman squinted at him. 'You can't fool me, Mr Tom Mackenzie.'

'You know who I am?'

'Get out of here, or are you a journalist who doesn't understand plain English?' she said, wielding the broom in a dangerous arc.

'You've seen Molly, haven't you?'

The old woman's eyes narrowed until they almost disappeared. 'What business is it of yours whether I've seen her or not?'

'I think it's of national importance,' Tom said smiling.

'You're an unscrupulous piece of scum, that's what you are. I think it's disgusting what you're doing to that poor girl. *Disgusting!*'

'I'm only telling it as it is.'

'That's your opinion, but you've twisted and turned the facts around until there's virtually no truth left. Why can't you leave that poor girl alone? Get yourself a proper job and get off my property.'

Tom held his hands up in resignation. He obviously wasn't

going to get anything other than insults out of the old woman. 'OK, I'm going!'

'Good! Get out of here,' she shouted and, with one final brandish of her broom, she chased Tom into his car.

'Aren't we staying?' Flora asked with a giggle as she turned round to see the woman wielding her broom.

'No,' he said. 'It's too expensive. You have to be a millionaire to stay here.'

'Like Molly?' Flora smiled.

'Just like Molly,' Tom agreed.

Molly hit the M5 and had been travelling for at least an hour before she had to fill up her new car for the first time. She pulled into the next station and shuddered as she saw *Vive!* in the newspaper rack. With the joys of driving her new car down the motorway, she'd almost forgotten about Peeping Tom and his front page but, now that it was staring her in the face again, she felt her anger rising up once more.

'Molly Bailey – I'm ashamed of you,' the voice of her father whispered in her ear.

Molly hung her head and bit her lip. She felt like a teenager with cheap, chipped nail varnish, stomping up the stairs to sulk in her bedroom. She'd never wanted to feel like that again, yet this stranger had thrown up all those feelings of adolescent insecurity again.

And that's when she made her decision. She was going to ring Tom Mackenzie and give him a piece of her mind.

The Bailey men might not have had any joy in finding Molly but at least they'd found The Swan, albeit after several wrong turns and getting stuck behind a very mucky, smelly tractor.

Being lunchtime, they'd decided that they might as well eat there, even though the menu was a tad more expensive than they would have liked.

Carolyn used the opportunity to sneak a call to Molly and was quick to tell her where they were.

'Don't worry,' Molly had said, 'I've left Gloucestershire.'

'Where are you heading?'

'Don't know yet but I'll make sure I don't slip up again.'

There was an awkward pause, both women wondering if anything would be mentioned about double-crossing jockeys.

'Listen,' Molly said, 'can you give me Tom Mackenzie's number?'

'What are you going to do?'

'Put him in his place,' Molly said. 'What else?'

Carolyn gave her the number, which she'd kept safely in her handbag since Tom had given it to her.

'Thanks,' Molly said. 'And you're OK, are you?'

Carolyn took a deep breath. Now was her moment to confess. 'Yes. I am. But—'

'Good!' Molly interrupted. 'Listen, Caro. I'm going to have to dash now. I'll catch up with you later, OK? Keep up the good decoy work.'

And she was gone, and Carolyn was left alone. 'But you're going to be an auntie,' she whispered into her mobile.

Chapter Thirty-Three

Tom's mobile phone started to ring just as he was about to cram a handful of chips in his mouth.

'Mackenzie,' he said shortly, inhaling the wonderful smell of hot vinegar which wafted up from his cone of chips, wondering who had the nerve to interrupt him.

'This is Molly Bailey.'

'*Molly?*' he said, aghast, almost dropping his chips.

'Yes.'

'Good heavens!' He flung the cone of chips into Flora's hand and pulled out a pad and pen from his trouser pocket.

Flora poked him in the ribs. 'Molly *Bailey?*' she whispered up at him.

Tom nodded, but he wasn't quite prepared for what happened next.

'I just wanted to ask you, why don't you use your column for something useful for a change? I've just had my car stolen and all you can think to write about is tittle-tattle about my private life! Well, I bet you didn't know that that thieving bastard jockey stole two and a half grand from my handbag!'

'Whoa! Hang on a minute,' Tom interrupted. 'I'm not sure I'm getting all of this.'

'You're not very quick for a reporter, are you?' Molly fired.

'Just a sec,' Tom said.

'If you think I'm going to speak slowly so you can write all this down, then you've got more nerve than I've credited you for,' she said.

'Declan O'Hara *stole* from you?'

'Two and a half thousand pounds.'

'But there's more where that came from, isn't there?' Tom said.

'That's not the point, is it? I had special plans for that money and he had no business to touch it.'

'What plans?'

Molly paused before answering. 'What would you care? You're only after stuff that's sensational.'

Tom raked his hands through his hair and frowned into the phone. 'I think you've got the wrong impression of me, you know.'

'Oh, have I?'

'Yes! Yes, you have! I'm only doing my job—'

'Well, your job—'

'—and if *I* didn't do it – somebody else would!' he finished, nodding his head in satisfaction.

There was a brief pause. Finally, Molly spoke. 'I rang to give you a piece of my mind and to tell you that what you're doing is immoral, inconsiderate and downright rude.'

'Is that all?'

'And I don't like your tone of voice. You really don't know how much damage you've done.'

'What have I done?'

He heard her sigh down the phone and suddenly began to feel a little bit guilty.

'I'm not sure yet, but your articles are being read by my friends and family.'

Tom started. The thought hadn't even crossed his mind. Naive as it might sound, he hadn't thought about Molly's relatives being amongst his readers. They'd always been a kind of faceless, opinionless crowd. Even when he received his emails, he didn't really think of the senders as being real people, apart from red-haired Rebecca from Bristol, of course.

'I'm sorry,' he said.

'Are you?'

'Yes,' he said and, for some reason, he recalled the photo he'd seen of Molly on the Internet winning the florists' award and remembered the large dark eyes and the sweetest of faces and, in spite of himself, he felt suddenly protective of her, imagining those lovely eyes filled with consternation. 'Look, if there's anything I can do?' he said in a slightly less urgent, less hungry-reporter-type voice.

'Why can't anyone understand what I'm trying to do? Is it so hard for people to be nice? Why's that so difficult? It shouldn't be unusual.'

'I agree.'

'Do you?' Molly said, not sounding as if she believed him for a second.

'Yes! That's why I want to know if there's anything I can do,' he said. 'Is there?'

'What do you mean?'

'Well, you said you had your car stolen, as well as your money. Maybe I can help. You know – put out an appeal in my column?'

'You'd seriously do that?'

'Why not?'

'I don't believe you.'

'You don't have to. I'll do it anyway.' There was a moment's silence. 'So you got yourself a new Beetle?'

'I knew it!' Molly said. 'There's not a good bone in your body. You're only after more information for your column. Well, you're not going to get it like that.'

'Shit!'

'Daddy?'

'She's hung up on me.'

'I don't think she liked your last question.'

'Have you been earwagging?'

'Of course. I'm the daughter of a journalist.'

Tom rolled his eyes.

'Why don't you stop following her, Daddy? Then she won't be mad at you anymore.'

'We're following her because she's an interesting person and newspapers always want stories about interesting people.'

'What makes her interesting?' Flora looked at her father with intense eyes.

'Well, she's rather unusual, don't you think?'

'Because she's giving all her money away?'

'Yes.'

'And that's unusual, is it?'

'It certainly is.'

'Why?'

Tom scratched his head. How could he explain human greed to her? How could he explain that sharing wasn't the norm in the world of adults; that you kept what was yours and that looking after number one was all that mattered. He sighed. 'People don't often give things away – for free. They usually want something in return.'

'Like at Christmas?'

'Exactly!' Tom nodded. 'Who would give a present to someone they knew wouldn't give a present to them?'

Flora looked puzzled for a moment. 'But they should, shouldn't they? If they're nice people.'

'Yes,' he said, smiling with pride at his daughter, 'they should.'

'And Molly's a nice person, isn't she?'

'She certainly is, and I'm going to ring her back – look – don't you just love technology? I've got her number in my phone now.'

'Clever!' Flora said, finishing the last of her father's chips.

'Molly?' There was silence. 'Are you there? I wanted to apologise. Molly?'

'I'm here. I don't appreciate you invading my privacy like this.'

'But I just wanted to say sorry.'

'Well, you have now so leave me alone.'

'Can I just explain some things to you about the job I do?'

'I'm not interested so you'd be wasting your breath.'

'The public loves you, Molly,' he said, deciding to carry on regardless. 'You do know that, don't you? I've been inundated with emails telling me how horrible I am in chasing you up and down the country. You've become the nation's daughter. Everyone's so protective of you yet, at the same time, they're desperate to read about you – want me to find out more about you. You're a national heroine and God only knows we need more of those,' he said. 'Molly?'

'I'm listening.'

'Where are you?'

'You don't give up easily, do you?'

'I'll never give up as long as there's a story to tell.'

'But what's so special about me? So I've got a bit of money to throw around – so what?'

Tom smiled. 'You don't realise how unique you are, do you? You're doing something quite extraordinary – you're being kind. *Kind* in a world filled with *un*kindness, you're generous where most people are seriously *un*generous, you're—'

'OK! I get the picture, but shouldn't that be my own private business?'

'You're also incredibly naive.'

There was a stunned silence.

'Molly? I've upset you again, haven't I? *Shit!*'

'Did she hang up again, Daddy?'

'Yes. She did.'

Chapter Thirty-Four

The Baileys were waiting to find out where Molly was via *Vive!*, and Tom was waiting for some email sightings of Molly to come in. The only person who seemed to be on the move was Molly herself and she'd reached Dorset by Saturday evening. After checking in to a small hotel in Lyme Regis, which had just had a last-minute cancellation and allowed dogs, she spread out her road atlas on the bed. Carlisle to Lyme; Cumbria to Dorset. It was a long way. Molly couldn't work out exactly how many miles she'd driven, nor did she know how many people she'd helped on the way but she was a good few pounds lighter now than when she'd started and that made her smile.

The public loves you, Molly. Tom Mackenzie's voice flooded her ears. Was that true? Did they love her? It was hard to imagine yet it never failed to amaze Molly how a little money could make all the difference. It wasn't that she was giving it away in order to be thanked; that wasn't part of her agenda, but she couldn't help thinking how very little it took to make a person smile.

After unpacking a few things, she pulled on a light jumper and went out for a walk with Fizz. She was desperate to see what he made of his first trip to the seaside and almost tripped over him several times on their way down the steep hill that led through the town down towards the beach.

By the time they had walked along the seafront, a cool breeze enveloped them but wasn't enough to deter Molly from climbing the steps up onto the great grey snake of the Cobb. No matter how hard Fizz pulled, there was no way Molly was going to let him off his lead here. The Cobb was dangerously high for a terrier pup, and a steep incline, from left to right, led straight into the sea.

She took in a great lungful of salty air. She'd better start stocking up on fresh air in case she had to hotfoot it to London in search of her mother, she thought, wondering how long a lungful lasted and how many she'd need in order to survive the Big Smoke.

She wondered how Legs was doing in London. Had he found the elusive Cynthia yet? And which part of London was she in, anyway? Molly couldn't quite imagine. Had she set up home in one of the beautiful wedding-cake houses in Belgravia and was she sloaning around Knightsbridge? No, Molly didn't think so. For a start, a Bailey divorce settlement wouldn't allow such luxuries. Still, she might have seen Cynthia on her recent disastrous shopping trip. How strange to think that she might have walked right by her in the street and not even known.

She still hadn't decided what she was going to do or say once she knew where her mother was. What *did* you say to someone you hadn't seen for sixteen years?

'So, how are things with you?' *No.*

'You'll probably notice I've grown quite a bit!' *Definitely* no!

'You know you left your cardigan behind?' Molly giggled in spite of herself.

She had often speculated on what Cynthia was up to but Marty had always refused to be drawn in.

'She left and she's not coming back,' he'd say, as if that was the end of the story. But it wasn't the end of the story for Molly. There were whole chapters left unexplained. She just wished that Marty could be a part of it too, and felt angry that she couldn't talk to him about it now with all this fuss being made over her lottery win.

Staring out across the darkening sea, she wondered, for the hundredth time, how two siblings could be so very different.

A steady stream of emails seemed to be pointing south.

'Devon!' Tom announced. 'Five sightings – look! Too late to leave now, though.'

Since being chased with a broom from Chartlebury Court, Tom and Flora had decided to bed down near Cirencester in the hope that the slight move south was inching them closer to Molly's new destination. He smiled smugly as he closed his laptop for the night.

'Did you send the article, Daddy?' Flora asked with a yawn.

'Went off this afternoon,' he said. 'Should be in tomorrow's issue.'

'It's a good article,' Flora said.

'I did my very best on it,' Tom said, joining his daughter in a yawn and thinking of the promise he'd made to Molly to help her. And he really did want to help her. It was as if Molly's crusade was becoming *his* crusade too and that they were linked in this strange mission. He rather liked the idea of that. Molly and Tom – helping the nation to happiness. He could imagine that as a headline.

'Do you think Molly will read it and forgive you?' Flora asked from somewhere beneath her duvet.

'I think she might,' Tom said, a smile curving across his unshaven face. 'I really think she might.'

It was Sunday morning, and a buttery sun had encouraged the crowds out onto the tiny stretch of sandy beach at Lyme Regis. Molly watched as tots tumbled in the sand, chubby fists pounding castle turrets out of bright plastic buckets whilst mums tried to grab a few moments' bliss in a paperback, and dads did their best not to get caught eyeing up the beach totty on parade.

For a moment, Molly thought what great fun it would be to walk amongst them, handing out fifty-pound notes. A smile spread across her face at the thought but, however tempting the idea was, she didn't want to cause a riot. Still, there was something very appealing about the idea. She'd muse on it for a while and see what she came up with.

Molly had completely fallen in love with fifty-pound notes. They were rather special, weren't they? You didn't come across them every day. They weren't common like five-pound notes or ten-pound notes. A fifty, with its poppy-red complexion, was a joy to behold – and to let go of, of course.

Heading back into town in search of some yellow gerbera, and still musing on the magic that was fifty, she couldn't help overhearing a young couple dragging their daughter away from a shop selling fossils.

'I've told you, Melanie, you've already spent your holiday money.'

'Come on, Beth, it's only seven pounds,' the father said, 'it's hardly going to break the bank, is it? And her birthday's next month. It isn't every day you get to buy a piece of history for seven pounds.'

The mother sighed. 'But she's spent all her money already, and I've only got ten pounds in my purse.'

'Excuse me,' Molly interrupted.

The mother and father turned round and stared at Molly with suspicion, as if she might be about to try and sell them something.

'I think you dropped this.'

They both looked down at the fifty-pound note that Molly held out to them.

'I don't think so,' the father said.

'But it was right behind you on the pavement,' Molly insisted.

'Must belong to someone—'

'I think it might be mine, actually,' the mother interrupted quickly.

'Are you sure, Beth? I thought you only had ten pounds left?'

Beth glared at him, taking the note from Molly's hand. 'Thank you,' she said in a small voice.

'That's OK,' Molly said. 'You'll be able to buy your daughter that fossil now, won't you?' Molly smiled, looking at the rosy-faced girl with bright-red pigtails.

Watching them venture back into the shop, Molly looked up and down the high street. 'Now,' she said, 'where do you find yellow gerbera in Lyme?' She walked up the steep street and suddenly halted outside a shop as she saw a copy of Sunday's *Vive!*. Her mouth dropped open as, instead of an obligatory blonde wearing a string vest, she saw an inch-tall headline:

Mollymobile stolen.

Molly smiled. Tom Mackenzie had kept his promise.

Chapter Thirty-Five

Donkeys really were the saddest-looking creatures, weren't they? No matter how much Molly called over to them, they stood in their field looking as if they were in some form of detention. Finally, after a good ten minutes of coaxing, a pale-grey donkey ambled over to her and allowed her to pet his dusty coat. Hanging over the fence, Molly let her dark curls fall over his pale face as she gave him a hug but it didn't seem to do any good. He still looked like Eeyore.

'Smith!' Molly announced, finding his name on the collar round his neck. 'Cheer up, sweetheart!' she whispered in his ear. 'You're beautiful!'

But, even with a torrent of praise flowing into his ears, he stood, heavy and silent, as Molly petted him.

She soon found out that there were about five hundred donkeys at the sanctuary, although not all of them were at the visiting centre, which was just as well because Molly would have been there for ever trying to distribute hugs fairly. She walked around the pathways that skirted the fields, gazing over at the sad-eyed creatures who didn't seem aware of the visitors desperate to get close to them.

She had slightly more luck at the feeding barn. There were no fences there: just man and donkey side by side. The sound of munching was quite deafening and made her want to laugh and cry at the same time as she walked in between the docile beasts.

How could anyone not love a donkey? she thought. How could anyone mistreat them or abandon them or work them to within an inch of their lives?

Walking into the gift shop, she picked out a few notelets to buy and took them up to a young girl at the till.

'How do I go about making a donation?' Molly asked.

'There's a box, here,' she said with a nod.

Molly smiled. 'I don't think it's going to fit in there. Is there someone I could speak to?'

The girl looked up at Molly and suddenly gasped, her hand flying to her mouth dramatically. 'You're *her*, aren't you?' Molly's eyes widened, and she felt herself blushing. 'You're *Molly*!'

'Shush!' Molly hushed, looking round the shop in case a local reporter was hovering with a notepad.

'God almighty! We were just talking about you the other day, saying we hoped you'd make it down to Devon, and here you are! It *is* you, isn't it?' she asked excitedly and Molly couldn't help but nod.

'Please,' she said, 'just keep it quiet.'

'Oh! I know! You're still trying to avoid that reporter, aren't you? Did you see him on *Susanna* the other day? He's rather dashing, you know.'

'No, I didn't see him.'

'Well, I wouldn't mind him chasing *me* round the country!'

the girl giggled, and then managed to recover herself. 'What's it like, then?'

'What's what like?'

'Being chased like that?'

'Like *this*, you mean. He hasn't given up yet.'

'You mean he could be here – *right now*?' the girl asked, looking around excitedly as if Tom Mackenzie might walk into the shop at that very moment.

'I don't think so,' Molly said. 'I'm smarter than him.'

The girls gave each other a conspiratorial smile.

'Anyway – about this donation?' Molly prompted.

The girl grinned. 'Come with me,' she said, leading her out of the gift shop.

Molly followed her, the sound of a braying donkey filling the yard.

Tom had just reached Axminster when his mobile phone went off. Quickly pulling over, he answered it.

'Tom Mackenzie.'

'It's Molly.'

Tom's eyebrows rose. 'Molly!'

'Don't get your hopes up,' she said quickly. 'I just wanted to thank you for today's article in *Vive!*.'

'I thought you might like it.'

'But it only goes some of the way to repairing the damage you've done, of course.'

'Oh,' he said, somewhat taken aback.

'I don't suppose you've had any calls about Old Faithful yet, have you?'

'Old—'

'I mean my car,' Molly corrected herself quickly.

'I'm afraid not,' Tom said. 'But it's early days yet,' he added, finding it hard to disguise a small chuckle at Molly's nickname for her car.

'I don't suppose I'd need two cars, though, would I?'

'Especially two yellow Beetles,' Tom said.

'Who said I had a yellow Beetle now?'

Tom smiled. 'But you have, haven't you?'

'Is that what people are telling you?'

'There've been quite a few sightings of a yellow Beetle in the Devon area in particular,' Tom added and was sure he heard her gasp. 'That's where you are, isn't it?'

'Look, I rang to thank you – nothing more – so please don't start up all your questioning again.'

There was a moment's pause.

'Are you OK?' Tom asked at last.

'Why do you ask?'

'You sound tired.'

'I am tired.'

'That's endless driving for you,' Tom said, trying to roll the stiffness out of his shoulders.

'You're not kidding. Do your shoulders ache?'

Tom laughed. 'They feel like concrete. I was just trying to loosen them up.'

'Me too,' Molly said and Tom tried to imagine her rolling her shoulders at the other end of the phone.

'A good long soak in the bath,' he said. 'That goes some of the way at the end of a long day behind the wheel.'

'Oh, that's the best, isn't it?' Molly said.

'Don't you get a bit fed up of moving around all the time?'

'No, I don't. I'm loving it. You wouldn't believe all the people I've met and the places I've seen.'

'Yeah?' Tom said.

'England's so beautiful.'

'It certainly is,' he agreed. 'And I have to thank you for allowing me to see so much of it for myself too.'

'What do you mean?'

'I mean, I hadn't really left my home county much before all this began.'

'Really?' she said. 'Me too!'

'I was kind of stuck in a Suffolk rut,' he said and he heard Molly laugh. It was the first time he'd heard her laugh and he liked it. 'Not that Suffolk isn't beautiful, you understand,' he added. 'Because it is but, I guess when you've grown up somewhere, you don't always see it, do you?'

'I know what you mean.'

'But your county's beautiful,' he said and there was a dreadful pause. Tom cleared his throat, worrying that he'd overstepped the mark in reminding her that he was practically stalking her. 'I mean, what I've seen of it.'

'It is,' she said and he breathed a sigh of relief that she hadn't hung up on him.

'I could never live in a city,' Tom said, desperately trying to keep the conversation going.

'No, I couldn't either,' Molly said.

'So, you're not heading to any cities in the foreseeable future?' Tom asked and then bit his lip. Had he pushed things? He waited for a reply. 'Molly?'

'What?' she said. 'I'm not telling you where I'm going.'

'I wasn't asking that.'

'Are you sure? You're a journalist. There's more than one way of asking a question.'

'Yes, I know. But I wasn't – really. I'm just enjoying talking to you. You know, finding out a bit about you.'

'Why?'

'Why? Because you're interesting,' he said.

There was a weighty pause when Tom felt sure Molly was about to hang up on him, and it would have served him right too, he knew. He sighed, knowing that her defences were up again. Still, he wasn't going to give up so easily.

'You know,' Tom said at last, 'I could be good for you.'

'Oh, really?'

'Yes!' he said. 'If you told me where you were – who you were helping and suchlike – my reports would add extra publicity for your campaigns.'

'But I don't want publicity. I just want to get on with this. You keep trying to turn this into some great crusade and it isn't. It's just me.'

Tom scratched his head. 'But you're not *just you* anymore. You're a national figure.'

'I don't think so.'

'But you *are*, and I want to help you – I really do.'

'If you really do, then just let me know if you find my old car.'

'Tell me where you are, Molly.'

'I'm not going to do that.'

'Why not?'

'Because I'm not a public person.'

'Yes you are.' There was a pause. Was she weighing up his words? Was she starting to believe him? 'Molly?'

'I'm still here.'

'Let me help you.'

'I don't need your help,' she said, and she hung up.

* * *

Sitting in the car park of the donkey sanctuary, Molly couldn't help wondering what had just happened. She'd been *chatting* to Tom Mackenzie – her public enemy number one – and it had been the sort of easy conversation she might have had with anyone. She frowned. She couldn't possibly be getting to like this man, could she? She shook her head, doing her best to dismiss the thought. She had other things to think about and yet she couldn't help mulling over Tom's words. He wanted to help her. He'd already proved to her that he could with his national appeal for Old Faithful, so maybe she should make use of his help for her good causes? No, she thought, shaking her head. This was *her* project and she didn't want anybody else getting involved in it. It wouldn't work – it would get out of hand, messy, confusing and competitive. This way, she alone was in charge. Anyway, it wasn't meant to be some grand scheme – it was just a whimsical way of spending the summer, which just happened to involve spending the best part of four million pounds. She still couldn't understand what all the fuss was about.

Leaving the donkey sanctuary, Molly pulled out onto the main road without really planning where she was going next. Bridport, Bournemouth, Bognor? There were so many places to discover and so many people whose lives could be made all the sunnier for a small injection of cash.

Before she could make her mind up, her phone rang. Pulling into a lay-by dwarfed by a sky-scraping hedgerow, Molly picked up her phone. If it was Tom Mackenzie ringing her back, she'd have to get tough with him.

'Hello,' she said somewhat abruptly.

'Ms Bailey?'

'Yes.'

'It's Malcolm McCleod from Marie Celeste. We have some news about your mother.'

Chapter Thirty-Six

Being a step behind *Vive!*, which was a step behind Molly, the Baileys arrived in Devon just after Molly had left.

'We don't want to stay here if we can help it,' Magnus growled from the back seat. 'Hideously expensive – even when it isn't holiday season.'

'Overrated too,' Old Bailey joined in with a knowing nod.

'Oh, have you been before?' Carolyn asked.

'No,' he said, looking surprised by her question.

'Then how do you know it's overrated?'

He frowned at her. 'What do people want with all those cream teas and fudge? Load of nonsense – just another way of getting money out of people.'

'But people wouldn't buy them if they didn't want them,' Carolyn pointed out.

'*Ah!*' Old Bailey said, waving a thick finger in the air. 'That's exactly it! These places make you *think* you want these things, but you don't! There's nothing wrong with a Tesco's-own tea bag and a digestive biscuit.'

'That reminds me – shall we have that flask now?' Marty asked from the front.

'Good idea,' Old Bailey said, and Marty pulled over at the first convenient lay-by.

Carolyn grimaced at the thought of what was to come: three men sharing a cup of tea from one plastic cup. Old Bailey had taken a handful of tea bags from the tea tray in the bed and breakfast the night before and had knocked on Marty and Carolyn's door to take theirs too.

'We're paying for these, you know,' he said when he saw her disapproval. What bothered her the most, though, was the fact that they expected her to join in.

'Marty,' Carolyn said, 'can't we stop for a proper cup of tea?'

'Don't you want some of this?' he said, offering her the yellowing top from the old flask which had already been swigged out of by Magnus and Old Bailey before reaching Marty's lips.

'No, thank you,' she said, trying her best not to retch at the thought.

'We've got to try and find Molly – you know that.'

'We can't keep stopping. We'll never catch up with her if we stop at every café en route,' Magnus added.

'*I'm only asking for a bloody cup of tea!*' Carolyn suddenly shouted, and the car filled with a stunned silence.

'*Carolyn!*' Marty said in shock.

'I'm not asking too much, *am I*? A ten-minute stop for a quick cup of tea. That's not expecting too much, is it?'

'Er – no,' he agreed. 'Dad?' he said, looking to Magnus to help bail him out.

Magnus's eyes narrowed. 'Perhaps a quick stop might be refreshing.'

'Granddad?' Marty said.

The car filled with silence once more as they waited for Old Bailey's answer. But he wasn't going to be budged on this one. He was a flask man. 'You know, young lady,' he said, looking sternly at Carolyn, 'you're beginning to remind me of that bloody Percy woman!'

Molly was shaking. All these years she'd longed to hear news of her mother and the minute she did, she froze, panicked and lied.

'You've made a note of the address?' McCleod asked.

'Yes,' she said.

'So you'll be heading to London straight away?'

'Yes,' Molly said, but the word sounded foreign and without meaning as she said it.

'So that wraps our business up, then?'

'I suppose it does,' Molly said. 'I can't thank you enough,' she added. 'You've been amazingly quick.'

'We like to do our best,' McCleod said, 'and Legs is the fastest in the business.'

'I've no doubt he is,' Molly said and, hearing McCleod coughing loudly into the phone, she said her goodbyes and hung up.

How strange. How very strange, she thought, looking at the tiny piece of paper she'd scribbled the address on. This was her mother's home and, according to the information Legs had gleaned, she'd been living there for almost nine years. Cynthia Bailey had become a city girl. Molly shook her head. What had happened to her mother to make her quit her beloved countryside?

As much as Molly longed to know, she was also absolutely terrified of finding out.

* * *

Tom sat frowning down at his mobile phone. He hadn't expected that phone call. He'd hoped, stupidly, that it was Molly. Instead, it had been bloody Anise.

'That was Mummy, wasn't it?' Flora said.

Tom nodded. 'If I'd known, I wouldn't have answered.'

'What did she say?'

Tom sighed and raked a hand through his thick hair. He needed a haircut as well as a shave. 'She wants you back home by the end of the week. She's back from her gallivanting early. Obviously bored of lying on a beach all day.'

'Is gallivanting what she does with JP?'

'Yes,' Tom said shortly.

'And what is it again?'

'Messing about.'

'Oh.'

'Anyway, you probably heard, I told her you're staying with me until my job's done.'

Flora nodded. 'I heard.'

'Is that all right with you? Or do you want to go home now?'

Flora shook her head and she grinned. '*No way*. I want to find Molly and I'm not going home till we've found her.'

Tom laughed and ruffled her hair. 'Me neither!' he said, and started the car up again before pulling out and heading for Lyme Regis.

Molly had been driving for most of the day but she wasn't exactly heading to London. Not yet. She didn't want to face her mother until she had formed some sort of idea of what she'd actually say to her. Her emotions were still too raw and too many questions were tumbling round her head. She needed time to think and so had found herself drifting through Dorset until she stopped at a picture-perfect village.

Half expecting to see the cast of a Thomas Hardy novel walking around, she wasn't at all surprised to see a wedding in full swing. Walking along the narrow lane and allowing Fizz to snuffle around the thick grassy verges, Molly watched the bride and groom posing for photographs. The bride, in a creamy-gold slim-fitting gown, looked elegant and serene, and the groom looked as if he'd walked straight out of a Merchant-Ivory film.

Molly thought back to Marty and Carolyn's wedding. It hadn't been anything on the scale of this one judging by the number of bridesmaids and the size of the bride's bouquet. She remembered Carolyn picking out the flowers in The Bloom Room.

'That's so beautiful,' she'd said, looking through the photograph album of bridal bouquets, 'but it's a bit on the expensive side even with our family discount.'

Yes, even when it came to his own wedding, Marty had budgeted until practically all the fun had been erased.

Looking over to the bride and groom, she wondered how long they'd last. She knew she was being an old cynic but it was hard not to be one when she thought about her parents' marriage and the ever-precarious one between Marty and Carolyn.

The photographer was waving his arms around like a windmill in a hurricane and Molly watched as one of the bridesmaids stepped forward, a huge smile bisecting her face.

'*Now!*' the photographer yelled, almost leaping off the ground with excitement as the bridesmaid sent a shower of confetti over the bride and groom. It swirled, light as blossom, on the summer air. Molly gazed at the sweet shower of pastel colours, the laughter of the wedding party ringing out in place of the church bells. It was the most beautiful thing Molly had ever seen.

And that's when she had an idea: the most wonderful, fun-filled, excruciatingly exciting idea.

Running back to her car, she gave Fizz a great squeeze before doing up her seat belt.

He looked up at her, his eyes large and softly adoring.

'London,' Molly said to him. 'We can't put it off a moment longer.'

Chapter Thirty-Seven

Despite the fact that she adored her new car, and the fact that Fizz was sitting beside her, Molly was beginning to feel quite lonely. She hadn't had a proper conversation since leaving Eleanora Howard's in the Cotswolds and she was beginning to wish that she had a travelling companion.

As if she'd sent a prayer up to heaven and God didn't have any queues, Molly saw a hitch-hiker. She'd never picked up a hitch-hiker in her life. She'd never dared.

'There are more strange people than sane out there,' her father had warned, his dark eyebrows drawn together over the bridge of his nose. 'You do *not* want them in your car.'

But this girl didn't look like an axe murderer or escaped convict, and it would be nice to have somebody other than a dog to talk to, and it was still a long way to London.

Pulling over, Molly took a good look at the girl. She didn't look more than about nineteen or twenty. She was wearing a faded black shirt and green combat trousers with more pockets than a snooker table. Her face was as pale as a Pre-Raphaelite's and she was wearing her long dark-blonde hair in pigtails. Definitely a student.

'Come on, Fizz, it's time you were relegated to the back seat,' Molly said, unclipping his belt and lifting him up before leaning across and opening the passenger door.

'Gosh!' the girl said in surprise. 'Thank you so much. I've been stuck here for *hours*. They don't seem to be very friendly with the lifts round here.'

Molly smiled as the girl heaved her rucksack into the back of the car.

'I'm Jo,' the girl beamed.

'Molly.'

'Hi, Molly,' Jo said, extending a hand with at least three silver rings on each finger.

'Welcome aboard,' Molly said as Jo scrambled in.

'This is such a great car!'

'Thank you!'

'And your dog's so cute too!' Jo said, leaning back to give him a pat on his snowy head.

'That's Fizz. I hope you haven't got any food in your rucksack because he'll find it if you have.'

'No, nothing in there,' Jo said, doing her seat belt up as Molly pulled out.

'You're heading to London, I take it?' Molly asked.

'Yes. That wasn't the original plan. I was meant to be going InterRailing with a friend but she's since found a man and doesn't go anywhere without him. And I didn't want to be travelling round Europe with a couple of lovebirds.'

Molly tutted. 'I *hate* it when girlfriends do that.'

'Me too. So I thought I'd try travelling round Britain but it isn't as much fun as I'd hoped.'

Molly smiled. 'I know what you mean!'

'Are you travelling too?'

'You could say that,' Molly said, realising that Jo was peering at her closely.

'You know, you look kind of familiar.'

'Do I?' Molly said, trying to sound light-hearted.

'Yes, you do.'

'Funny. Everybody says that.'

'Are you a TV presenter or something?'

Molly took her eyes off the road for a split second. 'You're joking, aren't you? You don't need to butter me up just because I'm giving you a free ride.'

'I know that,' Jo said, 'but it's bothering me now. I'm sure I've seen your face somewhere.'

Molly winced. It was only a matter of time, wasn't it? She'd tried to forget that Tom Mackenzie had somehow got hold of a photo of her winning some local florists' competition, and had published it in *Vive!* as if it were a 'wanted' poster. Should she own up and put the poor girl out of her misery or should she drop her off at the next service station and avoid the issue completely?

'Oh my God – you're *her*, aren't you?'

Too late, Molly thought. '*Her?* Her who?' she said quickly, hoping she could somehow bluff her way out of things.

'Her! You know – the only *her* everyone's talking about at the moment. That millionaire girl. *Molly!* I should have known as soon as you said your name! Molly Bailey! You're Molly Bailey!'

'Shush!' Molly hushed, waving a hand at her. This fame thing was really beginning to catch up with her today. First the donkey sanctuary and now this!

'You *are*, aren't you? I'm not wrong, am I?'

Molly sighed. 'You're not wrong.'

'Can I shake your hand? Blimey! I've never met a millionaire before. Maybe your luck will rub off on me. God knows I could do with some!'

Molly couldn't help but grin as she allowed her hand to be shaken.

'Fancy!' Jo said. 'Me, being picked up by Molly Bailey!'

'It's no big deal.'

'Not to you, maybe. But nothing exciting ever happens in my life! Just wait till I tell Sally!'

'Is she your ex-InterRailing partner?'

Jo nodded. 'I hope she's having a lousy summer holiday. Then I can get my own back when I tell her about this.'

There was a moment's silence, Jo sitting with a huge grin on her face. 'I must say, you don't seem very excited by it all.'

'By all what?'

'You're a celebrity!' Jo said, making it sound as if that was something everybody should aspire to.

Molly shrugged. 'I guess I've got other things on my mind at the moment.'

'How can you be so calm? God, if I'd won the lottery, I'd be screaming from the rooftops!' Jo's eyes were as wide as plates.

'That's exactly what I couldn't do,' Molly said. 'Besides, I don't feel that the money is really mine.'

'How do you mean?'

'Well,' Molly said, a slight sigh colouring her voice, 'I never really wanted money – so much money, I mean.'

'Are you mad?'

'Oh, no! Really – I only ever wanted enough to get by.'

'Nobody ever just wants to *get by*,' Jo stated. 'Everyone wants to be rich.'

'Not me. I feel that, in a strange way, I'm merely the custodian of this money. It's just passing through me. Do you know what I mean?' Molly said, echoing the words of Eleanora Howard.

Jo looked nonplussed. 'No, I don't think I do. I think you're absolutely crazy. Amazing, but crazy.'

Molly laughed. 'I'm not amazing really. Not with the kind of family I have.'

'And is that what you've got on your mind at the moment?'

'You could say that.' Molly chewed her lip. A few minutes before she'd been praying for company and someone to talk to, but was Jo the right person? She glanced quickly at her. She looked honest enough as she examined the split ends of her pigtails.

'My mother's in London,' Molly began.

'Yeah?'

'But I've not seen her since I was eleven.'

'Oh.'

'She left my dad, my brother and me.'

'I'm sorry,' Jo said. 'And you're going to meet her now?'

Molly nodded. 'I've just been given her address.'

'Gosh! Are you nervous?'

'Yes!' Molly laughed. 'The thought of meeting her again makes me feel quite sick!'

'Does she know you won the lottery?'

Molly shook her head. 'Not unless she's a *Vive!* reader.'

'Well, there are a few more of those now that that reporter has brought you to the public's attention. Did you know it's doubled its circulation?'

'Really?'

'Heard it on the radio – they were having a discussion about it.'

Molly shook her head. 'All this fuss.'

'Exciting though?'

'I just want a quiet life.'

Jo smiled. 'You wouldn't be doing all this if you wanted a quiet life.'

'I suppose you're right,' Molly said. 'And, do you know what?'

'What?'

'I've decided to play along with it.'

'What do you mean?' Jo asked.

Molly grinned. 'I've had this crazy idea – a kind of grand finale idea that I'm going to try and pull off in London. And it's going to involve *Vive!*.'

'Really? What is it?' Jo's bright eyes sparkled with excitement.

Molly bit her lip. 'I'll tell you later,' she said. 'Let's get to London first.'

The next phone call Tom received had been better news and he'd been quick to respond, arriving at the donkey sanctuary, near Branscombe, within twenty minutes. He was a little bit anxious about leaving the safety of his car, knowing that Flora would make a beeline for the animals. Tom had always been rather wary of animals, ever since a squirrel had run up his trouser leg in Regent's Park, and he wasn't too enamoured by the idea of meeting a couple of hundred donkeys.

'Come on, Daddy!' Flora yelled in excitement. 'Let's go!'

'Business first, Flo,' Tom said. 'We've got to meet Amber.'

They made their way over to the visitor centre and were greeted by a rather excitable girl in the gift shop.

'Tom Mackenzie!'

He extended his hand and she grabbed hold of it, her cheeks flushing scarlet. 'Amber?'

'Yes!' she said, sounding rather breathless.

'This is Flora, my daughter.'

'Pleased to meet you!' Amber said, shaking Flora's tiny hand.

'Hello,' Flora said, instantly warming to Amber.

'You're far better looking in real life than on television!' Amber gushed.

Tom didn't know what to say. Instead, he looked round the shop, desperate to change the subject, and that's when he saw the single yellow gerbera that was lying next to the till. 'I see Molly's left her usual calling card.'

Amber laughed. 'I teased her about leaving one for each donkey.'

'So what else did Molly leave behind?' Tom enquired.

'Ah!' Amber tapped her nose. 'Well, it was a confidential donation. We can't disclose that, I'm afraid. I'm not even meant to have called you. She made me promise but I'm sure she won't mind. She seemed to adore the donkeys and I'm sure she'd like to see us prospering from her visit – publicity-wise.'

'So what *can* you tell me about Molly?' Tom asked.

Amber beamed. 'I was just going to make a cup of tea,' she said. 'I hope you haven't got to rush off anywhere?'

Tom shook his head and gulped as she turned on her heels, her bum wiggling seductively in a pair of very tight jeans.

'Daddy,' Flora said, tugging at his sleeve, 'I haven't seen a single donkey yet.'

'No,' Tom said, 'neither have I.' But, he thought, there were definitely some very attractive asses about.

Chapter Thirty-Eight

'Do you mind if we have the radio on?' Jo asked Molly.

'Help yourself,' Molly said. 'I haven't worked it out yet.'

Jo fiddled with it and music blared out, causing Fizz to wake up and give a bark.

'Oh no, it's that new DJ – Krista Karen, or someone,' Jo complained.

'Never heard of her.'

'Stupid name. Stupid woman,' Jo said, and they listened as she filled the airwaves with her breathy voice.

'We're talking about our new national heroine, Molly Bailey,' Krista trilled.

Molly almost crashed the car. '*What?*'

'*Shush!*' Jo said.

'So, if you're out there, Molly, give us a ring. We'd love to hear from you. Now, let's take another call. Hello, is that Marsha?'

'Hi, Krista!'

'What's your question for Molly, Marsha?'

'I'd like to ask Molly, if she *had* to spend the money on

herself, what would she buy and why?'

'A good question,' Krista said. 'Did you get that, Molly? Give us a call if you'd like to tell Marsha, and the rest of us, what you'd spend your money on if you had to spend it on yourself.'

'This is ridiculous!' Molly laughed. 'They're talking about *me*!'

'Let's take another call,' Krista said. 'I have Paul on line two. Hello, Paul?'

'Hello, Krista,' a very well-spoken voice said.

'I believe you have a request – another *Molly song*?'

'I do.'

Molly's eyes widened. 'A *Molly song*? What on earth is a *Molly song*?'

'I think we're about to find out,' Jo giggled.

'It's "I'd Like to Teach the World to Sing",' Paul said in his softly spoken Oxbridge voice.

'And why do you think that sums up Molly?' Krista asked.

'Because she's one of the few people who's giving something back to the world.'

'Oh! I can't listen to any more of this,' Molly said.

'Shush!' Jo snapped again. 'Hear the poor man out.'

'If we all followed Molly's lead, the world would be a better place,' Paul finished, and the sound of the New Seekers filled the car.

'Good grief!' Molly laughed.

'I think it's wonderful!' Jo enthused. 'They're talking about you! They're playing your songs. They're—'

'Completely mad!' Molly interrupted.

'Mad about *you*!' Jo said.

*   *   *

Eighty-odd miles away, after finally escaping from Amber at the donkey sanctuary having been asked far more questions by her than he himself had had the chance to ask, Tom and Flora were singing along to 'I'd Like to Teach the World to Sing', and wondering which song they should nominate as a *Molly song*.

'"Money, Money, Money"!' Flora suggested.

Tom laughed, thinking of Flora dancing to his Abba album. 'Shall we ring in?'

Flora nodded enthusiastically. 'Yes!'

'Here,' he said, passing her his mobile. 'They'll say the number again in a minute.'

'You know, you really shouldn't hitch-hike,' Molly said to Jo as they got back in the car after filling up with fuel and chocolate.

'Well, you shouldn't go around picking people up.'

Molly nodded. 'Point taken.'

Jo unwrapped a king-size Mars Bar and proceeded to dissect it, layer by layer, with nimble teeth as she sneakily switched the radio on again.

'Really, Tom? You must be exhausted with all that driving,' Krista Karen was saying.

'Oh my God!' Jo squealed. 'It's Tom Mackenzie! You should ring in, Molly!'

Molly stared at Jo in horror. 'No way!'

'Why not? He sounds ever so nice.'

'Why does everyone keep saying that?' Molly asked, annoyed. 'Anyway, I've spoken to him already.'

'You have?'

'Yes.'

'And?' Jo leant forward as if to get closer to Molly's answer.

'It didn't go very well,' Molly said quietly, thinking of Tom's continual hounding of her.

'Wait a minute – didn't you say you were going to get *Vive!* involved in something – once you were in London?'

'Yes, I did.'

'Well, why not ring in to the radio station and tell him about it now?'

'There's no need to. I've got his mobile phone number – I can ring him once we're in London.'

'But this would be so much fun, Molly!' Jo persisted.

Molly was beginning to wish she hadn't picked Jo up. She didn't want fun – not just at the moment. She was going to ring Tom, yes, but not yet, not until she'd found her mother.

She looked at Jo. 'Do you mind if we don't?' she asked. 'It's just, I've got other things on my mind at the moment.'

Jo nodded. 'That's OK,' she said, but there was disappointment in her eyes.

They did their belts up and pulled out of the service area.

'He does sound nice though, doesn't he?' Jo said, a little smile decorating her face.

Molly cocked her head and listened to the laughing voice of Tom Mackenzie.

'This is the weirdest story I've ever covered,' he was telling Krista Karen.

'And you have an accomplice, I hear?'

'Yes – Flora – my daughter. Say hi, Flo.'

'Hi, Krista!' a young voice chirped across the airwaves.

'Oh, sweet!' Jo said.

'I didn't know he had a daughter,' Molly said, her forehead furrowing.

'It's the school holiday,' Tom explained, 'so Flo's come with me for the ride.'

'Single parent?' Jo asked. 'I bet Krista doesn't ask him what all the nation's women want to know.'

'And your *Molly song*, Tom?' Krista asked.

'Well, Flo and I have been thinking long and hard about this but we've come up with "Money, Money, Money" by Abba.'

'An excellent choice,' Krista said.

Molly tutted. 'Very predictable.'

'But he sounds so sexy,' Jo grinned. 'Have you seen his picture in the papers?'

Molly nodded, remembering the dark-blond hair and pale-grey eyes. 'Not my type,' she said unconvincingly.

'Right!' Jo nodded. 'You could ski off his cheekbones.'

'And you could murder him for his cheek.'

'Is he cheeky?'

'He's been following me round the country, bombarding me with questions – I'd rate that as pretty bloomin' cheeky.'

Jo laughed. 'Well, I, for one, would adore someone giving me that sort of attention.'

'You can have him. With my blessing!'

Jo sighed. 'But he doesn't want me. He wants you.'

Molly sighed. It was all rubbish and she wasn't going to listen. Instead, she focused on the road ahead, only half aware that Jo was up to something.

'What are you doing?' Molly asked a moment later, seeing that Jo had picked up her mobile.

'Do you mind if I make a call?'

'Go ahead,' Molly said.

Jo smiled. 'Ta very much.'

Molly made a mental note to buy Jo a mobile phone. She

really should have one if she was travelling round on her own.

'It's ringing!' Jo said at last.

Molly gave half a glance, thinking that Jo looked extremely excited at making a simple phone call.

'Who are you call—'

'Hello, Tom? Tom Mackenzie?' Jo said.

'Jo! What are you doing?'

'I'm Jo – I'm a friend of Molly's. We just heard you on the radio.'

'*Jo!*'

'Yes, that's Molly. I'm with her right now.'

Jo glanced at Molly. 'He wants to talk to you.'

'I'm driving,' Molly said. 'And I don't really have anything to say to him.'

'Oh, go on! Just say hello.'

'Jo, I'm really not—'

But Jo wasn't taking no for an answer and pressed the phone up to Molly's ear.

'Hello, Molly?'

Molly sighed. 'Hello,' she said. 'I'm sorry but I didn't know Jo was ringing you.'

'That's OK. Always good to hear from friends of yours.'

Molly took a deep breath.

'Go *on*!' Jo said. 'Talk to him!'

'We heard you on the radio,' Molly said.

Jo rolled her eyes. 'I told him that already!'

Molly glared at her.

'Hope you liked our song,' Tom said. 'It was Flora's idea.'

'Your daughter?'

'Yes. She's right here.'

'Hello, Molly!' a young voice chirped.

Molly smiled. 'I didn't know you had a daughter.'

'She's been with me on this whole journey. My ex thought it a good idea to take off for the entire summer holiday with her fancy man so Flo and I are getting to spend some proper time together.'

Molly couldn't help grinning at the way he'd managed to inform her that he was a single man. 'And she doesn't mind being dragged the length and breadth of the country?' she asked him.

'She's loving it, aren't you, Flo?'

'Don't stop, Molly!' Flora's voice called. 'We love following you!'

There was a pause.

'Molly?'

'Yes?'

'You OK?'

Molly nodded and then remembered she was on the phone. 'Yes.'

'You sound distant.'

'Look, if you're trying to find out where I am then you've got another thing—'

'No, no! I mean, you sound – you know – thoughtful.'

'Oh, right,' she said.

'Is all well in the world of Molly?'

Molly looked at the road ahead. She was heading to London. She was going to meet her mother – the woman she hadn't seen for so many years.

'Everything's fine,' she said at last.

'You're planning something, aren't you?'

'What do you mean?'

'I can tell. Something's changed, hasn't it?'

Molly bit her lip. Was this some journalistic trick? Was he trying to get her to confess something that he was just second-guessing?

'I...' She paused, and there was a part of her that wanted to tell him – there really was. There was something in his voice that let her know that he would listen – *really* listen to her. 'I have a plan, yes,' she said, 'but I can't tell you yet.'

'But you *will* tell me?'

'Yes,' she said.

'Promise?' he said.

Molly found she was smiling. 'Yes,' she said.

'Then I'll wait for your call, Molly Bailey. Take care.'

'Bye,' she said.

'Blimey,' Jo said, removing the phone from Molly's ear and switching it off.

'What?' Molly asked, feeling her cheeks flush.

'My arm would've dropped off if you'd been any longer!'

Chapter Thirty-Nine

Marty picked up a copy of *Vive!* first thing on Monday morning and threw it down on the dining table at the bed and breakfast.

'She's been to some donkey sanctuary near Branscombe,' he said, landing heavily in an old wooden chair.

'Well, that's it, then,' Magnus said, his voice weary.

'What do you mean – *that's it*?' Old Bailey asked, eyes narrowed as his mouth worked over his third slice of toast. He never normally ate such a hearty breakfast but he was paying for it so he was damn well sure he was going to eat everything that was presented to him.

'Animals,' Magnus said.

'I think you might be right,' Marty nodded, and Carolyn couldn't help but smile. She'd heard about Molly's animal antics before. Throughout her childhood, Molly had never been able to hold on to a pound whereas Marty would fill his piggy bank to bursting point. If Molly had any money, she'd join Greenpeace, the Young Ornithologists' Club or Llamas in Need. Marty would often ask, 'What about a rainy day,

Moll?' and his sister would answer, 'Charities have rainy days *every* day.'

Yes, Carolyn thought, the Baileys would be lucky if there was any money left after Molly's trip to the donkey sanctuary.

'So what should we do now?' Magnus asked. 'We can't have come all this way for nothing.'

Marty pursed his lip. 'It seems to me that she's got a definite route in mind. This Mackenzie fellow's mentioned it too. And she could very well be heading for London.'

'What's she going to do there?' Old Bailey asked.

'I don't know! How am *I* meant to know?'

'She's your sister!' Old Bailey barked back as if forgetting that he was related to Molly as well.

'I'm only telling you what I've read.'

'Well, I think it's a good idea,' Magnus said sagely. 'We need to find some way of getting ahead of Molly instead of arriving after she's already left.'

'But how are we going to find her in London?' Old Bailey asked. 'It isn't exactly Penrith, is it?'

'No, it isn't,' Marty agreed. 'But I rather have a feeling that she's going to make herself known pretty soon.'

Carolyn glared at Marty. 'What makes you think that?'

'Just a feeling,' he said. 'I am her brother, aren't I?'

Molly and Jo had booked into The Portland Hotel and were working their way through heavily buttered croissants and hot chocolate. They hadn't been able to part company when they'd reached London the night before. Instead, they'd booked into the hotel and Molly had treated them both to a slap-up meal in Chinatown.

Molly liked Jo. With her fabulously long blonde pigtails,

she reminded Molly of a yellow iris. She also helped to take Molly's mind off why she had come to London and that could only be a good thing.

'So,' Jo said, croissant flaking down the front of yet another black T-shirt, 'what are we doing today?'

Molly smiled, liking the fact that they had become a 'we' already. 'I thought we'd take a look round,' she said.

'Sounds good.'

Molly nodded. 'Yes.'

'But,' Jo said, wiping her mouth with a napkin, 'when are you going to see your mother?'

Molly took a mouthful of chocolate and blinked hard. Jo had an unnerving habit of going straight to the heart of an issue, Molly had noticed. 'Tomorrow,' she said, 'definitely tomorrow.'

'They say tomorrow never comes,' Jo pointed out.

'It will,' Molly said.

The Baileys left Devon as soon as Old Bailey had cleared everyone's plate and asked for a third cup of tea.

'You know you'll need endless toilet stops now,' Marty said, huffily piling the overnight bags into the car.

'My bladder's stronger than an old leather suitcase,' Old Bailey snorted. Carolyn grimaced. Images of Old Bailey's bladder first thing in the morning were more than she could stomach. She'd already had a bout of morning sickness, hidden from Marty by putting breakfast TV on full volume.

Carolyn stared at Old Bailey as he climbed into the car. He was wearing that disgusting shirt with the frayed collar and middle button missing through which his enormous belly shone pinkly to the world. His trousers were no better.

Carolyn could only guess at their original colour. They'd been stitched and patched to within an inch of their life. There was barely a scrap of the original material left. How could he bear to put his legs into them? And his socks! They looked more like fishnets.

Getting into the passenger seat and doing her seat belt up for what seemed like the hundredth time that summer, she sighed, wondering what London had in store for them and wondering if she had enough money in her bank account to treat herself to a seriously short haircut in a fancy London boutique.

Molly had never heard of The Monument before and, halfway up the three hundred and eleven stairs, was beginning to wish that she and Jo had stayed on the tour bus. After walking the length of Oxford Street, Regent Street, and doing a tour of both Hyde Park and Green Park, Molly was shattered. She'd never done so much walking in her life and she was exhausted from carrying Fizz around all day to prevent tourists stepping on his little white paws. But the climb up The Monument was worth it. The view over the River Thames to Tower Bridge and Canary Wharf quite took their breath away. In the other direction, they could just make out the London Eye and, directly underneath them, were what appeared to be a thousand offices. Molly frowned at the ugliness of the buildings. There wasn't a single beautiful one amongst them. All were ugly lumps of concrete.

Jo snapped some pictures as Molly dared to gaze down to the street below. They were dizzyingly high and she was glad that there was a safety cage around them to prevent accidents. Pulling out a tissue from her pocket to wipe away a speck of city dust, a chewing-gum wrapper fell from her pocket through the railings. Watching as it twisted and turned on its long descent to street level, Molly smiled, remembering the shower of confetti at the Dorset wedding.

Searching for the other part of the wrapper, Molly surreptitiously let it take flight through the railings. It fell, graceful as an airborne ballerina.

'What are you looking at?' Jo asked, startling Molly.

'Nothing,' she said, hoping Jo didn't think she was some kind of perverted litterbug.

'Shall we go and get something to eat? I'm starving.'

Molly nodded and took one last look down the grand white column of The Monument. She could feel her heart accelerate, and bit her lip to prevent herself from smiling too much.

She'd found the perfect platform for her grand finale.

Chapter Forty

Tomorrow did come. Waking up in her hotel room, Molly's first thought was that tomorrow was now today, and today was the day when she'd try to find her mother. For a moment, she had an overwhelming desire to snuggle back down under the fresh cotton sheets and slip into sleep again, but she didn't. With a quick push, she was up and out of bed.

Padding through to the bathroom, she threw herself under the shower, letting the hot water plaster her curls to her face and turn her flesh red. Even in the height of summer, Molly adored hot showers. She'd pay for it someday, she knew, with varicose veins or whatever, but the feeling was just too sensational to worry about possible side effects and, for a few brief minutes, it helped to calm her down.

After drying and dressing, Molly called on Jo and they went down to breakfast together.

'Moll,' Jo said, buttering a croissant the size of a human head, 'I can't thank you enough for this holiday. I'd never have been able to stay here under my own steam.'

Molly smiled.

'Are you OK?' Jo asked, flicking a blonde pigtail over her shoulder.

Molly nodded. 'I'm fine.'

Jo cocked her head to one side in a manner that reminded Molly of Fizz. 'You still nervous?'

Molly looked up and held her gaze. 'I haven't stopped shaking since I woke up.'

'Do you want me to come with you?' Jo asked.

'Thanks, but no. I have to do this on my own.'

Jo poured some more tea out.

'What will you do today?' Molly asked.

'Thought I might have a look round the galleries. Find something to do for free, you know.'

Molly nodded. She knew, only too well, what that felt like. Reaching into her handbag she grabbed hold of an envelope, which she slid across the table. 'For you,' she said.

Jo's mouth fell open. 'What's this?'

'Just a little thank you.'

Jo opened the creamy envelope and smiled as a yellow gerbera fell onto the breakfast table. 'Molly!' she gasped. 'I can't take this.'

'Of course you can!'

'It's too much!'

'I thought you said you could never have *too much*?'

'But I didn't mean for you to—'

'I know you didn't,' Molly laughed. 'But I've really enjoyed your company and I just wanted to thank you.'

'Boy, I've never seen a thank-you present like this before,' Jo said, her eyes still wide as she gazed at the envelope stuffed with cash.

'There's a cheque in there too – to help towards university.'

'Really?'

Molly nodded again.

'You shouldn't have – I mean – you're too kind – I don't know what to say!'

'You don't have to say anything,' Molly said, reaching across the table and giving her hand a light squeeze. 'Now,' Molly said, with a deep intake of breath, 'I've got to get going.'

After eating a horrible service-station sandwich for breakfast, Tom looked down longingly at his mobile phone. His fingers were itching to ring Molly's number. It was quite incredible, he thought, how, if he rang her number, the beam would leap up into the sky to some invisible satellite where it would about-turn and beam back down to find Molly. If only he could follow that beam and find Molly too, he thought. Where was she?

He took a mouthful of orange juice to wash away the taste of plastic cheese.

'I think we should head to London,' he told Flora.

'Can we visit the Egyptian mummies?'

'If we've got time,' Tom said.

'If we leave now, we could visit them today.'

'Possibly,' Tom said, not relishing the idea of a museum visit, 'but don't build your hopes up. We may have work to do.'

'You're *always* working, Daddy,' Flora said.

'But I thought you liked this job.'

'Oh, I do. And I hope we get to meet Molly soon. Do you think we will?' Flora asked.

'Yes,' he said. 'I do.' Tom looked thoughtful for a moment.

Ever since Molly had rung him, he'd been in the strangest of moods. And then last night...

He shook his head. It had been the craziest thing. He hadn't dreamt of Juliette Binoche or Nicole Kidman. He hadn't even dreamt of fame and fortune for himself. Oh, no. He'd dreamt of Molly Bailey.

Molly parked in a backstreet in Holborn and, after placing Fizz on his lead, left the car in what she hoped was the right direction. London wasn't the best of places to be in during midsummer. Heat seemed to rise in columns from the street, and the barking of car horns was deafening. Once again, Molly wondered what had brought her mother to such a place.

Taking out her A–Z, Molly crossed a wide road and found herself in a street worthy of a Dickens novel. The shopfronts were beautiful in a scruffy sort of way. Each looked as if it could do with a couple of cans of paint, but they had all the more character for it. There was a bookshop, a very expensive-looking shoe shop, a hairdresser's, a gallery and a florist's. A florist's! Why hadn't Molly guessed? She didn't even need to see what number it was because she knew it was where her mother was.

For a moment, she stood on the opposite side of the road as if she'd been nailed into place. Fizz looked up at her, waiting for her to make up her mind.

'In a minute,' she said, more to herself than to him. 'Just give me a minute.'

Molly couldn't believe what she was looking at. This was her mother's home and it was the spitting image of her own florist's up in the Eden Valley. Like Molly, it seemed Cynthia's objective in life was to make colour where there was none, but

Molly had never thought for a moment that her mother had a florist's. It was too bizarre. It was too close. It was inevitable, she supposed.

She crossed the road with Fizz tripping alongside her and, taking a deep breath, entered the florist's.

There was nobody around but Molly could hear voices in a room at the back of the shop. She took in the flower displays, much the same as in The Bloom Room, and realised that her heart was thumping and her mouth was quite dry.

'Can I help you?' a woman's voice suddenly asked.

Molly turned round and saw a woman emerge from behind an enormous fig tree. She had fine silver hair like a delicate halo, and conker-brown eyes stared out of a rosy face. Other than the hair, it was like staring at her very own reflection.

'Mother?' Molly said tentatively.

'Molly!' Cynthia's eyes widened and her mouth slid into a beautiful smile. 'I can't believe it!'

Molly tucked her fingers into tight balls to stop herself from shaking.

'How did you find me?' Cynthia asked. 'I mean, how long have you known I was here?'

'Only a few days,' Molly said, not really wanting to confess that, after sixteen years of silence, she'd had to resort to hiring a private detective.

'Why didn't you call me?' she asked, and Molly could see that her eyes had filled with tears. 'You should have called me.'

'Why didn't *you* call *me*?' Molly asked, and then blushed. She hadn't meant to come out with such a question.

Cynthia's mouth opened a fraction but no words came out.

'I wanted to talk to you – so many times,' Molly said, in a

voice that was strangely controlled. 'Where were you? Where did you go?'

'Here,' Cynthia said. 'I was here.'

'Not all the time.'

'No,' Cynthia said. 'You're right. For the first few months, I didn't even leave Cumbria. I wanted to keep an eye on you all – make sure you were OK before I left.'

'And how did you know when we were OK?' Molly asked, tears from long ago springing into her eyes. 'How did you decide that?'

'Molly! Don't.'

Molly bit her lip and cast her eyes down to the floor. She shouldn't have said that. This wasn't what she'd thought would happen at all.

There was a moment's silence when words seemed too painful to be used. Molly felt ashamed and wished she could take back what she had said.

'And who's this?' Cynthia asked at last, blinking away her own tears as she walked across the shop to bend down and pat Fizz.

'I just got him,' Molly said quietly, realising that her questions weren't going to be answered simply because she'd asked them. 'His name's Fizz.'

'He's gorgeous. I remember you always wanted a dog, didn't you?'

Molly nodded, her mind somersaulting into the past for a brief moment.

'A dog makes a family complete,' her mother had once said.

'Not when you go abroad,' her father had replied.

'But we never do,' her mother had answered.

Molly looked at her mother now. Her rosy skin was creased

with delicate lines around her eyes, and her hair didn't seem to be as thick as Molly remembered.

'I went grey years ago,' Cynthia suddenly said, standing up again.

Molly's eyes widened.

'In case you were wondering. I don't like to dye it.'

'Oh.' Molly wasn't really sure how to respond.

'You've let yours grow, I see. It suits you long,' she said, her skin forming fine, whiskery lines at the edges of her eyes as she smiled again.

Before they could summon the courage to say anything more, a voice yelled from behind the floral partition behind the counter.

'Who is it, Cyn?'

'Come and see,' she called. 'Come through, Molly,' she said, quickly wiping her eyes with the cuff of a sleeve before taking Molly's hand as if it were merely moments, and not years, since she'd last held it.

They walked through to the back, passing great silver buckets of flowers, the familiar perfumes making Molly feel homesick yet at ease at the same time.

'Come and see who's here,' Cynthia said, as they entered a small kitchen.

Molly saw a tall, fair-haired man with his hands in a sink, washing-up.

'Robert,' Cynthia said, 'this is Molly.'

'*Molly!*' he said, his voice exiting his mouth like an ignited firework.

'Yes! I can't quite believe it either.' Cynthia smiled before turning to Molly. 'Molly, I'd like to introduce you to Robert, my husband.'

Molly watched as he took his hands out of the soapy water and dried them on a towel slung over his shoulder.

'Very pleased to meet you, Molly,' he said, shaking her hand.

'And you,' Molly said, looking up into his kind face. But he was no longer looking at her – he was looking at Cynthia. For a few brief seconds, Molly watched as they communicated in a silent language that she couldn't follow at all.

Finally, Cynthia nodded. 'Molly,' she said, 'Robert is Marty's father.'

Chapter Forty-One

Robert discreetly offered to take Fizz for a walk and Cynthia led Molly up to their flat above the shop.

'You mean Marty isn't a Bailey?' Molly asked a few minutes later, a mug of tea placed in her hands by her mother. It wasn't as if she needed a dose of caffeine; her brain was stimulated enough.

'He's been brought up like a Bailey,' Cynthia said, 'but not by me.'

'Did Dad know he wasn't a Bailey?'

Cynthia nodded. 'He never spoke about it, but he knew.'

'And all the time you were in love with Robert?'

'Don't be angry with me, Molly.'

'I'm not angry! I'm just...' Molly looked round the room in exasperation as she tried to find the right vocabulary, '...bewildered!' she finished.

'I know it's a lot to take in but he's still your brother.'

'But you left him! With a father that wasn't his.'

'That's all in the past now.'

'But it's still a part of us,' Molly said, not meaning to

sound so angry but failing miserably.

Cynthia looked down at her hands neatly folded in her lap. She was perfectly calm, and Molly found it slightly unnerving.

'Am *I* a Bailey?' Molly asked.

'Yes!' her mother said, sounding somewhat startled by her question.

'And are you going to tell Marty?'

'If he asks me – yes. But I'm not sure he'd want to know the truth, and I don't think Magnus would want him to know either.'

Molly stood up and walked over to the window, looking out into the street. Her mother had swapped family life in the beautiful Eden Valley for an ugly little flat above a shop in London. And the man she loved. Molly still couldn't get her head around it.

'But Marty is just so *Bailey-like*!' she said, turning back to face Cynthia. 'Yet I'm so like you – Dad's always said so – and yet you weren't around.'

Cynthia shrugged. 'Molly, you want me to explain things to you that I can't.'

There was a pause when nothing could be heard but the ticking of the clock above the mantelpiece. Cynthia had always loved clocks; had always been careful to mark the passage of time. Molly couldn't help but notice the home furnishings, even after the bombshell her mother had dropped. She'd even noticed that they'd bought the same lamp from Laura Ashley.

'Where are you staying?' Cynthia asked.

'The Portland.'

'You can stay here, if you like.'

'It's OK. I won't be in London much longer.'

Cynthia nodded, a hint of disappointment in her eyes. 'I've

been following your travels in *Vive!*,' she said at last.

'Have you?'

Cynthia nodded. 'I would have done the same thing.'

'I know,' Molly said. 'I could sense that. I knew it was the right thing to do.'

'But you haven't finished yet, have you?'

Molly gazed at the woman before her; a woman she hardly knew and yet knew like her own self.

'No,' Molly said. 'Tomorrow.'

'Yes,' Cynthia nodded, as if she already knew.

There was another pause. Molly could feel her heart pounding as adrenalin was pushed round her body at an alarming rate. Half of her fear lay in what she might find herself saying next. She didn't appear to be in control of things and that scared her. She tried to think of something safe to say – something that wouldn't upset either of them.

'Do you still keep in touch with Auntie Clara and Jess?' Molly asked, suddenly remembering her trip to Bradford. It seemed an age ago since she'd climbed the stairs of the Moor View flats.

'Of course,' Cynthia said, getting up and picking a photo frame up from a highly polished sideboard. 'Here. Jess's wedding.'

Molly took the silver-framed photo and stared at the strangers in it. There was her mother, her hair still dark but streaked with silver, as if she'd walked through a cobweb. Next to her was Auntie Clara, her skin creased in a smile as she beamed at Jess.

'Jess!' Molly said.

'She's quite the lady now,' Cynthia said, 'you wouldn't recognise her.'

'No,' Molly said, and she felt as if she could cry again for all the years that had been lost. She didn't know these people and yet she wanted to so much.

As if reading her mind, Cynthia scribbled something on a piece of paper and handed it to her.

'Give them a call – they'd love to hear from you.'

Molly looked at the two phone numbers and nodded. 'I will,' she said. 'And when did *you* get married?' she asked, noticing a stunning ruby ring on her mother's finger. It looked like one of her favourite roses.

'Twelve years ago next month.'

Molly tried not to gasp. All this time, she'd had a stepfather and she hadn't even known. 'He seems nice,' she said, not knowing what else she could say.

'He is. He's good and kind and patient. And he loves me.'

Molly was sure that those words weren't chosen as opposites to the ones Cynthia would choose to describe Magnus, but it was hard not to make comparisons.

'Did you ever love Father?'

Cynthia stared at Molly, her forehead crinkling in dismay. 'Of *course* I did. We had you together, didn't we?'

'Are you sure?' Molly asked, and immediately regretted it when she saw the pained expression on her mother's face. 'I'm sorry,' she said quickly. 'It's just, I can't seem to get my head round this. I don't understand.'

Cynthia sighed and sat down again. 'How can I explain my life to you? How can I expect you to know what went on when I don't even understand myself? I didn't plan for any of it to happen,' Cynthia said. 'And I did try to make it work with your father. I spent years trying.'

'I know,' Molly said, her voice like a little girl's.

'It wasn't working. It was best for me to go, but the condition was that you two stayed with him.'

'Why?'

'Because you were settled and because we didn't want to split you. I couldn't have offered anything to you. I had no home and no job to go to. You were better off with your father.'

Molly blinked and stared at her. 'You could have called us.'

Cynthia nodded. 'I know,' she said, her voice very low. 'But I knew that, every time I talked to you both, I'd want to come back.'

'And you didn't want that, did you?' Molly said, her voice tinged with bitterness.

'I couldn't. You know what it was like with your father, don't you? You were there.'

'It was never exactly *The Waltons*, was it?' Molly said.

'Then you agree that my leaving was the best thing to do?' Cynthia asked, as if seeking her daughter's approval after all these years.

Molly looked up at the ceiling and then down at the floor as if searching for an answer to her mother's question. 'I don't know,' she said at last, and then she heard the sound of feet and paws on the wooden staircase. Robert was back. Their time was up.

'Hello,' Robert called, crossing the room to kiss Cynthia. Molly wondered if he always did that when he'd only been gone for an hour or so or if he was trying to show Molly that he really did love her mother. 'I've shut the shop,' he said.

'Good,' Cynthia nodded. 'I'll get us something for lunch then.'

It was a strange, quietly polite meal, as if they were all

trying to work out what the other was thinking but not daring to find out through questioning.

It was a wonder Molly could eat anything at all with all the thoughts that were running through her head, like why had she needed a private detective to try and find her mother? Did she really not want to be found? How long had she known Robert? And had she been seeing him whilst married to Magnus?

'More bread?' Cynthia asked.

'Yes,' Molly smiled politely, as if her head was empty of all thoughts other than food. But there was no getting away from the fact that, for the past sixteen years, there'd been a huge gap in her life where her mother should have been and she'd tried to fill it with flowers but it hadn't quite worked. Now, sitting opposite her at a tiny pine table, she didn't know what to say.

'So you have a florist's too, Molly?' Robert asked.

'Yes. In the Eden Valley.'

'It's beautiful up there, isn't it?'

Molly nodded, but she didn't want to talk about the Eden Valley. 'I couldn't live anywhere else,' she said, and then bit her lip. It sounded as if she was snubbing their home.

'I thought that once,' her mother said. 'But you'd be surprised how easy it is to change, given the right circumstances.'

Molly watched as another secret look passed between Cynthia and Robert. It was the kind of look that she'd never shared with Magnus.

'And have you a young man?' Cynthia suddenly asked.

Molly felt herself blushing. 'Oh, no,' she said.

'Nobody special?' her mum persisted. Could she tell,

Molly wondered? Was it possible that she knew?

'Well,' Molly said at last, her blush fading away to leave a lovely glow behind, 'there might be. We'll have to wait and see.'

It was mid-afternoon when Molly left her mother's. Robert had given her a hug and had left them to it.

'Where are you going?' Cynthia asked.

'I'm not sure.'

'You're not far from the British Museum here.'

'Oh,' Molly said. It was as if she was sharing a conversation with a stranger on the streets.

'Thank you for finding me,' Cynthia suddenly said, wrapping Molly in a warm embrace.

Molly blinked back the tears. It was a warmth that she hadn't felt for years. 'I'm glad I found you.'

'You'll visit again soon, won't you?'

Molly stood back and nodded. 'Yes,' she said.

'Good,' Cynthia said.

It was an awkward moment. Molly wondered why she couldn't stay longer but perhaps a short visit was best. They'd seen each other, and found out that they still cared about each other. That would have to do for now. They'd have the rest of their lives to fill in the gaps.

'Oh! There's something I'd like to give you before you go,' Cynthia said.

Molly watched as her mother bent down amongst the silver buckets. 'I don't know how many you'll be needing for tomorrow,' she said, standing up with an armful of yellow gerbera, 'but you're welcome to all I've got.'

* * *

Molly left her mother's shop feeling completely dazed. She'd only been there for a few hours and there were so many questions she still had but she couldn't expect them all to be answered immediately, not after sixteen years of silence.

After placing the gerbera in her car and pouring an outrageous number of coins into the parking meter, Molly walked the streets with Fizz with no real direction in mind. Her head ached with the stress of the afternoon and she managed to find a pretty square with a fountain and rested for a while on a bench. Watching the patterns the water made, Molly could feel her heartbeat return to something that was approaching normal at last. She felt her eyes closing. How easy it would be to slip into sleep now, she thought. But she mustn't. She mustn't lose sight of her plan. She had to keep on going and that meant one thing – ringing Tom Mackenzie.

She got out her mobile and dialled his number quickly before she could change her mind.

'Tom Mackenzie,' his voice was loud in her ear.

'It's Molly Bailey.'

'Molly?'

'Yes.'

'I was wondering when I'd hear from you again.'

'Were you?'

'Yeah, I was. How can I help?' he asked. 'That is why you rang me, right?'

'You're unbelievable!'

'Why? Because I knew you'd need me sooner or later?'

Molly rolled her eyes and tutted. 'What made you think that?'

'Common sense. But I'm right, aren't I?'

'You might be.'

'So how can I help?'

Molly sighed inwardly. As annoying as he was, she had to admire him. 'I'm in London.'

'I thought you might be.'

'Really?'

'And you want me there too?'

'This isn't an invitation,' Molly said.

'So what is it?'

'It's information for your newspaper.'

'The grand finale?' Tom asked.

Molly's mouth dropped open. 'How did you know?'

'Just a lucky guess.'

'Has Carolyn being talking to you?' Molly asked, knowing that she hadn't even told Carolyn about her plans.

'No. Not since the duff information which sent me into deepest Wales.'

Molly stifled the urge to laugh. 'I'm sorry about that.'

'No you're not.'

'No. I guess I'm not. You were becoming a bit of a pain.'

'But you need me now, eh?'

'How come everything you say sounds so self-satisfied?'

Tom laughed. 'I admit, it's hard being right all the time.'

There was a pause.

'So come on, then. What's the big plan? What's Molly going to do next?'

'Something monumental,' she said, 'seven o'clock tomorrow evening.'

'Monumental?'

'Work that one out,' she laughed, and hung up.

Chapter Forty-Two

Of course, Tom was in London when Molly rang him. He didn't tell her that, though. They'd reached London in very good time, in fact, allowing Flora her much anticipated visit to the British Museum. That's when Tom's phone had gone off. It had been rather embarrassing. Several people had glared at him, as if only a philistine would have their phone switched on in such a revered building, but he was glad he hadn't turned it off. And it had only taken him about half an hour to work out Molly's cryptic clue. He'd been flicking through a cheap guidebook to London when he'd come across a photo of The Monument.

'Bullseye!' he'd shouted, causing another crowd of tourists to glare at him in consternation, Flora included.

So Molly's grand finale was to take place at The Monument. He'd email his report in to *Vive!* as soon as he could. They were holding the front page for him, and this was exactly what they'd been waiting for.

* * *

Putting her mobile back in her handbag, Molly left the square and followed a sign to the British Museum. It was time she did a bit of sightseeing and it didn't take her long to reach it. She and Marty had only ever been to London once as children and that had been under pressure from their mother. It hadn't been a pleasant trip. There was anxiety in the air as their father had pushed them round the Natural History Museum, not really very sure what they should be doing. And the gift shop had been a nightmare. He'd been most disappointed when they hadn't wanted to buy a guidebook to remind them of their trip and to read on the train back home, and had looked horrified when they'd picked up a pair of rubber dinosaurs.

'What are you going to do with that?' he'd asked Molly, his dark eyebrows knitting together in anger.

'Love it,' Molly had replied.

She sighed at the memory as she crossed the forecourt of the British Museum and then remembered something: Fizz. What was she going to do with Fizz? She looked around, wondering if it would be safe to tie his lead to the railings, but she didn't like the idea of that. And then she saw two Chinese girls sitting in the late afternoon sunshine. They looked kind and honest – not the sort to run off with a stranger's dog.

'Excuse me,' Molly began, 'do you speak English?'

The girls nodded. 'Not good but OK,' one of the girls said.

'I wonder if you'd mind looking after my dog for me whilst I have a quick look round? I'll only be about half an hour, and I'll pay you,' she said, taking a fifty-pound note out of her pocket.

The girls gasped. They were obviously students.

'Would you? I'd be very grateful.'

'Yes!' one of the girls said enthusiastically.

'His name's Fizz,' Molly explained. 'And he's very well behaved. Is that OK? I'll see you in about half an hour?' She wrote down her mobile number. 'Ring me if there are any problems,' she said and, with a smile, she walked towards the great columns and up the steps, and found herself in the startlingly white entrance hall, the sun pouring through the honeycombed glass roof. It was still busy, despite the day drawing towards its close, so Molly knew she'd have to move fast if she wanted to see what she came in for: the Elgin Marbles.

Tom looked up from his museum guidebook. It was no good; he couldn't make head nor tail of the floor plans. They'd just have to amble round at leisure and hope they wouldn't get lost.

He'd already lost Flora once as she'd run off in excitement towards the mummies. After the petrol station incident he'd reprimanded her rather loudly, causing a pink flush of cheeks which he immediately felt guilty about but there were so many people around, and Flora was so tiny that she was liable to be swept away by a tide of tourists and never be seen again.

There was one couple in particular who seemed to be shadowing them: an American woman who looked like a hippopotamus in a leisure suit, and her husband who was wearing the sort of cap that, for some inexplicable reason, really grated on Tom. No matter which turn Tom and Flora took or which room they chose to explore, the American couple never seemed to be far behind. God almighty, the museum was the size of a small country yet there they were at every turn.

Tom and Flora had wandered through endless stretches of

galleries, heaving themselves up and down endless staircases and peering into endless cabinets. It was all so daunting. It reminded Tom of his disastrous trip to the Louvre in Paris when he'd spent all of half an hour there before suffocating under a blanket of boredom and deciding to spend the rest of the day in a smoky bar on the Left Bank.

That's what museums did to him: the first ten minutes were wonderful; full of promise, expectation and excitement, but then something happened. Expectation died and was quickly replaced by a feeling like no other: it was as if he'd aged a hundred years. He adopted what he came to call 'museum leg' where the slightest movement was an agony of tiredness. Then there were his eyes, frozen with fatigue, and his mouth as parched as if the sun had set up home there.

No, as long as he was alive, he'd be forever trapped into visiting museums and being thoroughly bored by them.

'It's good here, isn't it, Daddy?' Flora beamed up from examining some Death Pit jewellery.

'Marvellous,' Tom said, secretly hating it all. He couldn't be doing with all the regimental order and the information plaques. What fascinated him the most wasn't what was on display but the stories behind the displays: the people who had once been housed in the sarcophagi. Where were all the bodies now? And who had discovered them? That's what really interested him. Someone had got out of bed and left home one morning with the explicit task of digging up a mummy. What a weird job. And he'd thought his job was strange enough. At least he didn't get cursed in his. Well, unless you counted Molly Bailey's recent diatribe.

However, there was one exhibition that did hold Tom's attention for more than three seconds. The shabti.

'They're like dolls,' Flora said, peering at the tiny coloured figurines.

'I can't believe the Egyptians thought these would perform tasks in the afterlife! Wouldn't that be the worst? You spend all your life working and, just when you think you're being laid to rest, you have to go and irrigate some field.'

'Did they really think a doll could become a servant?' Flora screwed up her nose in disbelief.

'If they put a spell on it – yes.'

'If I put a spell on my toys, would they do my homework for me?'

Tom smiled. 'It'd be worth a go.'

'If they sell shabti in the gift shop, I'm going to buy one for you, Daddy, and make it do your work for you. Then we can spend more time together.'

'Don't we spend enough time together, then?'

'Well, we are *now* but we don't have much time when I'm at school and you're at work.'

Tom smiled at his little philosopher. It was true, though. In his job, he was always thinking about what could be turned into an article. Even now, his mind was working overtime on shabtis. He realised that he had some clout now as a journalist: that the public were following him; believed in him, and he knew that the British Museum could do with some positive publicity. Surely he could knock up a modern interpretation of the shabtis?

And then it occurred to him: he wanted to do something to help others. That wasn't the norm, was it? Didn't profit always reign supreme with him? Did this mean that he'd finally been Mollied?

* * *

Molly travelled through Ancient Egypt to arrive in Greece in a great grey room which housed the Elgin Marbles. Even the light seemed grey, which, to Molly, seemed an appropriate colour for something so old.

Highly strung horses and headless riders galloped round the room, muscles and tendons straining. Wrestling centaurs caught her eye and filled her imagination with mythological mayhem.

But what was so infuriating was the metal railing separating viewer and stone. Sculpture, Molly believed, was made to be touched, and her fingers ached to trace the curls of the soldiers' hair and the wheels of the horse-drawn chariots.

Tom was beginning to lose his patience. He'd been squashed, scraped and sneezed on as Flora had chosen a postcard of an exhibit he couldn't even remember seeing.

'Flora,' he said, putting an arm firmly on her bird-like shoulder, 'time to go, I think.'

'Can we just take one more look at the sarcrofiguses?'

Tom frowned. He was hot and tired and wanted a shower and drink.

'It's just over there,' Flora said. 'No stairs,' she added, seeming to read her father's mind.

'OK, but quickly.' He followed her through, looking at the sarcophagus lids, which were so huge that they reminded him of the giant's grave in Penrith. God, that seemed like an age ago now. He wondered how many miles they'd driven since then but tried not to think about the petrol cost and the bed and breakfast bills.

He looked at his watch. The museum would be closing soon. They'd better make a move.

But when he looked up he couldn't see Flora anywhere.

* * *

Molly was transfixed by a large horse's head sitting on a plinth like a leftover prop from *The Godfather*. No body, no dignity and only half an ear; Molly felt almost ashamed to look at him.

She wasn't the only one to be mesmerised either. A young girl was standing beside her. Molly turned and smiled down at her.

'Amazing, isn't it?' Molly said, nodding towards the horse's head.

'Yes. But he looks so sad.'

'A head shouldn't be on a plinth.'

'Where's his body?' the girl asked, looking round the room in case she'd missed it.

'I don't know.'

'He looks strange,' the girl said.

'He doesn't want to be here,' Molly said. 'I don't think any of it does.'

'Why not?'

'Because they don't belong here. They were collected by the Earl of Elgin when he was in Greece. He sent them back to England and they ended up here. But the Greeks want it all back.'

'Then we wouldn't be able to look at it,' the girl pointed out.

'No, we wouldn't. Not unless we travelled to Greece.'

'Do you think it's wrong to keep it?' the girl asked.

Molly nodded. 'I do. There are people who believe that, if it wasn't for the Earl of Elgin, the marbles would have been destroyed, but,' she paused, 'I still don't think it's right to take what isn't yours. It's different if it had been given to the museum as a gift from the Greeks but it's stolen really.'

'Will the Greeks steal it back?'

Molly smiled down at the girl. 'Not with all this security. And imagine carrying something like this. It's not the easiest thing to shift, is it?'

'God! Flora!' a man's voice suddenly filled the room, causing everybody in it to turn round.

'Daddy!'

'I thought I'd lost you again! Where have you been?' The man bent down and wrapped his arms round her. 'I thought you were talking to Ramesses II?'

'I got bored of Ancient Egypt, so I came in here.'

'But you forgot to take me with you!'

'It's all right,' the girl assured him. 'I met a kind lady.'

The girl's father looked up at Molly and it was only then that she realised who it was. It was Tom Mackenzie.

Her heart did a quick flip and her mouth went quite dry. Would he recognise her? And, if he did, what would he say to her? It had been one thing to speak to him on the telephone but she wasn't sure she was ready for a proper meeting just yet. Her job wasn't done. Molly Bailey's mission wasn't yet complete. She still felt suspended in a parallel universe and didn't feel ready to come back down to earth and explain herself just yet.

'Look at the horse's head, Daddy,' the girl said and Tom turned away for a moment.

Molly took her chance and fled, her light feet carrying her quickly down the long room and out of the door into Ancient Egypt. She heard him calling after her but he was obviously not keen to pursue her at the risk of losing his daughter again.

Running out of the museum, she fled down the steps, flung another fifty-pound note to the bemused Chinese girls, grabbed Fizz's lead and ran.

* * *

Tom grabbed Flora's hand and ran out of the museum as fast as he could but at the top of the steps a wall of flesh stopped his passage. It was the Americans.

'Excuse me!' Tom all but shouted.

'Pardon?' the American woman drawled, stepping back onto Tom's right foot.

Tom yelled out in pain.

'*Oh my Gard!*' the American woman exclaimed. 'Is there something I can do?'

For a split second, Tom was very tempted to say, 'Well, you could start by losing ten stone,' but bit his tongue.

'She's gone!' Flora said. 'Where did she go?'

'She couldn't have gone far.'

'I can't see her anywhere.'

'Damn it,' Tom said under his breath and received a reprimanding look from Flora.

'It's all my fault.'

'You couldn't possibly have known, Flo. Don't worry about it.'

They stood in silence for a moment, looking down into the forecourt of the museum, but they couldn't see her.

'How could she vanish so quickly?' Tom said.

'It's like Cinderella!' Flora said.

'But there's absolutely no clue where she's gone.' Tom shook his head in annoyance. He'd come so close to her at last but he'd lost her yet again. Well, at least until tomorrow.

Tom sighed as he and Flora left the British Museum and, as they walked down the shallow steps, something occurred to him. It had been Tom Mackenzie the man and not Tom Mackenzie the journalist that had wanted to talk to Molly.

Chapter Forty-Three

The Baileys were having breakfast in a cheap hotel in Victoria. Marty had already been out to buy a copy of *Vive!* and was sat reading it out over his cornflakes.

'Well, I was right,' he said, finishing Tom Mackenzie's report. 'She's bowing out at seven o'clock tonight at The Monument.'

'We'll have to make sure we get there before her, then, won't we?' Magnus said.

Marty nodded. 'That might be easier said than done. With this sort of publicity, think of the number of people who might show up.'

'Shush! Listen,' Old Bailey suddenly hushed, and the four of them listened to a radio that was blaring from the kitchen.

'So it looks as if Molly's finally decided to give us Londoners some loot,' the voice was saying. 'If you haven't yet heard, Molly Bailey plans to be at The Monument at seven o'clock this evening. It promises to be a night to remember!'

Marty sighed. 'That's it, then. There'll be no chance of stopping her.'

'We can still go, though,' Carolyn chipped in. She, for one, was not going to miss Molly's big moment.

'We can go and see exactly what she's up to!' Magnus said. 'Stupid girl, what does she think she's doing? She's making nothing but a spectacle of herself.'

'I'm not sure Granddad should come, though,' Marty said. 'It's going to be very crowded.'

'*What?*' Old Bailey barked over his second round of toast. 'Not come!' he said, turning a dangerous shade of purple. 'I've come all the way from bloody Penrith. I'm not going to miss this!' he grumbled, winding his scarf around his scrawny neck.

'Blimey, Molly. You must be gobsmacked!' Jo said, as they left the hotel that morning. Molly hadn't told Jo about her encounter with Tom and Flora at the British Museum. She knew Jo would just tell her off for running away and, right now, Molly had enough to be coping with.

'I *am* gobsmacked!' Molly said. 'I've lost a brother, but gained a stepbrother, a stepfather and an estranged mother.'

'Blimey!' Jo said again. 'Not quite what you'd expected.'

Molly nodded. 'I know.'

'What was she like, then – your mother?'

'She was…' Molly began, but seemed lost for words, '…content.'

Jo's face scrunched up in bemusement. 'How do you mean?'

'Everything about her life – the way she spoke, the way she walked,' Molly tried to explain. 'She just oozed contentment. I've never ever seen that in anyone before.'

'When are you going to see her again?'

'I'm not sure. Soon. We said soon.'

'So what now?' Jo asked.

Molly nodded, as if pushing all thoughts of family to the back of her mind so as to focus on the here and now. 'I've got to get ready for this evening.'

'You know, you've still not told me what you're up to.'

Molly smiled. 'I've got a favour to ask you.'

'What?'

'Will you help me? I think I'm going to need an extra pair of hands tonight.'

Jo grinned and there was a naughty light in her eyes. 'You bet I will!' she said.

'I suppose we should make the most of being in London,' Marty said as they left the hotel. 'It's not often we're down here,' he added, taking Carolyn's hand.

Carolyn almost leapt at his touch. It was the first romantic gesture in days. At once, she started to get excited. 'How about Covent Garden?' she suggested. 'I've always wanted to go there.'

'What about Dad and Granddad? We don't want to do too much walking today.'

'They don't have to. We could go there on our own, couldn't we?' she suggested, hoping that this would be their chance to talk; that this would be her moment to break her news.

'Caro! We can't just leave them.'

'Why not? They're grown men. We don't have to babysit them.' Carolyn's voice rose to match his. 'And then,' she added, her voice softer and sweeter, 'we can do exactly what we want.'

Marty turned back and watched his father and

grandfather ambling along the pavement, moaning at the crowds.

'Maybe you're right,' he said.

Carolyn beamed. 'Great!' she said, kissing him on the cheek. Maybe he wasn't completely beyond redemption after all.

'Caro!' he complained. 'Kissing in the middle of the street!'

She tutted at his response. 'Come on,' she said, 'let's go shopping.'

After arranging to meet Magnus and Old Bailey for tea, Carolyn and Marty left for Covent Garden. Summer sunshine flooded the streets and brought the tourists out in full force. Carolyn, who was feeling surprisingly well after an initial bout of morning sickness, was in the mood to shop and, as they peered in a row of windows, Marty cleared his throat. 'Caro,' he began.

'Yes?'

'I've been meaning to apologise for the last few days. I know it's not been easy for you to put up with three Bailey men at once.'

Carolyn was about to say, no it bloody hasn't been, but thought better of it. He was making an effort, and she knew just how hard it was for him to do that.

'And I'd like to make it up to you.'

'You would?' She looked up at him and caught a smile so rare, it was like being given a gift.

'I'd like to buy you something,' he said, gesturing to the row of shops.

Carolyn bit her lip. She'd already seen half a dozen items she knew would look great in her wardrobe. 'Marty – *thank you*!'

'Is there anything you've seen?'

Carolyn smiled and nodded. She felt like a little girl again. 'Yes,' she said. 'As a matter of fact, there is.'

'Where?'

Carolyn pointed to a shop they'd passed a couple of minutes ago and they retraced their steps.

'There!' she said, pointing to a divine floaty dress in summer-sky blue. 'What do you think? Isn't it beautiful?'

Marty nodded. 'It's lovely,' he said.

'Shall I try it on?' Carolyn asked, her voice vibrating with excitement.

'How much is it?'

'We'll find out after I've tried it on,' she said.

'Hang on a minute,' Marty said suddenly, pointing to a little white plaque by the mannequins. 'Are those the prices?'

Carolyn's eyes followed his finger. She knew what was coming. Reality had kicked in and she was about to kiss the dress goodbye. 'I don't know,' she said, shrugging her shoulders.

'That's outrageous! I've never seen anything so ridiculous in my life!'

'Marty – we're in London. That's what you pay for designer goods.'

'It's not what *I* pay! I'm sorry, Carolyn, but you must have confused me with a rich man.'

'Then why did you say—?'

'I'm *not* paying that for a silly piece of material. Look! There's barely anything there! You couldn't blow your nose on it!'

Carolyn felt her shoulders slump and her anger swell.

'Marty – you're *impossible*! I just can't believe you sometimes!' she yelled, causing several heads to turn and a busker to stop busking. 'And you were right – it's not been easy being with you three men for the duration of the summer. It's been an absolute nightmare if you must know.'

'Caro!'

'You've not considered me at all. You don't know what's going on with me, do you? Well, I've had enough. I've put up with this for long enough, and it's got to stop.'

'Hey!' Marty shouted.

But it was too late: she'd already fled into the crowds and disappeared.

Tom looked at the front page of *Vive!* and grinned. *Molly at The Monument*. Beautifully simple and highly effective. But it wasn't the only reason he was smiling. He'd been offered a permanent position at *Vive!* that morning. It would take some thinking about, though. It would mean moving house for a start and he wasn't sure he wanted to do that. He saw little enough of Flora as it was.

Maybe he should remain freelance. He had made a name for himself now and it would be easier to get work and he liked being his own boss. Not for one minute had he missed the claustrophobic atmosphere of life on the local rag. Still, he didn't have to make his mind up today. He and Flora were going to enjoy themselves. A trip to Madame Tussauds, lunch at Planet Hollywood and a quick tour on a London bus before camping out at The Monument. That was the plan – until his phone rang.

'Tom Mackenzie.'

'Hello, Mr Mackenzie, I'm ringing from *City Beat*. Would

you be available for a radio interview today?'

He looked down at Flora who was poring over a tourist guide and looking very excited.

'As long as it doesn't take too long,' he said, watching their day together slowly ebbing away before his very eyes.

Chapter Forty-Four

It was three hundred and eleven steps to the top of The Monument and Molly was thankful that Jo had come with her. She'd never have made it up to the top on her own with Fizz and her huge rucksack full of money and gerbera in tow. As it was, they had to keep resting, making sure they stopped at the tiny slit windows under the pretence that they were admiring the view of St Paul's Cathedral and not because they were so unfit.

But, finally, they reached the top, and what a view greeted them. London was painted in the pearly blues and soft whites of summer. The River Thames winked gently as it stretched its way under Tower Bridge; and Canary Wharf, the Millennium Wheel, church spires, offices, cranes, cars, buses and boats all jostled for attention.

'Wow!' Jo yelled. 'This is brilliant! You're so clever, Molly! I can't believe you've done this.'

'Neither can I!' Molly said, gazing down at the ground, which was a dizzying distance below. She'd booked the whole place, making a one-off payment, and telling them that she was filming something. Luckily, no questions had been asked. The custodian obviously hadn't seen a copy of *Vive!*.

'There may be a few dozen extras showing up around seven o'clock,' she'd said quickly. 'But they'll be remaining outside.' The man had just nodded and taken her cash. In fact, she was surprised that there wasn't anyone around when they'd turned up, but they had got there incredibly early.

'I just hope we don't need the toilet,' Molly giggled. 'We've got a long wait.'

'At least it's warm up here.'

Molly nodded. 'Warm and still,' she said, thinking of the disaster they might have had on their hands had it been windy.

Jo pulled out a couple of cushions she'd been carrying in her rucksack. They'd bought them that morning and now sat down and opened a couple of packs of sandwiches.

'This is the weirdest holiday I've ever had,' Jo said through a mouthful of lettuce and tomato.

'Me too!' Molly agreed. 'And I can't believe it's nearly over.'

Jo stared at Molly. 'What will you do?'

Molly pulled Fizz towards her and gave him a hug. 'Go home, I guess. But it's going to be so strange.'

'What about Tom?' Jo said suddenly. 'Aren't you going to see him? Oh, you've *got* to see him, Molly!'

Molly looked thoughtful for a moment, as if she was still trying to work that one out.

Jo grinned. 'It would be a shame not to see him after all this, don't you think? Anyway, I'm sure he'll find you. He's probably somewhere down there right now.'

'Yes,' Molly said, not daring to peep over the railings to find out. 'I have a feeling he is.'

* * *

Tom and Flora arrived at The Monument at half past six. Tom had hoped to get there earlier but, after the *City Beat* interview, he'd been waylaid by a few other phone calls which had cut into his day with Flora.

'Good heavens!' he said as he saw the number of people jostling round The Monument. 'Don't let go of my hand,' he told Flora. 'I don't want a repeat of the British Museum here.'

'Do you think she's there?' Flora asked, peering high into the sky.

'Must be,' Tom said. 'If she arrived now, she'd have a bit of a fight to get through this crowd.' Tom craned his head and gazed up at the golden flame on the top of The Monument, which was shining as if it really was fire. This is where it all began: the Great Fire of London. And this was where Molly's journey was going to end. So where was she? Tom thought about trying to blag his way into the building but he knew his story would be at ground level. Anyway, he wanted to know what it would feel like to be one of Molly's people.

'Do you think she's scared of heights?' Flora asked.

'I'd hope not,' Tom said. 'It's an awful long way up.'

'I wish I could see her,' Flora said.

'Yes,' Tom said. 'Me too.'

When Carolyn finally reached The Monument, she gasped. How on earth was she meant to find Marty in this crowd? Checking her watch, she saw that it was ten to seven. Marty was bound to be here, but where?

'Marty?' she called. '*Marty!*' A few heads turned to look at her for a second.

She hadn't made it back to the hotel in time to meet up with the Bailey men and it was going to be impossible to find them now.

'Damn!' she said, pulling out her mobile phone and tapping Marty's number into it. 'Marty? It's Caro. Where are you? What? Oh! Yes, I can see that. OK. Don't move. I'm on my way!' She pushed her way through the crowd to find Marty. It was time he knew the truth.

'Well?' Jo said. 'By my watch, it's time to stick your head over the parapet!'

Molly nodded but didn't say anything immediately.

'What's wrong?' Jo asked.

'I don't know,' Molly said. 'I'm suddenly rather nervous.'

Jo flashed a big grin and bent forward to give Molly a hug. 'This,' she said, 'is going to be brilliant.'

'Brilliant's rather scary, though, isn't it?'

'Of course! Everything worth having, and everything worth doing, usually scares the shit out of us!'

Molly smiled and suddenly they were both laughing.

'Come on, then!' Molly said, standing up and opening her rucksack. 'Let's give the crowds what they came for.'

'It's her!' somebody shouted in front of Carolyn, and a huge roar went up, rippling and growing through the crowd until Carolyn's ears trembled. She could see Marty now. He was only six or seven rows ahead of her.

'Marty!' she yelled. '*Marty!*' Carolyn was pushed forward and crashed into his back.

'Caro! Where have you been? We've been so worried.'

'Where's Magnus and Granddad?'

'I managed to persuade them not to come. But why didn't you meet us?' he asked.

Before she could answer him, a great whoop sounded from the crowd. Carolyn looked up to the skies and saw a shower of money and sun-yellow gerbera raining down on them like confetti at a wedding.

'Where is she? Can you see her?' Carolyn asked, gazing up at The Monument, but they were almost at its base and couldn't see Molly from their vantage point.

'Jesus!' Marty intoned. 'They're – they're – *ten*-pound notes! Look! And fifties too!'

Carolyn watched in despair as Marty leapt into the air, arms flailing as he attempted to catch as many of the falling notes as he could. But Molly had it sussed. She was moving round the enclosed balcony like a clockwork figure, making sure that everyone got a fair crack at catching something.

'Help me, Caro!' Marty shouted in exasperation, pushing the people in front of him as the money fell from the top of The Monument. 'Help me! We've got to get as much as we can!'

'Marty!' Carolyn shouted, but he didn't seem to hear. '*Marty! Stop! STOP!*'

Marty stopped, a solitary ten-pound note in his hand.

'It's no use,' Carolyn said, her voice quiet and subdued.

'But we've got to try – for God's sake – look at all this money – *wasted*!'

'But it *isn't* wasted. Don't you get that? Just look at the joy on these people's faces. Molly knows *exactly* what she's doing.'

There was something in Carolyn's voice that seemed to get through to Marty at last. She could see the change in his expression. First, he turned round to look at the crowd, watching their faces: each and every one filled with happiness. He looked up at The Monument. And then, he turned to look at Carolyn.

'Don't you see?' she asked. 'Just leave it.' Carolyn felt tears welling up in her eyes and, for the first time in a long while, she didn't bother to try and hide them from Marty.

'Caro? I'm sorry,' he said, stepping forward and placing his arms round her. 'I'm sorry. What can I say?'

Carolyn pulled away. Had she heard him right? Or was he simply caught up in the madness of the moment? Was he just agreeing with her to stop her from causing a scene?

'What can I say?' he repeated, leaning forward and kissing her forehead.

'You can say that you're never going to behave like this again. That you're going to stop making life miserable by counting every penny and scrimping and saving. That you're going to start having a bit of fun and enjoying what we work so hard to earn,' she finished, sniffing loudly and grabbing a crumpled tissue from out of her handbag.

'Is that all?' he asked, making a stab at humour.

'No,' Carolyn said. 'I want you to promise that we can have a decent holiday with the money Molly's given us.'

Marty's forehead crinkled. 'You mean Molly's given us a cut of her winnings?'

Carolyn nodded. 'Don't go getting excited. It's enough to pay off the mortgage and a bit more, but it's not millions.'

'Why didn't you tell me?' Marty asked, his eyes stretched in surprise.

'Because I wasn't sure how you'd react, and I wanted you to realise that there's more to life – more to our relationship –

than money, because it's not going to be just us two for much longer.'

Marty's mouth fell open. Despite the noise of the crowd, he'd heard Carolyn's words as if she'd shouted them through a loudspeaker.

'You mean you're pregnant? You're going to have a baby?'

'*We're* going to have a baby,' Carolyn corrected.

'Oh my God! How long have you known? When's it due? Why didn't you tell me?' His words fell out of his mouth like broken teeth and Carolyn couldn't help but smile.

'I've not known long. It's due in February, and I didn't tell you because you've been so wrapped up in Molly.'

'But that's *why* I've been wrapped up!'

'What do you mean?'

'That's why I've been scrimping and saving and worrying – because we want a family! God almighty, Caro, didn't you realise? *I worry!* I worry about the future, of us all having enough – I worry about—'

'But there's no need! We'll manage! We always have, haven't we?'

'I know,' Marty admitted, 'but, when the time came, I didn't want *you* to scrimp. I want you to have everything you need – no cutting the corners for once. I just want to be sure we're all all right.' He took her hand in his and gave it a gentle squeeze. 'I know I've not been the easiest of people to live with and I know I've made things tough on you, but it was only so that we'd have enough for when this happened.'

Carolyn wiped her eyes, blew her nose again, and smiled. 'You know what I've always wanted—' She stopped. She wasn't used to starting a sentence in front of Marty with those words.

'What? Tell me? Name it and it's yours!'

'Well, it's rather girly and silly, I know, but I've always wanted one of those big old-fashioned prams. You know – the ones with the big hood and silver handles.' She looked at Marty. Was it her imagination or had he turned slightly green around the gills?

'It's yours!'

'Really?'

'Yes.'

'Oh, Marty! I'm so excited!'

'Anything else? You can have anything you want for this baby. Just as long as it isn't twins. We'll have to go easy on the spending if it's twins.'

Carolyn grinned as a shade of old Marty peeped through. He'd never change completely, she thought, but at least he was moving in the right direction.

'Caro!' he said, his eyes suddenly very wide.

'What?'

'You've had your hair cut!'

'I know!' Carolyn's hand flew up to her head. 'Do you like it?' she asked anxiously.

'It's – it's so short!' he stammered, momentarily lost for words. 'It's amazing! You should have done it years ago.'

Carolyn rolled her eyes but said nothing. She'd won, and that was enough.

'Blimey!' Jo cried. 'That's the lot. It's all gone.'

Molly peered into the enormous rucksack and saw that Jo was right.

'What do we do now?' Jo asked.

'Face the crowd, I guess!'

'What if they want more?' Jo asked, suddenly nervous.

'There's no more where that came from,' Molly said. 'They've had the lot.'

'Well, I'm ready if you are,' Jo said, fastening up the rucksack and flinging it over her shoulder.

With Fizz in her arms, Molly and Jo almost flew down the three hundred and eleven steps. As they reached the bottom, the ticket officer turned round and glared at her. 'Is this something to do with this film of yours?' he asked, his face pale and suspicious.

'That's right!' Molly trilled, just a little out of breath.

'Rather a lot of extras if you ask me. Must've cost a fortune!'

'A fair bit,' Molly said, 'but worth every penny.'

One after the other, Molly and Jo pushed through the turnstile and walked out into the crowd.

'*There* she is!' someone yelled.

'*Molleeeee!*'

'Where's the rest, Molly?' a lady shouted.

'Yeah! Got any more?'

'It's all gone!' Molly shouted back, shaking her empty rucksack at them in case they doubted her.

'*Molly!*' A wild, banshee scream filled her ears as a woman pushed through the crowd. Molly stood stock-still.

'Molly!' the woman cried again, flinging her arms around her neck and smothering her in hot kisses. 'You're a saint. I *love* you!' the mad woman cried, strangling Molly with a passion until she felt sure she'd drown in affection. Molly coughed loudly and the woman released her grip, edging back as far as the crowd would let her. 'This country needs more people like you, Molly. It really does!'

'Give us a kiss, Moll!' a red-faced man in a pink-striped shirt shouted.

'Molly – over here!' a curly-haired pensioner shouted.

Cameras flashed at her, hands slapped her back. There was even a man selling 'Molly Makes the World Go Round' T-shirts. It was brilliant!

'Three cheers for Molly Bailey!' someone shouted from the sea of heads.

'Hip-hip.'

'Hooray!'

'Hip-hip.'

'Hooray!'

'Hip-hip.'

'*Hooooraaaay!*'

It was all so overwhelming. Molly felt tears pricking the back of her eyes as she scoured the faces of the crowd. Everybody seemed to be looking at her, waiting to see what she would do next. Indeed, Molly wasn't quite sure herself. She hadn't thought that far ahead.

She looked at a few of the faces nearby but there weren't any answers there. And then, something strange happened. It was as if the crowds suddenly parted, or a shaft of sunlight picked her out, because Molly saw her almost instantly. She'd been there all along. Molly hadn't dared to expect her but, in her heart of hearts, there'd been a tiny seed of hope.

Her hair, as silver as if it had been kissed by the moon, was worn loose and long. Her large chocolate eyes, a perfect mirror of Molly's.

'Molly!' Cynthia took a hesitant step forward, her face creasing up into the largest smile Molly had ever seen, and, all of a sudden, she found a pair of arms around her.

'I'm so proud of you,' Cynthia said in a voice barely audible above the crowd's excited shouting, even though her mouth was only an inch away from Molly's ear.

Molly moved back slightly, a warm glow filling her body.

'You'll come and see me soon, won't you?' Cynthia asked.

'Of course I will,' Molly said.

And then Cynthia was gone.

'Wow!' Jo said, grabbing Molly's shoulder from behind. 'Was that your mum?'

Molly nodded.

'What a perfect ending!' Jo sighed. And she was right.

Of course, Molly was arrested. Breach of peace, they told her down at Bishopsgate police station. But she didn't mind much. It would make great copy for Tom's final Molly report.

Leaving the station with Fizz, she pushed her way through the small crowd of people who'd followed her.

'What are you going to do now, Molly?' someone asked her.

'Yeah! Is this it, then? The end of the road for Molly's millions?'

Molly turned around at the familiar voice and there, standing at the front of the small crowd, was a tall man with tousled hair and a cheeky grin. It was Tom Mackenzie. Their eyes locked for a moment and Molly could feel herself blushing at the intense, grey-eyed gaze that fell on her. And then she laughed.

'I think it's time I gave everyone a break from chasing after me. I wouldn't want people to grow bored.'

'Oh, I don't think there'd be any chance of that. Besides, it hasn't been that bad,' Tom said, stepping forward from the crowd. 'I haven't minded driving the length and breadth of

Britain with a child and laptop in tow.'

Molly laughed again and smiled down at Flora beside him. 'I didn't ask you to follow me.'

'I know,' Tom said. 'Anyway, I guess you've run out of money by now?'

Molly paused before answering. 'Er – not quite,' she said somewhat cagily as they moved away from the crowd and walked up the street.

'What? You mean you've not given it all away yet?'

'Only a very silly girl would give it *all* away,' Molly said. 'There's a little bit put by for a rainy day. You have to take care of number one, don't you?'

'Of course,' Tom said.

There was a moment's silence and then Flora tugged her father's sleeve and whispered something to him.

'Listen, Molly,' Tom said at last, 'talking of taking care of number one, I wanted to apologise.'

'What for?'

'For being somewhat unscrupulous in my reports about you – in the early days. I, er – I was only thinking of number one. It made good copy, you know? I wasn't thinking about you.'

Molly chewed her lip. She'd been waiting for an apology from Tom Mackenzie for some time but, now she had it, she wasn't sure how to respond.

'I've been meaning to say something for ages,' he continued. 'I feel terrible about it all, I really do.'

'Do you?'

'Of *course* I do. I hate what I wrote. I was blinkered by my job. I wanted a good story – I wanted to strike gold – and I just didn't think about the people I might hurt. I'm sorry if I ever hurt you,' Tom said, his voice slightly hesitant. 'I really am.'

Molly smiled to herself, thinking she must be the only girl in the world to receive a heartfelt apology from a reporter. Of course, he could still be bluffing. He might only want to receive her forgiveness in order to make himself feel better. It was easy to apologise for something that had already happened; he'd made his money from her, so what did he have to lose? But there was something about his tone of voice that struck Molly as being completely sincere. He sounded like a little boy who knew he'd been naughty and was desperate to receive approval once more, and only she could give it to him.

'It's all right,' she said at last. 'It's all in the past, isn't it?'

'I'm forgiven, then?'

Molly felt a smile creeping over her face. 'What can I say?' she said, stringing him along for as long as she dared.

'You could say, "*Yes*, Tom, all is forgiven".'

'I could, couldn't I?'

'*Yes!*'

'OK then, you're forgiven. But on one condition.'

'What's that?'

'You make your last report a good one.'

'You've got it!'

They crossed the road together, the last warm rays of the sun filtering down through the office blocks, making their skin glow like ripe peaches.

'So what are you going to do now?' Tom asked.

'That's funny,' Molly smiled. 'I was going to ask you the same thing.'

Tom sighed. 'It's been a rather chaotic few weeks, hasn't it?'

Molly nodded. 'A holiday then?'

'Just what I was thinking. Is there anywhere you can recommend?'

Molly looked at him. His eyes were soft and smiling. 'Well,' she said casually, 'I've always loved the Lake District at this time of year.'

'Really?'

'Yes,' she said, 'and the Eden Valley is especially beautiful.'

'I'm afraid I don't know the area very well. Can you recommend any bed and breakfasts? Maybe in the Kirkby Milthwaite area?'

Flora tugged on her father's hand. 'That's where Molly lives, Daddy!'

Tom's eyes widened. 'Oh, yes! I'd quite forgotten.'

'You've got a very bad memory for a reporter!' Molly smiled. 'How on earth do you manage to make a living if you can't remember anything?'

'I just make it all up. Surely you know that as an ardent *Vive!* reader?'

Molly narrowed her eyes at him. If she didn't like him so much, she'd have thumped him in the belly by now.

'And you must be Flora,' Molly said, turning her attention to Tom's daughter at last. 'Did you know that Flora is the name of the goddess of flowers?'

Flora smiled, looking suitably impressed, just as her father's mobile began to ring. Tom cupped his ear so that he could hear it above the sound of the traffic.

'Really?' he said. 'Are you sure?'

They stopped walking for a moment and Flora bent down to give Fizz a fuss as her father finished his call.

'Who was that?' Flora asked a moment later.

Tom's face wore a stunned expression. 'You're not going to believe it.'

'What?' Molly and Flora asked.

'That was a lady from the Andre Levinson show. They want to know if we're interested in appearing on it.'

'Me and you?' Molly asked.

'Yes! Flo too.'

Flora beamed. 'Really, Daddy?'

'Yes!'

'What do you say, Molly? Do you want to be seen with me in public?'

Molly frowned for a moment. 'It would be *very* public,' she said.

'I know.'

'And we'll probably be asked all sorts of embarrassing questions,' Molly added.

'Yes,' Tom said, his brow creasing in thought. 'We can always rehearse,' he suggested.

'Do you think so?'

'Yes. It might take a while but I'm sure we could both find the time to work out our story. Flora could help, couldn't you?'

Flora nodded. 'I'm really good at asking embarrassing questions!' she grinned.

'Yes,' Tom said, 'you are, aren't you!'

'Like, are you going to be Daddy's new girlfriend, Molly?'

Tom's eyes doubled in size and Molly's face flushed red.

'*Flora!*' Tom shouted.

'It's what you'll be asked on TV,' Flora insisted.

'She's right,' Molly said. 'We probably will be asked that.'

Tom pretended to strangle Flora before turning to Molly. 'Well, what will we say?' he asked, a naughty light dancing in his eyes.

Molly looked at him for a moment and then looked down

at Flora. 'What do you think, Flora?' she asked.

Flora looked pensive for a moment before answering with great earnestness. 'I think you'd better rehearse. But don't worry,' she added with an impish smile, 'we've got the rest of the summer holidays to get it just right.'